William Shaw Russell

Pilgrim Memorials

and guide to Plymouth. With a lithographic map, and eight copperplate engravings

William Shaw Russell

Pilgrim Memorials
and guide to Plymouth. With a lithographic map, and eight copperplate engravings

ISBN/EAN: 9783337291877

Printed in Europe, USA, Canada, Australia, Japan

Cover: Foto ©Andreas Hilbeck / pixelio.de

More available books at **www.hansebooks.com**

PILGRIM MEMORIALS,

AND

GUIDE TO PLYMOUTH.

WITH A

𝕷𝖎𝖙𝖍𝖔𝖌𝖗𝖆𝖕𝖍𝖎𝖈 𝕸𝖆𝖕,

AND

EIGHT COPPERPLATE ENGRAVINGS.

BY

WM. S. RUSSELL,

REGISTER OF DEEDS, AND KEEPER OF THE PLYMOUTH COLONY RECORDS

> Yea, when the frowning bulwarks
> That guard this holy strand
> Have sunk beneath the trampling surge
> In beds of sparkling sand,
> While in the waste of ocean
> One hoary rock shall stand,
> Be this its latest legend —
> HERE WAS THE PILGRIM'S LAND.
> *Oliver Wendell Holmes.*

FIFTH EDITION.

BOSTON:
CROSBY & AINSWORTH.
NEW YORK: OLIVER S. FELT.

1866.

PREFACE TO THE SECOND EDITION.

THE following pages are designed to afford the means of ready access to the more prominent events and interesting localities connected with the landing of the Pilgrims, to which the attention of visitors is naturally directed on their first arrival at Plymouth.

Under the different heads, as arranged in the index, full descriptions will be found of the Forefathers' Rock, the ship Mayflower, Burying Hill, Leyden Street, Coles' Hill, the first burial-place, Clark's Island, Pilgrim Hall, and other points of antiquarian interest, which, with a lithograph map of Plymouth village, having explanatory references appended, and eight copperplate engravings, tending to illustrate " the very age and body of the time," it is hoped, will in some measure answer the inquiries of visitors, and accomplish the object designed by this publication.

The present edition has been considerably enlarged, to admit the introduction of many additional incidents, of an interesting character, connected with Pilgrim History, with a view to render the work more generally attractive to the public.

WM. S. RUSSELL.

PLYMOUTH, August, 1855.

PREFACE TO THE THIRD EDITION.

SINCE the last edition of this work was published, important accessions to Pilgrim History, have been made, deserving of attention on the present occasion.

The long-lost Manuscript History of Plymouth Colony, by Gov. William Bradford, has been found, and now appears in print among the valuable publications by the Massachusetts Historical Society. Although the early historians of New England copied largely from this manuscript before its loss, much remained of value, particularly in reference to the marriages and deaths among the passengers by the Mayflower.

Other valuable information respecting the Pilgrims, has through the exertions of the Hon. Henry C. Murphy, Minister Resident of the United States at the Hague, been obtained from the Records of the City of Leyden, which information was never before known to Antiquarians on this side of the Atlantic.

Under these circumstances, an appendix, comprising selections from the above-named writings and some local matters of interest, has been prepared, which it is hoped may tend to confer fresh interest on the History of Pilgrim times.

EXPLANATION OF ENGRAVINGS.

1st. Lithographic Map of Plymouth Village.

2d. View of Plymouth from the Burying Hill.

3d. Landing of the Pilgrims at Plymouth, Dec. 11,* 1620.

4th. Faç Similes.   Brewster, Bradford, Winslow, Standish and Allerton came in the Mayflower; the others came in the Fortune or Ann, excepting Constant and Thomas Southworth, who came about the year 1628.

5th. This house shows the best style of building in the latter part of the seventeenth century.   The lot on which it stood was owned by Robert Hicks, merchant, in 1645. It was afterwards owned by Edward Gray, who sold it to John Richards, in 1677.   The house was taken down in 1826, and was the oldest in town.   The Universalist Church stands on the same lot.   In this house the mother of the celebrated patriot, James Otis, was born, in 1702.   She was the grand-daughter of Edward Doty, who came in the Mayflower.

6th. The Fuller Cradle belonged to Dr. Samuel Fuller, who came in the Mayflower, and is now owned by Jacob Noyes, Esq., of Abington, whose late wife, Mrs. Olive Noyes, was a descendant.

7th. The apple-tree was planted by Peregrine White, the first Englishman born in New England, about the year 1648, who died in 1704, in the 84th year of his age. It still produces apples, and the orchard in which it grows is now owned by his descendants, near the lot which he occupied, in Marshfield.

* Dec. 21, New Style.

8th. The originals of the following Fac Similes have been collected since the previous edition of this work, viz. Samuel Fuller, John Alden, George Soule, Senr., who came in the Mayflower; Timothy Hatherly, an original Merchant Adventurer, and justly called "the Father of Scituate;" James Cudworth, an early settler of the same town, and highly distinguished both in civil and military life; John Brown of Plymouth, afterwards of Swansey, who occupied various civil stations in the colony, and whose signature, above copied, was subscribed to a document of the Commissioners of the United Colonies; Thomas Willet, so well known in early colonial times, and who was the first mayor of New York after its capture from the Dutch nation; Kenelme and Josias, brothers of Gov. Edward Winslow; Josiah, the son of said Edward, and the first native Governor of Plymouth Colony, highly distinguished for valuable services rendered both in civil and military affairs, especially during the critical period of Philip's War.

1*

INDEX.

A

B

C

PILGRIM MEMORIALS, ETC.

A BRIEF ACCOUNT OF THE PILGRIMS, PREVIOUS TO THEIR ARRIVAL IN AMERICA.

"We have an advantage over all nations in being able to trace our history from the beginning. We have no fabulous age, but it has more romance than any which has ever been written." — SALTONSTALL.

IT is well known that the removal of the Pilgrims from England to Holland, whence they afterwards sailed to America, was one of the results of that great religious movement, during the latter part of the sixteenth and the first part of the seventeenth centuries, which for a long time convulsed and eventually revolutionized England itself.

It was at the closing period of Queen Elizabeth's reign, in the year 1602, a period of ardent excitement in relation to the great objects of human pursuit; when the progressive influence of the Reformation earnestly engaged the attention of every thoughtful mind; when the recently-discovered art of printing facilitated the dissemination of knowledge, and new discoveries by successive navigators had widely enlarged the bounds of commercial enterprise; that we first trace our Pilgrim Fathers, in the north of England, manfully contending against the principalities and powers, which denied them "the liberty wherewith Christ had made them free."

Though few in number, their strong faith, earnest zeal and fervent love, created a bond of union and an intensity . of purpose, which never deserted them throughout their perilous career ; whether hunted at home by the adherents of hierarchical oppression, exposed to the dangers of the deep, seeking a precarious subsistence in a strange land, or exploring the bleak shores of Cape Cod, amidst the rough blasts of a cheerless winter.

In a publication of Mr. Joseph Hunter, F. S. A., an assistant keeper of Public Records, in England, which appeared in August, 1849, additional light has been thrown on the early state of the Pilgrim church, and the place of its meeting has been satisfactorily identified, as will be seen from the following extracts, taken from that valuable ·publication, page seventh : "But a passage in Bradford's account of Brewster enables us to fix not only the town or village at which the church held its meetings, but the very house in which they assembled ; and, to proceed at once to the removal of this uncertainty, I add that it is manifest to any one who has an intimate knowledge of those parts of the kingdom, that the seat and centre of the church, while it remained in England, was at the village of *Scrooby*, in Nottinghamshire, and in the principal mansion of that village, the house which had been for centuries a palace of the Archbishop of York, but which was in those days held under one of the many leases of episcopal lands granted by Archbishop Sandys.

"*Scrooby* will be found in the maps, about a mile and a half south of Bawtry, a market and post town situated on the borders of Yorkshire and Nottinghamshire. The nearest point of the county of Lincoln is distant six or seven miles."

The same writer states, on page eleventh, that "The house fell by degrees into decay. No portion of it is now standing; yet the site may be traced by a few irregularities in the surface of the ground."

Mr. Bartlett, in his late work, published in London, in 1853, called the "Pilgrim Fathers," when describing this celebrated building, says: "Not a wreck of this sumptuous building now remains; but its position is evidently discernible; and in the annexed view the farm-house, with a row of willow-trees, marks its site." And again, he observes, after describing several unimportant features comprised in the locality: "Beyond these insignificant relics there was no trace of the stately 'Manor of the Bishops,' where these lordly prelates, attended by a splendid retinue, went forth to hawk and to hunt, and returned to feast and to revel, in its days of pride; and where, in its decay,— strange contrast! — the little band of sufferers for conscience' sake, stealing through by-paths from the neighboring villages, assembled under the hospitable roof of Brewster, to practise in secret that form of worship which the persecution of their enemies prevented them from celebrating openly. This now vacant spot was the nucleus of the Pilgrim Church; and here was linked and riveted that solemn fellowship, and unity of purpose and spirit, which subsisted through manifold perils, until it had laid the foundations of a mighty empire on the distant shores of America."

It is highly gratifying thus to learn, from unquestionable authority, a fact so important as that above stated, the identification of the spot and building where the Pilgrim

2

church first worshipped in England; a fact so long concealed from all previous inquiry, the development of which
at this late day may justly inspire the hope, that diligent
and persevering investigations in future, on kindred subjects,
will be crowned with similar success.

In the year 1607, not long after the actual organization
of the church, under the care of John Robinson and William
Brewster, the precise date of which organization seems not
to have been accurately ascertained, as appears from Mr.
Hunter's remarks, they concluded to remove from their
native country to avoid the persecution which assailed them
on every side.

In the year 1608, after the failure of a previous attempt,
they arrived at Amsterdam, in Holland, and, in less than
one year, again removed to the city of Leyden, at which
place they continued and ably sustained public worship,
under the ministrations of their accomplished and venerated
pastor, till their embarkation at Delft Haven, in the ship
Speedwell, of sixty tons burthen, on the twenty-second of
July, 1620,* from whence they reached South Hampton, in
England, to join the Mayflower; and on the fifth day of

---

* " Without entering into particulars, it is sufficient to state, as illustrative of the trade of Holland, that in 1690, when it had attained to a
maximum, Sir William Petty estimated the whole shipping of Europe at
2,000,000 tons, of which he supposed the Dutch to possess 900,000 tons ;
and it is believed that this estimate was rather within, than beyond the
mark." — McCullock's Gazetteer, Edit. 1833.

It is, perhaps, well deserving our attention, as illustrating the growth
of commerce in America, that our present tonnage exceeds that owned by
all Europe at the time of embarkation, when our rivers, bays and oceans,
possessed no better means of water communication than a birch canoe, or,
by way of improvement, a log of the larger class, dug out, with much
labor, by some Indian shipwrig t.

August both vessels sailed from that port, to execute the long-cherished purpose of emigration to America.

> " By heartless bigots basely spurned,
> From tyrant power resolved they turned,
> And sought in western wilds to meet
> Some spot to rest their weary feet ;
> Some spot to rear their house of prayer,
> Beyond the *mitre's* angry glare ;
> To fix the reign of conscience free,
> Despite of *Rome's* imperial *see ;*
> That *Church* and *State* no more combined,
> With iron grasp the soul should bind ;
> Where freedom winged might raptured roam,
> And find at last a genial home."

They had not proceeded far, however, before Mr. Reynolds, of the Speedwell, complained that his ship was in so leaky condition that he feared to proceed further ; and, on the thirteenth of August, both vessels put into Dartmouth. The Speedwell, having undergone what were deemed adequate repairs, both vessels put to sea again on the twenty-first of August. After proceeding about one hundred leagues beyond the land's end of England, Mr. Reynolds again complained of his ship, and the danger of foundering, if they proceeded on the voyage, when both vessels entered the harbor of Plymouth. On a second examination of the Speedwell, no particular injury seemed to have been sustained, and the general weakness of the ship was assigned as the cause of difficulty, though it afterwards appeared that the deception of Reynolds and others was the main cause of the serious and repeated delays to which they had been subjected, and which proved highly injurious to their future interests. It was now determined to dismiss the Speedwell, and such part of the whole company as could not be accom-

modated in the Mayflower.* It was decided that Mr. Cushman and his family, and others, about twenty in all, should
return to London. Another sad parting scene occurred, and
the *Mayflower*, on the sixth day of September, once more
spread her canvas to a favorable breeze. But the fair prospects, which cheered the pilgrims when leaving the shores of
England for the last time, were soon clouded; contrary
winds opposed their progress; fierce storms assailed them;
the upper works of the ship were injured, and she became
leaky; one of the main beams was wrenched from its place;
serious doubts existed whether it would be practicable to
pursue the voyage; and a consultation of the principal seamen and passengers was held. But the ship proving strong
under water, the beam was restored to its proper position by
means of a screw, strongly secured by the carpenter, and
they continued their voyage. "And so, after many boister-
ous storms, in which they could bear no sail, but were forced
to lie at hull for many days together, after long being at sea,
(on the ninth of November) they fell in with the land, called
Cape Cod, the which being made and certainly known to
be it, they were not a little joyful."

* Though it is not improbable that, as respected some of the passengers
appointed to return in the Speedwell with Mr. Cushman, reference was
had to their relative ability to aid in the arduous labor of establishing the
intended colony, there seems no reason to conclude, as some historians
have intimated and asserted, that they were *timid* or *discouraged*. The
spirit, not of fear, but of a sound mind, appears to have generally pervaded the whole body of emigrants; and Robert Cushman was the last
individual among them on whose character for self-devotion, intelligence
and courage, the slightest breath of suspicion should rest.

FOREFATHERS' ROCK.

'A rock in the wilderness welcomed our sires
From bondage far over the dark rolling sea ;
On that holy altar they kindled the fires,
Jehovah ! which glow in our bosoms for thee."

ANONYMOUS.

" In grateful adoration now,
Upon the barren sands they bow.
What tongue of joy e'er woke such prayer
As bursts in desolation there !
What arm of strength e'er wrought such power
As waits to crown that feeble hour ! "

SPRAGUE.

THE Forefathers' Rock, so attractive to the curiosity of visitors, excepting that part of it which is now enclosed within the railing in front of Pilgrim Hall, retains the same position it occupied two hundred and thirty-five years ago, when the founders of New England first landed on our shores, and introduced the arts of civilization, the institutions of religion, civil government and education, upon the basis of just and equal rights ; which, from that memorable day to the present time, have secured the general good of the whole community to an extent probably unexampled in any equal period of human experience.

" It is not a little curious that one loose rock on the shore of Plymouth harbor should have become so famous as is that called the ' Pilgrim Rock,' where there is not known in the township a single ledge save those the fisherman reaches with his lead at various points of the coast. ' Pilgrim Rock' is one of these boulders — itself an older pilgrim than those who landed on it. It is an extremely hard variety of Sienitic granite, of a dark gray color. The mica is

2*

in very small quantity, in fine black particles. The rock, by its rounded edges, bears evidence of its rolled character, as well as of the attempts to break specimens from it; which fortunately its extreme hardness renders seldom successful. The rock is now in two pieces, each piece about four feet through." * That part now at the water's side is about six and a half feet in diameter, and is situated on the south side of the store now occupied by Phineas Wells, at the head of Hedge's wharf, a few feet only from the same.

The visitor frequently inquires, Is this the *veritable* rock which first received the Pilgrims? Happily, we are able to answer his question with perfect confidence.

Besides the general and undisputed tradition which designates it as that on which the fathers landed, it was ascertained to be the same on an interesting occasion in the life of Elder Thomas Faunce, the last ruling elder in the first church of Plymouth; who was born in the year 1646, and died in the year 1745, at the advanced age of ninety-nine years. In the year 1741, the elder, upon learning that a wharf was about to be built near or over the rock which, up to that period, had kept its undisturbed position at the water's edge, and fearing that the march of improvement might subject it to injury, expressed much uneasiness. Though residing three miles from the village of Plymouth, and then in declining health, he left home, and, in the presence of many citizens, pointed out the rock we have described as being that one which the Pilgrims, with whom he was contemporary and well acquainted, had uniformly declared to be the same on which they landed in 1620. Upon this occasion this venerable and excellent man took a

* Extract from a Geological account of Plymouth.

..nal le. ?e of this cherished memorial of the fathers. The circumstances above related were frequently mentioned by the late Hon. Ephraim Spooner, deceased, who was present upon the occasion connected with Elder Faunce. He was deacon of the church of Plymouth forty-one years, and fifty-two years town-clerk, and died March, 1818, aged eighty-three years. The same information was communicated by Mrs. Joanna White, widow of Gideon White, deceased, who was intimately acquainted in the family of Elder Faunce. She died in 1810, aged ninety-five years. And the same account has been transmitted by other aged persons, now deceased, within the recollection of many now living.

On the anniversary celebration of the landing of the fathers, in 1817, the late Rev. Horace Holly, deceased, delivered the customary address, and upon the morning of that day had some hours' conversation with Deacon Spooner, above mentioned, in relation to early times; and, among other interesting reminiscences, learned from him the incidents above narrated. Deacon Spooner had, for many years, been accustomed to read the hymn "Hail, Pilgrims," line by line, according to an ancient practice of the church, and on this occasion officiated for the last time. Mr. Holly, inspired by his theme and the interview, in the course of his eloquent address, happily observed: "Our venerable friend knew and conversed with Elder Faunce, who personally knew the first settlers; so Polycarp conversed with St. John, the beloved disciple of our Saviour."

In the year 1775, some ardent whigs, to render available the patriotic associations connected with the rock, undertook its removal to the town square, with the intention to place over it a liberty pole, as an excitement to vigorous efforts in

the approaching revolutionary struggle, and to quicken the
zeal of such persons as hesitated to join the standard of in-
dependence.   In this attempt at removal the rock split
asunder, which excited, as tradition avers, great surprise
among the citizens present, and by some was construed into
a favorable omen, indicating the final separation of the colonies from the mother country.   This unexpected accident
led to some hesitation among the excited group assembled,
and the conclusion was to lower the under part of the rock
into its original bed, from which it had been elevated, and
the other part was drawn by twenty yoke of oxen to the
town square ; when the far-famed liberty pole was speedily
erected over it, on which an appropriate poetic effusion of
some ardent son of liberty was placed, urging the citizens to
renewed efforts in the cause of their country.

These circumstances, in connection with the increasing
curiosity of visitors, each of whom sought a small fragment,
if no more, have sensibly diminished the size of the rock,
rendering it necessary to prevent such depredations in future, lest the " first stepping-stone to those who should come
after " might at last fail of a " local habitation and a name."
These considerations, it is hoped, may in some degree relieve the disappointment occasionally expressed by strangers,
on first viewing this rock.   It should further be recollected
that a mammoth rock of granite would have been inconven-
ient for the purpose of landing, particularly to the women
and children who shared in the glorious event.   It has long
been a subject of regret that this enduring memorial of the
landing has remained in its present apparently neglected
condition, and we doubt not that New England, aided by her
patriotic sons throughout the nation, will cheerfully bestow
the means required for such improvements around it as the

public wishes and feelings demand, and for the final erection of an appropriate monument in honor of the fathers. Under the head of "Pilgrim Society," the reader will find some account of the progress of this matter.

On the fourth of July, 1834, that part of the rock which had been taken to the town square, was removed and placed in front of Pilgrim Hall, enclosed within an iron railing, prepared for its reception, on which is inscribed the names of the forty-one individuals who subscribed the compact on board the Mayflower, at Cape Cod harbor, Nov. 11th, 1620.

The honor of first stepping upon the rock is claimed by the descendants of Mary Chilton, in her behalf, and also by those of John Alden, in his favor — resting upon tradition in both families. It is evident that neither of them had the honor of *first* landing upon it. This occurred on the 11th of December, 1620, old style, corresponding to December 21st, new style, when the shallop of the Mayflower, having left on the 6th of December the harbor of Cape Cod, coasted along the shore, and was finally driven by storm into Plymouth, and found shelter at Clark's Island. The shallop at this time had on board ten of the pilgrims, who had signed the compact, whose names were as follows : Capt. Standish, Master Carver, William Bradford, Edward Winslow, John Tilley, Edward Tilley, John Howland, Richard Warren, Stephen Hopkins, and Edward Dotey, from which it appears that John Alden was not among the number who first stepped on the rock. Besides the ten pilgrims above named, there were eight seamen, making in all eighteen persons. The Mayflower arrived and anchored about one and a half miles from the town, between Clark's Island and Beach Point. When the passengers went on shore, in the ship's boat, it is not improbable that some rivalship occurred between Mary Chilton and John Alden, as to which should first land on the rock; and the young gallant doubtless yielded his claim to the lady, as might have been expected of the modest youth, who afterwards became the favored choice of Priscilla Mullens.*

* Tradition states that Capt. Standish, after the death of his wife, proposed a matrimonial alliance with Miss Mullens, the daughter of William Mullens, and that John Alden was engaged as the messenger to announce his wishes. But the lady, it seems, not so much enamored with the military renown of Standish as by the engaging address of the youthful advocate, dexterously hinted her opinion to that effect ; by which course an end was put to all hope on the part of the distinguished military leader of the Pilgrims.

Without intending to discredit this ancient tradition, which has so long held its claim undisputed in the families descended from Alden and Chilton, there seem to be sufficient grounds for entering a protest against the unbounded license assumed by fiction, originating from various quarters, both in a verbal and written form, in relation to this amusing incident of early times. The following facts are therefore stated as aids to truth in the matter. Rose, the wife of Standish, died Jan. 29th, and William Mullens, the father of Priscilla, Feb. 21, 1621. Edward Winslow married the widow of Wm. White, May 12, 1621, it being the first marriage which occurred after the landing. John Alden and Miss Mullens were probably married in the spring of 1622, or the preceding fall.

Bearing in mind these facts, it seems hardly *credible* that Standish, so soon after the decease of his beautiful and excellent wife, — for such tradition assures us she was, — that within a month, " nay, not so much," he should propose a renewal of the matrimonial bonds, so suddenly severed, in the saddest hour of even Pilgrim experience. It is gratifying in this case that tradition and the facts of history may pleasantly harmonize under the guidance of rational probabilities, leaving us to infer that no leave was asked of Mr. Mullens, in person or by proxy, to visit his daughter ; but that the embassy of Alden was to the maiden herself, some time after; that, as no cattle were imported into the colony till the year 1623, of course no animal of that species was here found, to be " covered " with a " handsome piece of broadcloth ; " that, as the town of Barnstable was not settled till the year 1639, some eighteen years subsequent, when all the parties were happily settled in the same neighborhood in old Duxbury ;

The conclusion, therefore, of the late Samuel Davis, Esq., may be safely adopted, when he says : " We are disposed, however, to generalize the anecdote. The first generation doubtless knew who came on shore in the first boats; the second generation related it with less identity; the fourth with still less : like the stone thrown on the calm lake, the circles, well defined at first, become fainter as they recede: For the purpose of the arts, however, a female figure, typical of faith, hope, and charity, is well adapted."

The late Dr. Dwight, President of Yale College, who visited Plymouth in the year 1800, expresses himself, respecting the rock, in the following manner : " No New Englander who is willing to indulge his native feelings, can stand upon the rock where our ancestors set the first foot after their arrival on the American shore, without experiencing emotions very different from those which are excited by any common object of the same nature. No New Englander could be willing to have that rock buried and forgotten. Let him reason as much, as coldly and ingeniously as he pleases, he will still regard that spot with emotions wholly different from those excited by other places of equal or greater importance."

therefore the bridal party and the novel cavalcade, which figure so largely in the story, on proceeding to and returning from the nuptial ceremonies of the *transported* lovers, are matters assignable to some after period, when time and circumstances rendered them entirely suitable and appropriate. We are justified in assuming that a " flirtation " actually occurred at the commencement of " good old colony times," and that *Cupid* and *Mars* were in open conflict — that Miss Mullens was irresistibly attractive in person, manners and character, since a military hero was *fairly* conquered, never before known to surrender, being severely but not mortally wounded ; as a certain skilful lady, who came over in the ship Ann, in the year 1623, and became his second wife, was able to effect a perfect cure.

"This rock has become an object of veneration in the United States. I have seen bits of it carefully preserved in several towns of the Union. Does not this sufficiently show that all human power and greatness is in the soul of man? Here is a stone which the feet of a few outcasts pressed for an instant, and the stone becomes famous; it is ·treasured by a great nation; its very dust is shared as a relic. And what has become of the gateways of a thousand palaces? Who cares for them?" *

"Beneath us is the rock on which New England received the feet of the pilgrims. We seem even to behold them, as they struggle with the elements, and with toilsome efforts gain the shore. We listen to the chiefs in council; we see. the unexampled exhibition of female fortitude and resignation; we hear the whisperings of youthful impatience, and we see, what a painter of our own has also represented by his pencil, chilled and shivering childhood, houseless but for a mother's arms, couchless but for a mother's breast, till our own blood almost freezes. The mild dignity of CARVER and of BRADFORD; the decisive and soldier-like air of STANDISH; the devout BREWSTER; the enterprising ALLERTON; the general firmness and thoughtfulness of the whole band; their conscious joy for dangers escaped; their deep solicitude about dangers to come; their trust in Heaven; their high religious faith, full of confidence and anticipation:— all these seem to belong to this place, and to be present upon this occasion, to fill us with reverence and admiration." †

The growing curiosity of the public, so often expressed by visitors, to learn every circumstance connected with the

---

* De Tocqueville's work on America.
† Webster's Centennial Address, Dec. 22, 1820.

history of Forefather's Rock, induces the author to present the following additional statements and remarks, prepared after a very thorough reëxamination of existing records, which are fully confirmed by traditionary information obtained from many aged persons, in frequent conversations, within the last fifty years. These statements were published in reply to a communication which appeared in the *Old Colony Memorial* of January 15th, 1853, signed, "A Descendant of John Alden." This writer appears to have misapprehended not only some traditional testimony, but the true application of one or more historical facts, leading him to inferences not warranted by a just estimate of the whole evidence applicable to the matters under consideration.

"JOHN ALDEN, MARY CHILTON, AND PLYMOUTH ROCK.

"I have attentively perused the communication of your intelligent correspondent, which appeared in the *Memorial* of January 15th; and though it contains many interesting facts and remarks, in connection with the conflicting traditionary accounts respecting John Alden and Mary Chilton, I cannot but regard some of the *inferences* and *opinions* of the writer as liable to strong objections. Considering the subject, therefore, as opening a field of inquiry as yet not wholly exhausted, I shall venture to enter it as a humble gleaner of truth; not without the hope that something may be garnered from the scattered fragments of history and tradition applicable to the questions at issue, and tending to afford the means of just conclusions, in reference to a pleasing incident of early times, which should still be retained among Pilgrim reminiscences, unless fairly excluded

3

by testimony of an indisputable character. The tradition,
as stated by your correspondent to have been received by
the Hon. Beza Hayward, deceased, from Ann Taylor, is as
follows : — 'The late Hon. Beza Hayward, a native of
Bridgewater, a graduate of Harvard in the class of 1772,
a representative, senator, councillor, and finally register
of probate at Plymouth for many years, and until his
death, soon after leaving college, or before, kept a school in
Milton. While there he became acquainted with the widow,
Ann Taylor, then ninety-four years old (relict of John
Taylor, and grand-daughter of John Winslow, of Boston),
claiming, like himself, a descent from Mary Chilton. This
old lady communicated to him the following family tradition, which he often related in our presence and hearing,
and, as nearly as we can now recollect, in the following
words : " Mary Chilton, when going ashore in the boat,
said she would be the first to land — jumped out, and, wet-
ting her feet, ran to the shore." Nothing was said about a
rock, or other locality. Now, history helps us to a very
probable solution and explanation of this tradition, and one
entirely conformable to the terms of it and to the situation
of the place where it is recorded to have occurred. We are
told that the Mayflower anchored in Cape harbor, on Saturday, the 11th (21st) of November, 1620, and that on Monday, the 13th (23d), "the women were set on shore to
wash their clothes." Now, Mary Chilton, being a young
girl, what can be more likely than that she was one of the
women in the boat, and that she did what the tradition states
her to have done ? And this is understood to be all her
descendants have ever claimed for her.' This account of the
tradition, though in the main correct, varies in its phraseol-
ogy from that of the late Dr. Thatcher, whose wife was a

descendant of Mary Chilton. He states it in these words : 'But the following traditionary anecdote has ever been regarded as correct among the Chilton descendants. The Mayflower, having arrived in the harbor from Cape Cod, Mary Chilton entered the first landing boat, and looking forward, exclaimed, "I will be the first to step on that rock!" Accordingly, when the boat approached, Mary Chilton was permitted to be the first from the boat who appeared on the rock; and thus her claim was established.' Another version of this tradition is contained in Notes on Plymouth, written in 1815 by the late Samuel Davis, Esq., whose acquaintance with Pilgrim traditions was more extensive, probably, than that of any other person living within the last century. He says: 'There is a tradition as to the person who first leaped upon this rock, when the families came on shore Dec. 11th,* 1620. It is said to have been Mary Chilton. This information comes from a source so correct, as induces us to admit it; and it is a very probable circumstance from the natural impatience of a young person, or any one, after a long confinement on shipboard, to reach the land, and to escape from the crowded vessel; and we leave it, therefore, as we find it, in the hands of history and the fine arts.' He further states, 'This tradition, we have reason to believe, is in both families. We are disposed now to generalize the anecdote. The first generation doubtless knew who came on shore in the first boats; the second generation related it with less identity; the third and fourth with still less: like

* The error of this date is evidently corrected by the tenor of the extract itself, which shows that Mr. Davis meant to apply this tradition to a time subsequent, namely, after the Mayflower arrived at Plymouth harbor. Mr. Davis, we believe, afterwards discovered and corrected the evident mistake.

the stone thrown on the calm lake, the circles, well defined at first, become fainter and fainter as they recede. For the purposes of the arts, however, a female figure, typical of faith hope and charity, is well adapted.'

"The writer of this communication, for many years a member of the family of the late Hon. Beza Hayward, above referred to, recollects hearing him frequently relate the tradition, in the truth of which he fully believed ; but he uniformly spoke of it as applicable to the landing at Plymouth, never at Cape Cod ; and, if now living, would doubtless regard the *inference* and opinions of your correspondent, in this matter, not only as *far-fetched*, but strange and unwarrantable, in view of all the probabilities bearing upon the question. In fact, one might as well infer that because Gov. Bradford, in exploring Cape Cod, was unfortunately caught in a *deer trap*, therefore the landing of the Pilgrims, so called, must somehow have been at Long Point. The true import of President Adams' remarks, it is believed, recognizes the existence of the tradition in the Alden family, at the time they were written; and common opinion has, for more than half a century, assigned it a place there. It seems proper to state that the time of landing, December 22d, 1620, was fixed by the 'Old Colony Club,' formed in 1769, whose members were the first to celebrate the event. Soon after the common house was rendered fit for shelter, and probably before the end of January most of the passengers from the Mayflower were landed, though history does not particularly state the exact time or numbers as they came on shore. In your next paper I propose to offer some remarks on the views expressed by your correspondent respecting the rock of Plymouth, with some additional facts of history and tradition, which, it is believed, may be interesting to your readers, and deserving their consideration.

"OLD COLONY."

"JOHN ALDEN, MARY CHILTON, AND PLYMOUTH ROCK.

"MR. EDITOR: In your paper of last week I attempted to show that some of the views and inferences of your correspondent, in relation to the traditions for a long time said to exist among the descendants both of John Alden and Mary Chilton, were liable to many objections, and that a just estimate of probabilities, derived from the best sources of information, divested of the evident mistakes by which these traditions have so often been encumbered, would result in retaining as admissible history at least that which relates to the lady in question. It is now proposed to state the prominent historical facts and traditions relating to the rock of Plymouth, from which the reader may form such conclusions of its size, notoriety, and partial removal, as may seem warranted from the best light of careful investigation. The first designation of this rock, on record, is contained in a document in the second volume of Plymouth Town Records, page 181, dated in 1715, to which the writer's attention was some years ago directed by Isaac P. Davis, Esq., of Boston. This document describes the bounds of First-street (now Leyden-street), and New-street (now North-street), from which the following extract is made : — ' Thence to extend north twenty-one degrees westerly, to a stone and stake set in the ground within the easterly corner bound of New-street, said stake and stones being west eleven degrees northerly, thirty-six foots from the northerly part of a great rock that lieth below the way.' The distance above men-

3*

tiou ;d correspoι ls with the present situation of the rock.
We thus learn ·that in 1715 it acquired the name of a
' great rock,' — probably one reason why it was chosen by
the Pilgrims, as well suited for the desired purpose. This
brief description of the rock coincides with that received
many years ago from Mrs. Jane Palmer, late of Scituate,
deceased, by Mrs. Clark, of this town, now in her eighty-
third year, ·the widow of ·the late John Clark, and sister of
the late Robert Roberts, Esq., whose memory of ·past events
is remarkably clear and reliable. Mrs. Palmer was the
widow of John Palmer, and her will appears in the Probate
Records, book 42, pages 303 and 304, dated Oct. 28th,
1795, with a codicil, dated Jan. 28th. 1806, proved May 20th,
1808. The will of the husband is recorded in the same records, book 85, page 82, dated in 1782, and proved in 1794.
Mrs. Palmer was the second daughter of Isaac Doten, of
this town, and aunt of the late Major Benjamin Warren,
and was born November 10th, 1706, according to the first
town-book of births, &c., page 37 ; and therefore, at the
time of her decease, had reached something over the age of
one hundred and one years. Mrs. Clark states that this
aged couple lived together seventy years, and were married
about the year 1724 — a fact confirmed by the records above
named. Mrs. Palmer, living but a short distance from the
rock, recollected frequently seeing it when quite young,
before the building of any wharf had disturbed its quiet
repose at the water's edge. Its form was described as being
somewhat oval and regular, and favorable for the uses which
uniform tradition had always assigned it. The banks of
Cole's hill, and many garden lots in Leyden-street, were, at
this period, frequently marked by a small growth of pine
and cedar saplings, and ·occasional trees of moderate size.

"The next important movement respecting the rock, stands connected with the long-cherished and venerable name of Elder Thomas Faunce, and is generally so well known as hardly to require more than a brief notice. He was the son of John Faunce, who came over in the ship Ann, in the year 1623, and died Nov. 29th, 1653. Thomas Faunce, the elder of the church, was born in 1645 or 6, and died in 1745, at the advanced age of ninety-nine years. Hearing that a wharf was about to be built, in the year 1741, and that the rock, which from youth upward he had regarded as an object of high veneration, was in danger of molestation, he visited Plymouth village, for the last time, a 'distance of three miles from his residence at Eel river, at the age of ninety-five years, and related the early traditions received from his father and other contemporary Pilgrims, and, in the presence of many spectators, declared it the same as that on which the fathers had landed in 1620. The next document in order is ' A Plan of Plymouth, including bays, harbors, and islands, &c., by Charles Blaskowitz, one of the deputy surveyors for North America, and by him presented to Edward Winslow,'Jr., July, 1774.' Edward Winslow was born in 1746, was a graduate of Harvard University, an original member of the Old Colony Club, and eventually removed to Nova Scotia, where he died, and the above-named plan was presented by his sister, Penelope Winslow, to the late Isaac Lothrop, Esq.

"On this map several important historical points are briefly designated, namely, Captain's Mount, Clark's Island, and Plymouth Rock. That relating to the rock is as follows : ' No 1. The place where the settlers above mentioned first landed upon the main, Dec. 22d (N. S.), 1620, upon a large rock, which, in the course of time, being buried in sand, was, by their grateful posterity, dug up and transported to a more public situation, Anno Domini, 1775.'

" We next arrive at the revolutionary period of American history, the year 1775, when, in the language of a venerable patriot,* who served throughout the whole of that eventful struggle, and lived to rejoice in its glorious results, ' The citizens of Plymouth, animated by the spirit of liberty which pervaded the province, and mindful of the precious relic of our forefathers, resolved to consecrate the rock on which they landed to the shrine of liberty.'

" In attempting to raise it from the original bed, it split asunder, and the upper part was taken to Town Square, close by the large elm-tree nearest the market, serving as a support to the memorable liberty-pole erected on that exciting occasion, on which the following lines were posted, as appears from the memorandum attached to them, when first published in the *Old Colony Memorial* of May 4, 1822. ['The following lines were attached to the liberty-pole, erected in 1775, on Forefathers' Rock, and were the production of Mr. James Shurtleff, a cabinet-maker, and now living in Litchfield, Me.']

> ' To wake the sons of Plymouth to oppose
> The daring insults of our country's foes,
> This monumental pole erected stands,
> Raised by a few, but *patriotic* hands ;
> Friends to their country and their country's right,
> In which truth, honor, justice, all unite.
> For these our famed forefathers firmly stood,
> And purchased freedom with heroic blood.
> Let not their sons desert the glorious cause,
> But still maintain our Liberty and Laws,

* The late James Thacher, M. D., surgeon in the United States army during the whole of the war of the revolution.

Nor from what's *right* and *just* like cowards fly ;
We 'll rise like *heroes*, or like *heroes* die ! '

" Fr:m the above memorandum, made by Edward Winslow, Jr., we may justly infer that, after the interesting visit
of Elder Faunce, in 1741, and while the proposed wharf
was in process of construction, the *rock* became 'buried in
sand,' and so it remained till the ardor of the revolutionary
times released it from obscurity. We have always understood, from those who witnessed its removal in 1775, that it
was first perpendicularly raised some feet above its original
bed on the shore, and that blocks were placed under it,
which still remain there. This part of the rock was again
removed, July 4th, 1834, and enclosed within the iron railing
in front of Pilgrim Hall, from whence we trust it will, at
no distant day, be once more transported and reünited to its
kindred stock. Having thus brought our promised labors
to a close, and in some manner concentrated the history of
Plymouth Rock, we must be permitted briefly to quote your
correspondent, who says, when speaking of the rock, ' However this may be, we have little reason to think Mary Chilton ever saw it, or that John Alden, first or last, was ever
upon it.' Now this language appears too sweeping, and the
concurrent facts and traditions referred to in the present
communication, it is believed, will establish a different conclusion, rendering it highly probable that both of them
would hardly suffer so prominent an object, and used on an
occasion so interesting, to escape their frequent attention.
The founders of New England had a high vocation assigned
them in the order of Divine Providence, and wrought out a
glorious work for their posterity.

" When, in the progress of human events, that posterity

was roused to action by the notes of freedom and indepen-
dence which patriotism sounded along every hill-top and
valley, they naturally sought to rekindle the hallowed
thoughts that time had clustered around the speechless
rock, practically illustrating the beautiful creations of
poetic genius, and finding in the ancient haunts of Pilgrim
times, 'tongues in trees, books in the running brooks,
sermons in stones, and good in everything.' "

THE SHIP MAYFLOWER.

" Nobly the Mayflower bows
    While the dark wave she ploughs
        On to the West ;
    Till from the tempest's shock
    Proudly she lands her flock
    Where on Old Plymouth Rock
        Freedom found rest."   DAWES.

THE progress of time and the course of human events
have contributed to invest the fortunes of the Mayflower
with the deepest interest, and to confer upon this once
peaceful herald of freedom to our shores a celebrity achieved,
perhaps, by no other vessel known to the annals of maritime
enterprise. .

Her first voyage across the Atlantic was commenced
under circumstances of obscurity hardly attracting the
curiosity of the passing world, by men whose previous history had formed a school of the severest trials in defence
of Christian liberty, eminently adapted to prepare them for
the still sharper conflicts and perils which overhung the
dubious horizon of their future prospects. High and holy
as were their aspirations after righteousness, truth and free-

dom, the most vivid imagination among them must have utterly failed to comprehend the vast influence they were destined to exert on the whole current of human affairs.

> " They little thought how pure a light,
> With years, should gather round that day ;
> How love should keep their memories bright,
> How wide a realm their sons should sway.''   BRYANT

But results have followed in the wake of the Mayflower auspiciously affecting the condition of millions ; results which, if the past affords any just indications of the future, present but faint glimpses only of what are destined to appear in ages to come.

The Mayflower, of one hundred and eighty tons burthen, Capt. Jones, was chartered by the Merchant Adventurers of London to transport a part of the Leyden Church to America, the Speedwell having been purchased in Holland for the same purpose. The conditions upon which the Pilgrims contracted with the Merchant Adventurers of London, as they were called, for their transportation to America, indicate the exhausted state of their pecuniary means, and would probably never have obtained their assent under circumstances not imposed by absolute necessity. We place these conditions before the reader, that a just estimate may be formed of the " hard terms " upon which the emigration of our fathers depended. They were preserved in Hubbard's History, but no date is mentioned. Judging from the best sources of information, they were probably signed, after much delay, and the occurrence of various difficulties, some time in May or June of 1620.

" An^{a} 1620. July 1.
" 1. The adventurers† & planters doe agree, that every

person that goeth being aged 16 years and upward, be rated at $10^{£1}$, and ten pounds to be accounted a single share.

"2. That he that goeth in person, and furnisheth him selfe out with $10^{£1}$, either in money or other provissions, be accounted as haveing $20^{£1}$ in stock, and in y^e devission shall receive a double share.

"3. The persons transported & y^e adventurers shall continue their joynt stock & partnership togeather y^e space of 7 years, (excepte some unexpected impedimente doe cause y^e whole company to agree otherwise,) during which time, all profits & benifits that are gott by trade, traffick, trucking, working, fishing, or any other means of any person or persons, remaine still in ye comone stock untill ye division.

"4. That at their coming ther, they chose out such a number of fitt persons, as may furnish their ships and boats for fishing upon ye sea; imploying the rest in their several faculties upon ye land, as building houses, tilling, and planting ye ground, and makeing such comodities as shall be most usefull for ye collonie.

"5. That at ye end of ye 7 years, ye capitall & profits, viz., the houses, lands, goods and chatles, be equally devided betwixte ye adventurers, and planters, wch done, every man shall be free from other of them of any debt or detrimente concerning this adventure.

"6. Whosoever cometh to ye colonie hereafter, or putteth any into ye stock, shall at the ende of y^u 7 years be alowed proportionably to ye time of his so doing.

"7. He that shall carie his wife & children, or servants, shall be alowed for everie person now aged 16 years & upward, a single share in ye devision, or if he provid them necessaries, a duble share, or if they be between 10 year old and 16, then 2 of them to be reconed for a person, both in transportation and devision.

" 8. That such children as now goe, and are under ye age of ten years, have noe other shar in ye devision, but 50 acers of unmanured land.

" 9. That such persons as die before ye 7 years be expired, their executors to have their parte or sharr at ye devision, proportionably to ye time of their life in ye collonie.

" 10. That all such persons as are of this collonie, are to have their meate, drink, apparell, and all provissions out of ye comon stock and goods of said collonie."

These conditions, as we have previously observed, obtained at last but a reluctant assent on the part of those concerned in the enterprise of emigration, and Robert Cushman, their principal agent, as Gov. Bradford states, " answered the complaints that, unless they so ordered the conditions, the whole design would have fallen to the ground; and, necessity, they said, having no law, they were constrained to be silent."

The intelligent reader will not fail to perceive that the foregoing articles of agreement between the planters and adventurers, which, in fact, might very properly be termed articles of copartnership, contain no provisions from which it should be inferred that a community of goods, in the usual acceptation of that phrase, was ever intended or really existed among the Pilgrims; nor can it be affirmed with truth that any other feature of their civil or religious organization justifies such an assumption; therefore no sufficient grounds exist for the hasty and inconsiderate opinions

4

that such was the case, advanced by various historians, both of earlier and later times.

History affords but scanty information respecting the merchant adventurers. Many of them were doubtless influenced in their connection with the Pilgrims by the hope of gain, while Sherley, Hatherly, Collier, Thomas, Beaucham, Ling, and some others, were guided by far higher aims, in which considerations of profit held but a secondary place.

The celebrated Capt. John Smith, whose efficient services and romantic adventures in the early settlement of Virginia are so generally known, writes, in 1624, as follows : " The adventurers which raised the stock to begin and supply this plantation were about seventy, — some merchants, some handicraftsmen,— some adventuring great sums, some small, as their affection served. These dwelt most about London, knit together by a voluntary combination in a society, without constraint or penalty, aiming to do good and plant religion."

But, however pure might have been the motives which influenced the original members of this association, its subsequent history shows that certain ingredients of human imperfection were destined, in a few years, to render it unavailable for executing the purposes which it seemed at first designed to accomplish. The sad intelligence, conveyed by the Mayflower on her return to London, of the sufferings, sickness and death, involving the loss of one half of those who had originally embarked, produced a disheartening effect on the most zealous friends of colonial enterprize, and a strong feeling of distrust among others whose pecuniary interests were endangered. This state of feeling, in the course of a few years, led to open disaffection, while the necessary supplies required for the wants of an infant colony were refused, though promised to be furnished. This state of things growing still worse, as time progressed, a compromise between the parties was effected, by which the adventurers were paid the sum of eighteen hundred pounds sterling. This negotiation was entrusted to Mr. Isaac Allerton, by means of whose discretion, talents and perseverance, it was at last, through many perplexing difficulties, satisfactorily adjusted to the mutual advantage of all concerned. The document by which this desirable result was effected bears date November 26th, 1626, and was ratified in 1627, and may be found in the Mass. Hist. Collections, vol. 3d, 1st series, pp. 47, 48, and is subscribed by forty-two of the merchant adventurers.

The slow growth of the colony during the first ten years after the landing has often been ascribed to what has been termed the narrow bigotry and stern intolerance of the Pilgrims in religious concerns; but the true cause, we are fully persuaded, may far more justly be traced to the dissensions and conflicting interests continually existing among the merchant adventurers, which left the colonists almost single-handed to contend against the difficulties by which they were surrounded, and eventually leading to the withdrawal of that further coöperation and pecuniary aid which they had good reason to expect. On this subject the author before quoted — Smith — thus remarks: "These disasters" (referring to the hardships endured by the Pilgrims during the first winter) "made such disagreements among the adventurers in England, who began to repent, and rather lose all than longer continue the charge, being out of purse six or seven thousand pounds, accounting my books and their relations as old almanacs. But the planters, rather than leave the country, concluded absolutely to supply themselves, and to all their adventurers pay them for nine years two hundred pounds yearly, without any further account; where more than six hundred adventurers for *Virginia*, for more than two hundred thousand pounds, had not sixpence." This impartial testim:ny to the upright character of the Pilgrims, coming from so competent a judge, is deserving of special consideration.

The following laudable act of the Plymouth Colony General Court towards one of the merchant adventurers, who had fallen " to decay," is extracted from the Court Orders and Grants of Land : " 1660, Prence, Governor. It is ordered by the Court that twenty pounds shall be given and sent to Mr. Ling, one of the Merchant Venturers att our first beginnings, being fallen to decay and having felt great extremity and poverty, the said twenty pounds being bestowed on him towards his relief, which is to bee proposed to the several Townships of this jurisdiction, that if any one shall give voulentary it shall be put into such a way as may conduce to the end aforesaid ; and what such contribution will fall short of the said twenty pounds, that it bee made up out of the Countrey stocke by the Treasurer."

· As before stated, the Mayflower sailed from Southampton, August 5th, 1620,* discovered Cape Cod the 9th, and anchored in the harbor of Provincetôwn, the 11th day of

---

* " Behold the little Mayflower, rounding now the southern Cape of England, filled with husbands, and wives, and children, families of righteous men, under ' covenant with God and each other,' ' to lay some good foundation for religion,' engaged both to make and to keep their own laws, expecting to supply their own wants and bear their own burdens, assisted by none but the God in whom they trust. Here are the hands of industry ! the germs of liberty ! the dear pledges of order ! and the sacred beginnings of a home ! " — *D. Bushnell's Address, at New York, Dec. 22d, 1849.*

November, 1620, Old Style,— 21st, New Style,— having been ninety-eight days on the voyage to that place.

The proceedings at this time are thus related by Gov. Bradford : " This day, before we came to harbor, observing some not well affected to unity and concord, but gave some appearance of faction, it was thought good there should be an association and agreement, that we should combine together in one body, and to submit to such government and governors as we should by common consent agree to make and choose, and set our hands to this that follows, word for word :

" ' In the name of God, Amen. We, whose names are underwritten, the loyal subjects of our dread sovereign lord, King James, by the grace of God, of Great Britain, France, and Ireland, king, defender of the faith, &c., having undertaken, for the glory of God, and advancement of the Christian faith, and honor of our king and country, a voyage to plant the first colony in the northern parts of Virginia, do, by these presents, solemnly and mutually, in the presence of God and one of another, covenant and combine ourselves together into a civil body politic, for our better ordering and preservation, and furtherance of the ends aforesaid ; and by virtue hereof to enact, constitute and frame such just and equal laws, ordinances, acts, constitutions, and offices, from time to time, as shall be thought most meet and convenient for the general good of the colony ; unto which we promise all due submission and obedience. In witness whereof we have hereunder subscribed our names, at Cape Cod, the 11th of November, in the year of the reign of our sovereign lord, King James, of England, France and Ireland, the eighteenth, and of Scotland, the fifty-fourth, Anno Domini, 1620.' "

4*

[Mr. John Carver †	 8	* Edward Fuller,†	. . . 8
William Bradford,†	 2	* John Turner,	 8
Mr. Edward Winslow,†	. . 5	Francis Eaton,†	 8
Mr. William Brewster,†	. . 6	* James Chilton,	 8
Mr. Isaac Allerton,†	. . . 6	* John Crackston,	. . . 2
Capt. Miles Standish,†	. . 2	John Billington,†	. . . 4
John Howland,	. . . . . .	* Moses Fletcher,	 1
John Alden,	 1	* Deogry Priest,	 1
Mr. Samuel Fuller,	 2	* Thomas Williams,	. . . 1
* Mr. Christopher Martin,†	. 4	Gilbert Winslow,	. . . 1
* Mr. William Mullins,†	. . 5	* Edmund Margeson,	. . . 1
* Mr. William White,†	. . . 5	Peter Brown,	 1
Mr. Richard Warren,	. . . 1	* Richard Brittebice,	. . 1
* John Goodman,	 1	George Soule,	. . . . .
* Mr. Stephen Hopkins,†	. . 8	* Richard Clarke,	. . . 1
* Edward Tilly,†	 4	Richard Gardiner,	. . . 1
* John Tilly,†	 8	* John Allerton,	 1
Francis Cook,	 2	* Thomas English,	 1
* Thomas Rogers,†	 2	Edward Dotey,	 1
* Thomas Tinker,	 8	Edward Leister,	. . ——
* John Ridgdale,†	 2		101]

The above list of the signers of the celebrated compact, is taken from Prince's New England Chronology, vol. i., p. 85, Edit. 1736, which is preceded by the following remarks : "To this instrument Mr. *Morton* sets the *subscribers* in the *following order ;* but their *names corrected,* with *titles* and *families,* I take from the *list* at the end of Governor Bradford's folio manuscript. Only this I observe, that out of modesty, he omits the title of Mr. to his own name, which he ascribes to several others."

The figures opposite each name designate the number in each family. Those having an asterisk (*) prefixed, died before the end of March. Those which are marked with an obelisk (†) brought their wives with them. One of those attached to the name of Samuel Fuller was his servant,

William Bradford

Jno: Winslow

Willm Bressler

Myles Standish

Isaac Allerton

John Bradford

Tho: Prence

Nathaniell Morton

Thomas Cushman

Josr Winslow

Constnt Southworth

Tho: Southworth

1649

Tho Willett

Tobias ...

Kenelm Winslow

Mrs. ...

1675

John Tomson

1649

Margaret Bickes

1632

Samuell ...

1632

John Alden

1671

Georgy Somerson:

1649

...

James Cudworth

1653

named William Butten, a youth who died Nov. 6th, on the passage. George Soule was of Winslow's family. Edward Dotey and Edward Leister were of Stephen Hopkins' family. Christopher Martin, Richard Warren, Stephen Hopkins, John Billington, Edward Dotey, Edward Leister, and perhaps some others, joined them at London.

The number against the name of William White, does not include that of his son Peregrine, born in Cape Cod harbor.

John Howland was of Governor Carver's family; John Allerton and Thomas English were seamen. Dr. Young, in his Chronicles of the Pilgrims, page 122, remarks that "the list includes the servant who died; the latter ought not to be counted. The number *living* at the signing of the compact, was, therefore, only one hundred."

"So there were just one hundred and one who sailed from Plymouth in England, and just as many arrived in Cape Cod harbor. And this is the solitary number, who, for an undefiled conscience and the love of pure Christianity, first left their native and pleasant land, and encountered all the toils and hazards of the tumultuous ocean, in search of some uncultivated region in North Virginia, where they might quietly enjoy their religious liberties, and transmit them to posterity, in hopes that none would follow to disturb or vex them." The same day Mr. John Carver was appointed their Governor.

"These were the founders of the Colony of New Plymouth. The settlement of this colony occasioned the settlement of Massachusetts Bay, which was the source of all the other colonies of New England. Virginia was in a dying state, and seemed to revive and flourish from the example of New England.

" I am not preserving from oblivion the names of heroes whose chief merit is the overthrow of cities, provinces and empires, but the names of the founders of a flourishing town and colony, if not of the whole British empire in North America." — *Hutchinson*, xi. 462.

" This is perhaps the only instance, in human history, of that positive original social compact, which speculative philosophers have imagined as the only legitimate source of government. Here was a unanimous and personal assent, by all the individuals of the community, to the association by which they became a nation. It was the result of circumstances and discussions, which had occurred during their passage from Europe, and is a full demonstration that the nature of civil government, abstracted from the political institutions of their native country, had been an object of their serious meditation. The settlers of all the European colonies had contented themselves with the powers conferred upon them by their respective charters, without looking beyond the seal of the royal parchment for the measure of their rights, and the rule of their duties."*

Various excursions were afterwards made, in pursuit of some place for settlement, but without success, and conflicting opinions arose as to the measures it was most expedient to adopt; while the approach of winter, and the impatience of Capt. Jones, rendered their situation full of perplexity, and beset with perils.

Under these circumstances, on the 6th of December, another expedition was resolved upon, the day previous having been stormy. Ten men, who were willing to embark, were appointed, namely, Capt. Standish, Master Carver,

---

*John Quincy Adams' Oration, Dec. 22, 1802.

William Bradford, Edward Winslow, John Tilley, Edward Tilley, John Howland, and three of London, Richard Warren, Stephen Hopkins and Edward Dotte, and two seamen, John Alderton and Thomas English. Of the ship's company there went Master Clark and Master Coppin, the master-gunner, and three sailors. It was late in the day before the preparations for the expedition were completed, and the weather was extremely severe. After clearing from the ship, it required some time to get under way, on account of a sandy point, during which two of their men were sick, and Edward Tilley had nearly swooned. The gunner was also sick, and so remained all that day and night.

After clearing the sandy point, they coasted six or seven leagues by the shore, landed and spent the night; on the 7th visited several places, and probably passed the night at Great Meadow Creek, in Eastham; and on the 8th, about five o'clock in the morning, were suddenly attacked by the Indians. The attack was repulsed with great intrepidity on the part of the Pilgrims, and the Indians retreated with precipitation.

After returning thanks to God for their wonderful deliverance, they took to their shallop, and called the place *" The First Encounter."* The wind being favorable, they sailed along the coast of Barnstable Bay, about forty-five miles, but saw no river or creek convenient for landing. After sailing an hour or two, snow and rain commenced falling; the sea became rough, the hinges of the rudder were broken, and it could no longer be used, but two men supplied its place with oars. The ocean heaved with increasing agitation, and they were in great anxiety and danger. The night was fast gathering around them. At this trying moment, Master Coppin bid them be of good cheer, for he

saw the land; but, as they drew near it, the gale increased,
and heavy sail being set, in order to reach the harbor before
dark, the mast was split in three pieces, and the shallop
was threatened with destruction. "Yet, by God's mercy,"
says Gov. Bradford, "we had the flood with us, and struck
into the harbor. The pilot, who had bid the company be of
good cheer, was deceived; and when arriving at the harbor
exclaimed, 'Lord be merciful to us! my eyes never saw this
place before;' and he and the master's mate would have
run the shallop ashore in a cove full of breakers, had not
the seaman who steered bid them that rowed, 'if they were
men, about with her, or else they were all cast away;' 'the
which they did with all speed,' and, although it was dark
and rainy, they succeeded in securing a safe shelter under
the lee of a small island, where they spent the night." *

In the morning they marched over the island, but found
no inhabitants, making it their rendezvous, being Saturday,
the ninth day of December. "On the Sabbath day we rested,
and on Monday we sounded the harbor, and found it a very
good harbor for our shipping. We marched into the land,
and found divers corn-fields, and little running brooks, a
place very good for situation. So we returned (the 14th)
to our ship, with good news to our people, which did much
comfort our hearts."

During the passage from England a child was born,
named Oceanus, the son of Stephen Hopkins; and the only
death was, on the sixth of November, that of William Butten, a youth, and servant of Dr. Samuel Fuller. On the
6th of December, and while at Cape Cod harbor, Dorothy, the wife of Gov. William Bradford, fell overboard

* Clark's Island.

and was drowned. On the 4th of December, Edward Thompson, the servant of William White, died. About the last of November, Peregrine, the son of William White, was born.

The following bill of mortality was collected by Prince :

In December, ...	6
In January, ...	8
In February, . . ᷓ . .	17
In March, ...	13

Total, 44

Of the above-named were signers of the compact, .	21
The wives of Bradford, Winslow, Standish, and Allerton, ...	4
Also, Edward Thomson, a servant of William White, Jasper Carver, boy of Gov. Carver, and Solomon, a son of Christopher Marten, ...	4
Women, children, and servants, most of whose names are unknown, ...	16

44

After the month of March, and before the arrival of the Fortune in November, 1621, six more died, including Gov. Carver and his wife, making the whole number of deaths fifty, and the·number of survivors fifty.

Holmes, in his Annals, vol. 1, page 168, states that "Tradition gives an affecting picture of the infant colony during this critical and distressing period. The dead were buried on the bank, a little distance from the rock where the fathers landed ; and, lest the Indians should take advantage of the weak and wretched state of the English, the graves were levelled and sown for the purpose of concealment."

The prevalance of this great mortality among the first comers, as we learn from early writers on the subject, was not so much owing to an unhealthy climate, as to the use of unwholesome food, which had been injured during a long voyage across the ocean; and still more to the frequent explorations at Cape Cod, in quest of some suitable place of settlement, which occasioned colds of great severity and long continuance, where no relief could be had from sheltered habitations, comfortable firesides, and warm clothing, in the midst of an unusually variable winter.

Some interesting occurrences which happened on board the Mayflower — one of them, connected with John Howland, of honorable memory — were first published in the *Historical and Genealogical Register*, No. 2, vol. 2d, page 187. A letter of Charles Deane, Esq., of Boston, on the subject, copied below, will afford the requisite explanations. Thanks are justly due to him who rescues from the shadowy embrace of early times a single fact which illustrates Pilgrim history, particularly in a field of research already so much explored; where curiosity, however intense, should first acquire the virtue of full-grown patience; since, while asking for much, it rarely gleans but little, and must often obtain its reward in partial disclosures, where larger results were eagerly anticipated, and sometimes ends its persevering toil in hopeless disappointment.

" To the publisher of the New England Historical and Genealogical Register.

" DEAR SIR: The following are extracts from a MS of

Prince's Annals, in his own hand-writing, a fragment of which I have in my possession. Prince has drawn his pen once diagonally across the passages, and did not incorporate them into his work. They are, as will be seen by the initial, quotations from Bradford's Manuscript History (now lost),* which he (Prince) used in compiling his Annals.

"These incidents are interesting, as occurring on board the Mayflower, during her first voyage to New England, and are worthy of preservation; and, as no record of them is to be found in those writers who made use of Bradford's manuscript, it is quite certain that this brief portion of the latter is now for the first time printed.

"From a passage in Prince, page 72, quoting Bradford, it has been supposed that William Butten was the only person who died on the voyage; but the statement is that he was the only 'passenger who died on the voyage.' In the MS. alluded to, this event last named is recorded on the same page with the extracts below.   C. D.

"In a mighty storme, a lustie yonge man (called John Howland) coming upon some occasion above ye gratings was with a seele of ye shipe throwne into ye sea: but it pleased God y^t he caught hould of ye tope saile halliards, which hunge over board, & rane out at length: yet he held his hould (though he was sundrie fadomes under water) till he was hald up by ye same rope to ye brime of ye water, and then with a boat hooke & other means got into ye shipe againe, and his life was saved: and though he was something ill with it, yet he lived many years after, and became a profitable member both in church and comonewealthe.†

* Recently (1855) discovered in England.   † See Appendix, p. 204.

5

"And I may not omite hear a spetiall work of Gods providence. Ther was a proud very profane yonge man, one of y° seamen, of a lustie, able body, which made him the more hauty: he would allway be contemning y° poore people in their sickness & cursing them dayly with greeous execrations, and did not let to tell them that he hoped to help to cast halfe of them over board before they came to their journeys end, and to make mery with what they had: and if he were by any gently reproved, he would curse and swear most bitterly. But it plased God, before they came halfe seas over, to smite this yong man with a greeveous disease, of which he dyed in a desperate maner, and so was him selfe y° first y° was throwne over bord. Thus his curses light on his owne head: and it was an astonishmente to all his fellows, for they noted it to be y° just hand of God upon him."

In conclusion, it would afford high gratification to announce that any additional information had been received respecting the ship Mayflower, subsequent to the voyages already known to our history; but the most thorough investigation of Mr. Hunter, and other gentlemen in England, has thus far failed to accomplish satisfactory results; and, though numerous vessels called by her favorite name are found enrolled on the appropriate records of that period, none can be fairly identified as the one so memorable in our annals, which first bore the intrepid, triumphant founders of an empire to the shores of America and the home of freedom.

The Mayflower, after remaining thirty-four days, left Cape Cod harbor on the 15th of December, and anchored Saturday, the 16th, in Plymouth harbor, about one and a half miles from town, between Clark's Island and Beach Point. Here she remained during the winter, and afforded partial accommodations to the settlers, while preparing their houses on shore. In the spring, as Secretary Morton observes, " They now began to hasten the ship away, which tarried so long by reason of the necessity and danger that lay on them, because so many died, both of themselves and the ship's company likewise, by which they became so few as the master durst not put to sea until those that lived recovered of their sickness, and the winter was over." She sailed on the 5th of April, 1621, having been in Plymouth harbor one hundred and ten days, and arrived at London on the 6th of May — a short passage compared with the previous one, so full of delays, accidents, and dangers.

It was on board this ship that the celebrated compact was signed by forty-one individuals. The last survivors of the Mayflower, who signed the compact, were John Howland, who died in 1672, aged eighty years, and John Alden, who died in 1686, aged eighty-nine. Mary, daughter of Isaac Allerton, and wife of Elder Thomas Cushman, the son of Robert Cushman, died in 1699, aged ninety, and was the last of the one hundred passengers who arrived at Cape Cod harbor.

Mr. Savage observes, in a note to his invaluable edition of Winthrop's History of New England, " That the principal vessels which brought our fathers hither are remembered by their descendants with no small degree of affection. The Mayflower had been a name of renown, without forming a part of this fleet,* because in her came the devoted planters of Plymouth ; and she had also brought, in the year preceding this, some of Higinson's companions to Salem." It thus appears that Plymouth, Salem, and Bos-

---

* The fleet that brought over Gov Winthrop and his colony.

ton, have a direct and peculiar interest to all that pertains
to the successful history and fortunes of this vessel, which
aided in transferring so many individuals from England to
America.

Thomas Carlyle observes, in his recent work: " Look now
to American Saxondom, and at that little fact of the sailing
of the Mayflower, two hundred years ago. It was properly
the beginning of America. There were straggling settlers
in America before ; some material as of a body was there ;
but the soul of it was this. These poor men, driven out of
their own country, and not able to live in Holland, determined on settling in the New World. Black, untamed forests
are there, and wild, savage creatures ; but not so cruel as a
star-chamber hangman. They clubbed their small means
together, hired a ship, the little ship Mayflower, and made
ready to set sail. Ha! these men, I think, had a work.
The weak thing, weaker than a child, becomes strong if it
be a true thing. Puritanism was only despicable, laughable,
then ; but nobody can manage to laugh at it now. It is one
of the strongest things under the sun at present."

With the following inimitable description of the Mayflower, on approaching the New England coast, we close
this section :

" Methinks I see it now, that one solitary, adventurous
vessel, the Mayflower of a forlorn hope, freighted with the
prospects of a future state, and bound across the unknown
sea. I behold it pursuing, with a thousand misgivings, the
uncertain, the tedious voyage. Suns rise and set, and weeks
and months pass, and winter surprises them on the deep,
but brings them not the sight of the wished-for shore. I
see them now scantily supplied with provisions, crowded
almost to suffocation in their ill-stored prison, delayed by

calms, pursuing a circuitous route ; and now driven in fury before the raging tempest, on the high and giddy waves. The awful voice of the storm howls through the rigging. The laboring masts seem straining from their base ; the dismal sound of the pumps is heard ; the ship leaps, as it were, madly, from billow to billow ; the ocean breaks, and settles with engulphing floods over the floating deck, and beats with deadening, shivering weight against the staggered vessel. I see them, escaped from these perils, pursuing their all but desperate undertaking, and landed at last, after a five months' passage, on the ice-clad rocks of Plymouth, weak and weary from the voyage, poorly armed, scantily provisioned, depending on the charity of their ship-master for a draught of beer on board, drinking nothing but water on shore, without shelter, without means, surrounded by hostile tribes. Shut now the volume of history, and tell me, on any principle of human probability, what shall be the fate of this handful of adventurers ? Tell me, man of military science, in how many months were they all swept off by the thirty savage tribes enumerated within the early limits of New England ? Tell me, politician, how long did this shadow of a colony, on which your conventions and treaties had not smiled, languish on the distant coast ? Student of history, compare for me the baffled projects, the deserted settlements, the abandoned adventures, of other times, and find the parallel of this. Was it the winter's storm, beating upon the houseless heads of women and children ; was it hard labor and spare meals ; was it disease ; was it the tomahawk ; was it the deep malady of a blighted hope, a ruined enterprise, and a broken heart, aching in its last moments, at the recollection of the loved and left beyond the sea ; was it some, or all of these united, that hurried

5*

this forsaken company to their melancholy fate? And is it possible that neither of these causes, that not all combined, were able to blast this bud of hope? Is it possible, that from a beginning so feeble, so frail, so worthy not so much of admiration as of pity, there has gone forth a progress so steady, a growth so wonderful, an expansion so ample, a reality so important, a promise, yet to be fulfilled, so glorious?"*

LEYDEN-STREET AND TOWN SQUARE.

> "The murmuring brooks whose waters sweet
> Induced them near to fix their seat,
> Whose gushing banks the springs afford
> That eked along their scanty hoard ;
> There first was heard the cheerful strain,
> Of axe and hammer, saw and plane ;
> Around their humble roofs appeared,
> Through wasting care and labor reared."

THIS street received its present name in the year 1823, in grateful remembrance of the hospitality and kindness shown to the Pilgrims during their residence of eleven years in the city of Leyden.

It was originally named *First-street*, and afterwards is in the records sometimes called Great, and Broad street.

Among the principal considerations which determined the fathers of New England to settle in Plymouth, was its favorable position for defence against the aborigines, and the excellent springs of pure water which abound along its shores, and the precipitous banks of Town Brook. The tide

* Edward Everett's Oration, Dec. 20th, 1824.

flowed for some distance up this stream, and formed a convenient basin for the reception and safe shelter of the shallops and other vessels employed in their early enterprises of fishing and traffic. It may, in some measure, be owing to this circumstance that convenient wharves along the unprotected shores were not sooner constructed.

This stream proceeds from Billington Sea, which is about two miles distant from town. It furnishes a valuable water power in modern times; and in the days of the Pilgrims, and for nearly two centuries after, it abounded with alewives, almost at their doors, affording an important resource for the supply of their wants. On the banks and vicinity of this stream they constructed their humble dwellings, and spent the first winter after their arrival, and experienced the keenest sufferings and sharpest trials. Had not their voyage across the Atlantic been treacherously delayed, and protracted to an unusual length, they would doubtless have arrived in season to secure a shelter before the advance of winter.

They first constructed a frame building, twenty feet square, for their common house, and, soon after, other buildings for their stores and provisions. It stood partly on the lot occupied by the dwelling-house of Captain Samuel D. Holmes, on the south side of Leyden-street, near the declivity of the hill towards the water side. In the year 1801, when some men were digging a cellar on this spot, several tools and a plate of iron were discovered, seven feet below the surface of the earth, which were carefully preserved and highly valued by the late Isaac Lothrop, Esq., who died in 1808, and whose cherished veneration for the fathers will be long remembered by our citizens.

" Thursday, the 28th of December, so many as could

went to work on the hill, where we purposed to build our platform for our ordnance, and which doth command all the plain and the bay, and from whence we may see far into the sea, and might be easier impaled, having two rows of houses and a fair street. So in the afternoon we went to measure out the grounds, and first we took notice how many families there were, willing all single men that had no wives, to join with some family, as they thought fit, that so we might build fewer houses ; which was done, and we reduced them to nineteen families. To greater families we allotted larger plots ; to every person half a pole in breadth, and three in length ; and so lots were cast where every man should lie ; which was done, and staked out. We thought this proportion was large enough at the first for houses and gardens to impale them round, considering the weakness of our people, many of them growing ill with colds ; for our former discoveries in frost and storms, and the wading at Cape Cod, had brought much weakness amongst us, which increased so every day more and more, and after was the cause of many of their deaths."

The following transcript is from the first page of the first book of the Old Colony Records, being the oldest record contained in the same, and is, doubtless, an imperfect plan of the lots assigned, December 28, 1620, as before mentioned.

"The Meersteads* and Garden plotes of those which came first, layed out 1620.

---

* The word *Meersteads* but seldom occurs in the Plymouth Colony Records, and comes from *Meer* or *Mere*, a boundary, and *stead*, a place.

The North Side.	South Side.
	Peter Brown,
	John Goodman,
	Mr. Wm. Brewster.
	High way.

The Street.

	John Billington,
	Mr. Isaak Allerton,
	Francis Cooke,
	Edward Winslow.

Tuesday, the 9th of January, was a reasonable fair day; and we went to labor that day in the building of our town in two rows of houses, for more safety. We divided by lot the plot of ground whereon to build our town, after the proportion formerly allotted. We agreed that every man should build his own house, thinking by that course men would make more haste than working in common. The common house, in which for the first we made our rendezvous, being near finished, wanted only covering, it being about twenty foot square. Some should make mortar, and some gather thatch; so that in four days half of it was thatched. Frost and foul weather hindered us much. This time of the year seldom could we work half the week."

By the words, " The Street," in the above plan, Leyden-street is doubtless meant; and "High way" represents a street which run easterly of what is now called Market-street. This appears evident, from the fact that in 1684, when the King's highway was laid out, it run westward of the old way, and also from the account of our streets in 1627, as given by Isaac de Rasieres, in his letter, which the reader will find in the latter part of this book; from which it appears that the street south of Leyden-street commenced on the opposite side of Main-street, partly on the lot now occupied by William R. Drew, and partly on that owned by the late William Davis, Esq., and thence took a circular direction to join what is now called Summer, in early times called South-street.

Edward Winslow, in a letter sent to England, dated December 11, 1621, says, "We have built seven dwelling-houses, and four for the use of the plantation." The four lots above named probably included the common house, and the store-house, &c., adjoining. An allusion is made to the "*old store-house*," the only one known to the writer, in a deed of William Bradford to John Dyer, in 1698.

The seven dwelling-houses were doubtless found sufficient to shelter those who survived the first winter, comprising but about one half the number living at the time of the allotments, in December, 1620. It appears from a deed, dated in 1677, that the homestead of Stephen Hopkins was at the corner of Main and Leyden streets, and that of John Howland, whose wife Elizabeth probably inherited the same from her father, Governor Carver, was the lot now owned by the heirs of Barnabas Hedge, deceased.

The following occurrence may be interesting to the reader :

"On the 14th of January, those on board the ship proposed going on shore to join their brethren in keeping the first Sabbath. At six o'clock in the morning, however, they observed the common house on fire, but, on account of low water, could render no aid till three fourths of an hour afterwards. The thatch with which the roof was covered caught from a spark, and instantly burnt up, but the building was saved. Governor Carver and Mr. Bradford were sick at the time, and the room was crowded with beds, loaded muskets and powder, but they happily escaped without personal injury, though not without pecuniary loss."

In the common house, according to tradition received from an aged relative, by the late Isaac Lothrop, Esq., who died in 1808, as mentioned by the late Judge Davis, in a note to New England's Memorial, the celebrated sermon of Robert Cushman was delivered, some time in November or December, 1621 — being the first preached in New England; in which he enforced with great earnestness, the importance of self-denial, and pointed out the special duties devolving on those who undertake the settlement of new countries.

The first parsonage house was built in this street, and stood east of the present one, embracing the lots on which now stand the houses of the late Barnabas Churchill and James Bartlett, and was early occupied by the Rev. John Cotton, pastor of the first church. The lot on which the present parsonage house stands was given, March 1, 1664, to the first church, by Mrs. Bridget Fuller and Samuel Fuller, the excellent widow and son of Samuel Fuller, who came in the Mayflower, in 1620, and died in 1633. It is now occupied by Dr. James Kendall, senior pastor of the first church, who was settled in the ministry, January 1st, 1800, and is now in the eighty-sixth year of his age.

The following vivid delineation of the scene of suffering which occurred among the Pilgrims during the first winter, may justly claim the reader's attention. The author,* after referring to the heroic achievements of Thermopylæ, thus proceeds :

"And yet, do you not think that whoso could, by ade-

* Choate's Address at New York, December 22, 1843.

quate description, bring before you that winter of the Pilgrims, its brief sunshine, the nights of storms slow waning ;
the damp and icy breath, felt to the pillow of the dying, its
destitutions, its contrasts with all their former experience in
life, its utter insulation and loneliness, its death-beds and
burials ; its memories ; its hopes ; the consultations of the
prudent ; the prayers of the pious ; the occasional cheerful
hymn, in which the heart threw off its burthen, and, assert-
ing its unvanquished nature, went up to the skies — do ye
not think that whoso would describe them, calmly waiting in
that defile, lonelier and darker than Thermopylæ, for a
morning that might never dawn, or might show them, when
it did, a mightier arm than a Persian raised in act to strike,
would he not sketch a scene of more difficult and rare hero-
ism ?　A scene, as Wordsworth has said, ' Melancholy, yea,
dismal, yet consolatory and full of joy ; a scene even better
fitted to succor, to exalt, to lead the forlorn hopes of all
great causes till time shall be no more ! ' ' "

Town Square. — The first house of public worship was
built in this place.　History affords nothing definite respecting a place of public worship in Plymouth, previous to 1622,
though from incidental hints it may be inferred that the
common house was used for that purpose.　In 1622, a fort
was erected on the hill, and so constructed as to combine
both the means of defence and accommodations for public
worship, as is particularly mentioned by the early historians.*
In the year 1637, one of the planters gave, by will,
" somewhat " to " Plymouth meeting-house."　Richard
Church, the father of Colonel Church, and John Tomson,
who afterwards settled in Middleborough, were the archi-

* See, also, Isaaok De Rasiere's letter, in this book.

tects, and Captain Thomas Willet was one of the contracting committee. That it stood on the north side of Town
Square is inferred from the fact that in an ancient deed
land was sold there, which is alluded to *as the spot where
the old meeting-house stood.* This, observes the late
Samuel Davis, Esq., who possessed every advantage for
obtaining accurate information on this point, "This is all
the description we shall ever probably obtain of this *ancient
sanctuary,* where a *Reynor* and a *Cotton* broke the bread
of life, where a *Brewster* and a *Cushman* ruled in holy
things. It had a bell, but no dimensions are on record."

This house was taken down in 1683, when another was
built. It stood, not upon the old lot, but at the head of the
square, the front extending considerably lower down than
the present church; dimensions forty by forty-five feet. A
drawing of this church, by the late Samuel Davis, Esq., is
still in existence.

A third house was erected, in 1744, on and near the same
spot as the former, being seventy-one feet ten inches in
front, and sixty-seven feet eight inches deep. Its spire, one
hundred feet high, was surmounted by a brass weathercock.

The present Gothic house was built by the first church.
It measures sixty-one by seventy feet, and cost about ten
thousand dollars.

The Church of the Pilgrimage was erected in 1840, that
society having previously worshipped in their house on
Training Green, which was built in 1801. This house was
dedicated November 24th, 1840. The body of the church is
sixty-eight by fifty-nine feet, with a tower twenty-six feet
square. It contains ninety-two pews on the lower floor, and
eighty seats in the organ loft, and will accommodate about
seven hundred people. "It received its name in commemoration of the pilgrimage of our puritan fathers to this place,

6

and stands near the site of the church they first erected for worship."

The town-house, formerly the county court-house, was built in 1749, and was in that day esteemed one of the best models of architecture.*

The elm-trees in the square were set out in the year 1784, by the late Thomas Davis, Esq.

> " Let strangers walk around
>   The city where we dwell,.
> Compass and view thine holy ground,
>   And mark the building well."

BURYING HILL.

> The Pilgrim Fathers are at rest :
>   When Summer 's throned on high,
> And the world's warm breast is in verdure dressed,
>   Go, stand on the hill where they lie ;   ·
> The earliest ray of the golden day
>   On that hallowed spot is cast ;
> And the evening sun as he leaves the world,
>   Looks kindly on that spot last.   PIERPONT.

THIS hill was originally called Fort Hill, from the circumstance of its occupation for defensive purposes immediately after the landing. The first encounter of the Pilgrims with the natives, though resulting in defeat to the latter, natu-

* The old building had been used as a place of meeting by the Plymouth Colony Deputies, etc., before the union with Massachusetts, and afterwards by the courts of law ; but the time of its erection, though probably not far from 1660, is not satisfactorily ascertained. The entire frame of the old building, when taken down, was removed to the lot owned by William and Thomas Jackson, deceased, next to the Plymouth Bank. It was fitted up for the use of the courts while the new house was in process of construction, and remains there still, though the exterior has had modern improvements. The above statement was received from the late Mrs. Eunice D. Hodge, who had the tradition from the late Dr. Nath'l. Lothrop.

rally excited apprehensions of future hostilities from the same quarter. Under these circumstances, their first measure of precaution was the erection of a platform on the hill, on which their ordnance was placed, as a protection to the dwellings, which they designed to build in two rows directly below. The site of this ancient fort is distinctly marked, on the south-east part of the hill, which overlooks the bay and surrounding country in every direction — a point, no doubt, exactly suited to attract the military taste and practised eye of Standish. It was connected by a way, now called Spring-street, with Town Brook, near which excellent springs of fresh water abounded. In the year 1622, according to Morton and other historians,* " they built a fort with good timber, both strong and comely, which was of good defence, made with a flat roof and battlements, on which fort their ordnance was mounted, and where they kept constant watch, especially in time of danger. It served them also for a meeting-house. and was fitted accordingly for that use." These precautions were taken at the time of threatened hostility from Canonicas, the distinguished and powerful Sachem of the Narraganset Indians. In September, 1642, according to the town records, " it was agreed that every man should bring two pieces more, eight foot long, to finish the fortification on the fort-hill, and that Richard Church shall speedily build the carriage for another piece of ordnance." September 23d, 1643, "it is agreed upon by the whole, that there shall be a watch-house forthwith built of brick, and that Mr. Grimes will sell us the brick at eleven shillings a thousand." This is the first instance in which brick are mentioned. In September of the same year the whole township was classed in

---

* For an interesting description of this fort, and the order observed by the Pilgrims in attending public worship, see Isaac de Raisere's letter, pages 142 and 143 of this book.

a watch, six men and a corporal assigned to a watch, "when
Gov. Bradford, Mr. Prince, Mr. Hopkins, Mr. Jenney, Mr.
Paddy, Mr. Souther, were chosen the council of war.
Twenty-one individuals, living at Jcnes River and Wellingsly,
were appointed with others in town to keep watch twenty-four
hours, from sunset to sunset, in regard to the danger of the
Indians," — those in the town, according to order given
Nathaniel Souther and Thomas Southworth, appointed masters of the watch.   Arrangements were at the same time
made in case of alarm at Plymouth, Duxbury, and Marshfield, that, from the two former places, twenty men should
repair to the scene of danger, and ten from the latter.
Beacons were placed on Gallows hill, and Captain's hill in
Duxbury — and on the hill by Mr. Thomas' house in Marshfield — to be fired as signals in case of danger.   In the
month of February,* 1676, the apprehension of danger from

* Town Records, vol. I. p. 83.
February 19th, 1676.   "It was ordered by the Towne that there shall
be forthwith a fortification build upon the fort hill att Plymouth ; to he
an hundred foot square, the pallasadoes to be ten foot and an halfe longe ;
to be sett two foot and an half in the ground, and to he sett against a post
and a raile ; every man is to doe three foot of the said fence of the fortification ; the pallasadoes are to be battened on the backsyde one against
every two, and sharpened on the topps, to be accomplished by every male in
each family from sixteen yeares old and upwards, and that there shall be a
watch house erected within the said fence or fortification, and that the three
peec of ordnance shall be planted within the said fence or fortification.
    "Agreed with Nathaniel Southworth to build the said watch house,
which is to he sixteen foot in length and twelve foot in breadth and .eight
foot studd, to be walled with board, and to have two flores, the upper
flore to be six foot above the lower flore, and hee is to batten the walls
and to make a small paire of staires in it and to frame two small win-
dowes below, to make two gebles to the roofe on each syde one, to cover
the roofe with shingle and to build a chimney in the said house, and to
do all the work thereunto ; only the frame is to be brought to the place
at the Townes charge ; and for the said work he is to have eight pounds
to be paid either in money or other pay equivelent."   In the year 1679

ALLYN HOUSE.

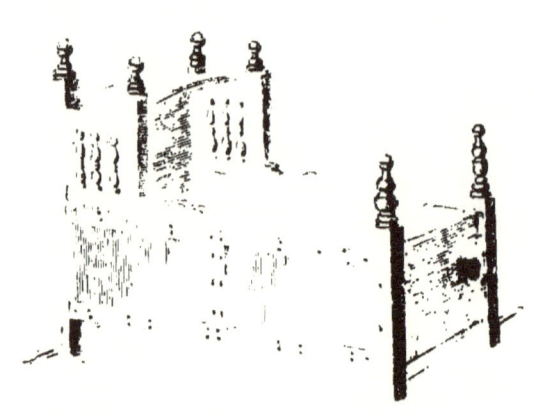

King Philip led to more extensive and formidable defences of this point than had been made at any previous period.

There exists no historical account of the time when this hill first became the place of sepulture. It has, however, been inferred, from traditions which have come down, that it was so used not long after 1622, when the fort was constructed and served for public worship as well as defence. The following inscriptions are from the oldest stones now on the hill. Why grave-stones were not sooner placed there, can now only be subject of conjecture. Perhaps a sufficient reason existed in the expense and difficulty of promptly procuring stones from England — and something should be allowed to the weighty cares and labors early required to hold possession of the country, demanding thoughts and energies which rendered other considerations of comparatively secondary consequence.

It seems proper in this place to remark that we are unable to designate the exact spot where many of the Pilgrims repose. Among these were Richard Warren, on the occurrence of whose death, in 1628, the author of New England's Memorial thus remarks: "This year died Mr. Richard Warren, who hath been mentioned before in this book, and was a useful instrument, and during his life bore a deep share in the difficulties and troubles of the first settlement of the plantation of New Plimouth;" his widow, Elizabeth, died in 1673, aged ninety-three; — Samuel Fuller, deacon of the church, and the first resident physician of New England, who died in 1633; — Stephen Hopkins, who

this watch house was granted to Samuel Jonney " to dwell in, or remove when he pleaseth." The remains of the old fort were sold to William Harlow, and formed part of his dwelling-house. The cannon were used in Revolutionary times for the defence of Coles' hill, and afterwards, as we learn, sold, to be wrought into more harmless forms of human use.

6*

died in 1644, — all of whom arrived in the Mayflower; —
Thomas Southworth, "a magistrate, and good benefactor to
both Church and Commonwealth," who died in 1669; —
Thomas Prince, for many years governor of the Colony,
and a strenuous patron of free schools, who died in 1673;
— Nath'l Morton, secretary of the Colony from 1645 to
1685, and the author of New England's Memorial, who
died in 1685: — names of high standing in our earlier
annals, — pillars of the colony, — devoted friends of law,
liberty, and religion.

The selection of epitaphs is necessarily restricted in a
work like the present one, and the following are copied as
of greatest interest in connection with the Pilgrims. A
white marble monument, with an appropriate inscription,
was, some years ago, placed on the site well known as the
grave of Gov. Bradford, by several of his descendants. It
stands on the easterly brow of the hill, and is eight and a
half feet from the ground, and of pyramidal form. This
point overlooks the middle street of Plymouth, at the lower
end of which stands a house, on or adjoining the spot consecrated as the *first buryal-ground* of the Pilgrims; which
street is distinctly marked in the preceding engraved view.

Alice Bradford, widow of Gov. Bradford, whose memory
history honors, and tradition still loves to cherish, was
doubtless buried near this monument. Her decease is thus
mentioned in the Old Colony Records: "On the 26th day
of March, 1670, Mistress Allice Bradford seni'r changed
this life for a better, haveing attained to four score years of
age or thereabouts. Shee was a godly matron, and much
loued while shee lived, and lamented tho' aged when she
died, and was honorably interred on the 29th day of the
month aforesaid: at New Plimouth."

Near this monument two of Gov. Bradford's sons are interred.

"Here lies the body of ye honorable Major William Bradford, who expired Feb. ye 20th, 1703–4, aged 79 years.

> "He lived long, but still was doing good,
> And in his country's service lost much blood.
> After a life well spent, he 's now at rest,
> His very name and memory is blest."

"Here lyes interred ye body of Mr. Joseph Bradford, son to the late honourable William Bradford Esq. Governour of Plymouth Colony who departed this life July the 10th 1715 in the 85 year of his age."

"Here lies the body of Edward Gray, Gent., aged about 52 years, and departed this life the last of June, 1681."

Mr. Gray was a distinguished and successful merchant and a valuable man in his day and generation. He lived in Rocky-Nook, and died there; and the same field near the water, on which his house and store stood, are still owned by his descendants.

Some years ago a grave-stone was placed over the remains of John Howland, by his descendant in the fifth generation, the Hon. John Howland, of Providence, President of the Historical Society of Rhode Island, who died Nov. 5th, 1854, aged ninety-seven years and five days.

"Here ended the pilgrimage of JOHN HOWLAND — and ELIZABETH his wife. She was the daughter of Gov. Carver. They arrived in the Mayflower, Dec. 1620. They had four sons and six daughters, from whom have descended a numerous posterity.

"1672, Feb. 23d. John Howland of Plymouth, deceased. He lived to the age of 80 years. He was the last

man of them that came over in the Mayflower, who settled
in Plymouth."

" Here lies buried the body of Mr. Wm. Crowe, aged
about 55 years, who decd January 1683–4."

" Here lies yᵉ body of Mrs. Hannah Sturtevant, aged
above 64 years.   Decᵈ in March 170$\frac{8}{9}$."

NOTE.— She was the daughter of Josiah Winslow, a brother of Gov.
Edward Winslow, and first married Wm. Crowe ; her second husband was
John Sturtevant.

" 1695.   Here lies buried yᵉ body of Mr. Thömas Clark,
aged 98 years.   Departed this life March 24, 1697."

It has long been supposed that Mr. Thomas Clark was
mate of the Mayflower; but tradition upon this point is not
entirely satisfactory.   The Christian name of the Clark who
was mate of this renowned vessel is not mentioned in history.   Thomas Clark arrived in the Ann, in 1623, at which
time he was 23 years of age; and, if he were mate of the
Mayflower, was 20 years old when she arrived in 1620.   It
is at least remarkable that no mention of him as such
appears in any record extant.

" Here lyes the body of Mrs. Hannah Clark wife to Mr.
William Clark Decᵈ Febʳʸ yᵉ 20th 1687 in the 29ᵗʰ year of
her age."

" Here lieth buried the body of that precious servant of
God, Mr. Thomas Cushman, who, after he had served his
generation according to the will of God, and particularly
the church of Plymouth for many years in the office of a
ruling elder, fell asleep in Jesus Dec. 10th, 1691, and in
the 84th year of his age."

Mr. Cushman was the son of Robert Cushman.   He
lived in the latter period of his life near Jones' river ; and

the place where he dwelt and the spring near it, is called Elder's Spring to this day. It is a short distance south of the Kingston landing, a few rods westerly of the railroad.

" 1645. Here lies buried the body of Mr. Thomas Faunce, ruling elder of the first church of Christ in Plymouth. Deceased Feb. 27, 1745, in the 99th year of his age.

> " The fathers — where are they ?
> Blessed are the dead who die in the Lord."

This venerable cotemporary of the Pilgrims was the last ruling elder of the first church, from whom most of the traditions respecting the first comers were received,— a source of information deserving of entire confidence.

* " Here lies the body of Joseph Bartlett, who departed this life, April the 9th, 1703, in the 38th year of his age.

> " Thousands of years before blest Abel's fall,
> 'T was said of him, being dead he speaketh yet.
> From silent grave methinks I hear a voice,
> Pray fellow mortals do'nt your death forget ;
> You that your eyes cast on this grave,
> Know you a dying time must have."

" Here lyeth yᵉ body of the honourable James Warren Esq. who deceased June yᵉ 29ᵗʰ 1715 in yᵉ 50th year of his age."

NOTE — He was the youngest son of Nathaniel Warren — and in the 3d generation from Richard, of the Mayflower. His decease is thus noticed in the Records of the first church : " Died, James Warren, Esq., in yᵉ 50ᵗʰ year of his age : an exceeding loss to the Church Town and County."

* It has generally been supposed that the grave-stone of Edward Gray was the first placed on the hill — the late Dr. Nath'l Lothrop, however, received information from an aged relative, from which it appears that Mr. Bartlett's was first *placed* there, though his death was some time subsequent to that of Mr. Gray.

" Here lyes ye body of Francis Le Baron Physician who departed this life Augst ye 8th 1704 in the 36 year of his age."

NOTE. — Dr. Le Baron was surgeon on board a French privateer, which was wrecked in Buzzard's Bay. He came to Plymouth, and having performed an important surgical operation, the selectmen petitioned the Executive of the Colony for his liberation as prisoner of war, that he might settle in this town. We believe that from this ancestor all of the name in the United States are descended.

" Here lyes buried the body of the Reverend Ephraim Little, Pastor of the Church of Christ at Plymouth, aged 47 years 2 m° and 3 D^s. Deceased Nov. ye 24th 1723."

NOTE. — Mr. Little was the first minister buried in Plymouth — after the lapse of one hundred and three years from its settlement. He left no children, and his widow was liberally supported by annual grants from the town during her life.

" This stone is erected to the memory of that unbiassed judge, faithful officer, sincere friend, and honest man, Coll. Isaac Lothrop, who resigned this life, on the 26th day of April, 1750, in the 43 year of his age.

> " Had virtue's charms the power to save
> Its faithful votaries from the grave,
> This stone had ne'er possessed the fame
> Of being marked with Lothrop's name."

NOTE. — Col. Lothrop was a descendant, in the fourth generation, from the Rev. John Lothrop, who settled in the ministry at Scituate, in the year 1634, and removed from thence to Barnstable, with most of his church, in 1639.

" Departed this life, 23^d June, 1796, in the 90th year of her age, madam Priscilla Hobart, relict of the Rev. Noah Hobart, late of Fairfield, in Connecticut, her third husband. Her first and second were John Watson, Esq., and hon. Isaac Lothrop."

"William Thomas, M. D. Died Sep. 20, 1802, aged 64 years."

Note. — Dr. Thomas was a descendant in the 4th generation from Wm. Thomas, who arrived in the colony and settled in Marshfield, about the year 1630, and died in Aug. 1651. He was in the Medical Staff of the army at the capture of Louisburg, in 1745 — and at Crown Point in 1758. Soon after the battle of Lexington, in 1775, he joined the first organized corps of the army, with his four sons, viz., Joshua, Joseph, John and Nathaniel, an instance of family patriotism of rare occurrence.

"Here lies the body of the hon. Josiah Cotton Esq., who died 19 August 1756, aged 76 years and 7 months."

Note. — He was the son of Rev. John Cotton, who was ordained minister of the first church of Plymouth in 1669, and afterwards of a church in Charleston, S. C., where he died in 1696, and grandson of John Cotton, minister of Boston. He was Register of Deeds for the County of Plymouth for more than forty years, and left a diary of great historical value.

"This stone consecrated to the memory of the Rev. Chandler Robbins, D. D., was erected by the inhabitants of the first religious society in Plymouth, as their last grateful tribute of respect for his eminent labors in the ministry of Jesus Christ, which commenced January 30th 1760, and continued till his death, June 30th 1799, Ætatis 61, when he entered into that everlasting rest prepared for the faithful embassadors of the most high God.

"Ah come Heav'ns radiant offspring, hither throng,
Behold your prophet, your Elijah fled ;
Let sacred *symphony* attune each tongue
To chant hosannas with the sacred dead."

Note. — Dr. Robbins was born at Branford, Connecticut, the 24th of Aug. 1738, and was son of the Rev. Philemon Robbins, then minister of that place.

"Sacred to the memory of Rev. Adoniram Judson, who died Nov. 25, 1826, Æ. 75. A faithful and devoted minister of Christ."

"Adoniram Judson, D. D., Missionary of the American Baptist Missionary Union to the Burman empire, who died at sea, April 12, 1850, Æ. 62 years."

The following lines, copied from the grave-stone of the late Samuel Davis, Esq.,* may appropriately find a place in the closing pages of inscriptions connected with the Pilgrims :

> "From life on earth our pensive friend retires,
> His dust commingling with the Pilgrim sires ;
> In thoughtful walk, their every path he traced,
> Their toils, their tombs, his faithful page embraced,
> Peaceful and pure, and innocent as they,
> With them to rise to everlasting day."

"In memory of seventy-two seamen, who perished in Plymouth harbor, on the 26th and 27th days of December, 1778, on board of the private armed brig General Arnold, of twenty guns, numbering in officers and crew one hundred and six persons in all, James Magee, of Boston, commander ; sixty of whom were buried on this spot, and twelve in other parts of the hill."

Plymouth harbor ordinarily affords the means of safety instead of danger to the mariner on approaching our coast, when the storms of winter naturally increase the perils connected with his hazardous pursuits. The number of shipwrecks, therefore, which have occurred here since the

---

* On the occasion of an anniversary celebration, some years ago, the Rev. Dr. Peirce, of Brookline, and Mr. *Davis*, were in conversation together, at which time several gentlemen entered the room, when the Doctor introduced his friend by observing, "Gentlemen, this is Mr. *Davis*, who can tell us where we all *came from ;*" — to which Mr. Davis promptly replied, "Gentlemen, this is Dr. *Pierce*, who can tell us where we are all *going to.*"

Pilgrims landed, has probably been less than at first sight might be expected.

Our annals present no instance of a disaster so trying in its circumstances, or involving so large a loss of lives, as that briefly stated in the preceding epitaph ; none so exciting to the feelings of the observer, or fraught with such striking alternations of fear, hope, and unutterable distress, to the sufferers ; a scene which age recalls and describes with a vividness and particularity of detail, showing how deeply its stern realities stand engraved on the memory of those who, after the lapse of nearly seventy-three years, still survive to rehearse the awful calamity.

The two following documents, which so minutely describe the disastrous fate of the brig General Arnold, have never appeared in any published history of the town, and are here presented, as containing the most full and accurate account now extant.

[*From the Boston Gazette, Jan.* 4, 1779.]

" On Friday, the 25th ult., at six A. M., the wind to the westward, sailed from this port the brig *General Arnold,* James Magee, commander ; and about meridian the wind chopped round to north-east, and looking likely for a gale, they thought best to put into Plymouth, and came to anchor in a place called the Cow-yard. On Saturday, the gale increasing, she started from her anchor and struck on the White Flat. They then cut both cable and masts away, in hopes to drive over ; but she immediately bilged ; it being low water, left her quarter-deck dry, where all hands got for relief. A schooner lying within hail heard their cries, but could not assist them. On Sunday the inhabitants were cutting ice most of the day before they got on board, when they saw seventy-five of the men had perished, and thirty-

7

four very much frozen, which they got on shore and on
Monday they got on shore and buried the dead. Great part
of her stores, etc., will be saved. Some evil-minded persons
have raised a report that she was plundered by the inhabitants, which is entirely false, as they behaved with the
greatest humanity. The following are the persons taken off
the wreck of the General Arnold, that *survived* the ship-
wreck : Capt. James Magee, John Steal, Jotham Haughton,
George Pilsbury, Peter Moorfield, Robert Hinman, Dennis
Flin, Thomas Farmer, ——— Stevens, John Bubbey, James
Hutchinson, Andrew Kelley, Francis Fires, Daniel English,
Robert Mitson, James Kent, ——— Robertson, James
Rughley, of Boston; James Williams, David Williams,
Chelsea; George Chockley, Bedford; Eleazer Thayer,
——— Potter, Providence; Wm. Russell, Vineyard; Abel
Willis, Edward Burgess, Jethro Naughton, ——— Coffin,
——— Merchant, William Gardner, ——— Chapman,
Martha's Vineyard ; ——— Dunham, Falmouth ; Barnabas
Lathrop, Barnabas Downs, Jun'r, Barnstable."

[*Extract from the Boston Evening Post, Saturday, Jan.* 28, 1779.]

" MESSIEURS PRINTERS : By inserting the following
you will oblige your humble servant,

" JAMES MAGEE.

" As I am informed a report has circulated through the
country that myself and people did not receive that relief
and assistance to which the distressed and unfortunate are
ever entitled, justice to the inhabitants of the town of
Plymouth, in which harbor I was unhappily shipwrecked,
indispensably requires of me to contradict so groundless a
report, and state the circumstances.

" Agreeable to the account before published, in the morning of the 26th ultimo, in the severest of all storms, the brigantine I commanded (called the General Arnold) dragged her anchors, and struck on a white flat, notwithstanding every effort and precaution to prevent it; in about twelve hours after she bilged. The quarter-deck was the only place that could afford the most distant prospect of safety, and a few hours presented a scene there, that to mention the particulars of which would shock the least delicate humanity. Some of my people were stifled to death with the snow; others perished with the extremity of the cold, and a few were washed off the deck and drowned. The morning of the 28th, so ardently wished for, discovered a spectacle the most dreadful; forty or fifty men, who the day before were strong and healthy, lying dead on the deck in all manner of attitudes. The survivors, finding themselves within a mile of the shore, entertained the most sanguine hopes of being taken off the wreck and rescued from the frozen and premature fate that awaited them; but, though constant and repeated attempts were made for this purpose by the good people of Plymouth during the whole day, we were so situated, that all human endeavors to relieve us were exerted in vain. Several of my men, imagining from this circumstance that death was inevitable, gave way to despair, and instantly yielded up the ghost. We continued in this deplorable and suffering condition until Monday, the 29th, at twelve of the clock, when the inhabitants of Plymouth were enabled to bring us off the wreck, and receive us to their houses, and administered everything to us that was necessary and comfortable, with that tenderness and social sympathy which do honor to human nature. The dead, amounting in the whole to seventy-two men, were carried on shore and decently buried as soon as possible ; some, indeed, who were alive were saved only to drag out a few miserable days in the extreme of pain, and then expire. An universal disposition was shown to secure everything belonging to the owners and people, and the minutest article, wheresoever found, was *sacredly* taken care of, of which I shall always retain a grateful remembrance as well as of that kind Providence which preserved my life."

The preceding letter, written soon after the terrific event which it so vividly describes, discloses traits of character highly honorable to the writer, indicating a sense of justice prompt to rebuke the misrepresentations of falsehood, unfailing courage and self-control in the hour of imminent danger, and sentiments of gratitude, deeply felt and warmly expressed.

Several facts have been preserved not mentioned in the letter of Capt. Magee. Some of his men having broached a cask of spirits, which they used so freely as to endanger their lives, he stove it to pieces, reserving only a small quantity, which he poured into their boots and his own, without suffering them to drink. Joshua B. Thomas, Esq., of this town, states that about thirty-five years ago, on a visit to Martha's Vineyard, he met with Mr. Merchant,* at that time a clerk of the court and a survivor of the shipwreck. Mr. Merchant was about ten years of age when the General Arnold was lost, and ascribed his preservation mainly to the reiterated efforts of Capt. Magee, urging him not to give up.

Mr. Thomas further states, that his aged mother, recently deceased, frequently adverted to the fact, that, in conversa-

* This name is usually written Marchant.

tion with Capt. Magee some time after, respecting the
disastrous fate of the General Arnold, he was entirely over-
come, and could not refrain from tears. The late Dr.
Thacher, in his account of this disaster, observes, "that on
Monday the inhabitants passed over the ice to the wreck.
Here was presented a scene unutterably awful and distressing. It is scarcely possible for the human mind to conceive
of a more appalling spectacle. The ship was sunk ten feet
in the sand ; the waves had been for about thirty-six hours
sweeping the main deck ; the men had crowded to the quarter-deck, and even here they were obliged to pile together
dead bodies to make room for the living. Seventy dead
bodies, frozen into all imaginable postures, were strewed over
the deck, or attached to the shrouds and spars ; about thirty
exhibited signs of life, but were unconscious whether in life
or death. The bodies remained in the posture in which they
died ; the features dreadfully distorted. Some were erect,
some bending forward, some sitting with the head resting on
the knees, and some with both arms extended, clinging to
spars or some parts of the vessel. The dead were piled on
the floor of the Court House, and it is said that Dr. Robbins fainted when called to perform the religious services."

Among those who perished were Dr. Mann, of Attle-
borough, Dr. Sears, Captain John Russell, of Barnstable,
Commander of the Marines, and Lieut. Daniel Hall. The
names of the two last are inscribed on a stone at the south-
east side of the hill. From the most authentic source it is
understood that Capt. James Magee was an Irishman by
birth, and married a near relative of the late General Simon
Elliot, of Boston. After the revolution he made three
voyages to Canton direct, and one of three years' duration
to the North-west Coast, and from thence to Canton. In the

7*

year 1789, on his third voyage to Canton, he commanded the ship Astræa, owned by Mr. Derby, of Salem, the super-cargo on board for the voyage being the venerable Col. Thomas H. Perkins, still living in Boston, the distinguished public benefactor of our times, who was warmly attached to him through life, and was with him at his death, which oc-curred in the year 1798, at the age of about forty-five years. It was thought that his constitution had been per-manently injured by his sufferings at Plymouth. He was in the practice of assembling the survivors to an annual dinner whenever he was at home, on the anniversary of their res-cue. He left three sons and six daughters, all of whom, with their mother, are now deceased. The last survivor of his daughters was the wife of the Hon. Jonathan Phillips, of Boston, who died recently ; and his only surviving de-scendant now is the daughter of Captain Charles Magee, married to a son of the Hon. Judge Walker, of Lenox, in this state.

REMAINS OF THE PILGRIMS EXHUMED FROM COLE'S HILL, THE FIRST BURIAL-GROUND OF THE PILGRIMS.

Under the appropriate head of Cole's Hill, the reader will find a full statement of the discovery and removal of these remains. They were collected by the town author-ities, and placed in a plank box, lined with lead, in a brick cell, upon the easterly brow of the hill, near the monument to Governor Bradford, where some appropriate structure is to be placed, designating the certain resting-place of some of the Pilgrim Fathers of New England.

" Here lies ye Body of Deacon George Morton who Dec^d August ye 2^d 1727 in ye 82^d year of his Age."

NOTE. — This is the earliest grave-stone on the hill bearing the name of Morton Ephraim Morton, father of the above (and son of George, who came o er in the Ann, in 1623), was born on the passage, and died in 1693. No stone marks the place of his burial, or that of his brother Nathaniel, Secretary of the Colony, who died in 1685 ; they were probably buried near the spot indicated by the above epitaph.

"Here Lyes y^e Body of Ephraim Morton who Dec^d Feb^{ry} y^e 18th 173$\frac{1}{2}$ in y^e 84th year of his Age."

NOTE. — He was a son of Ephraim Morton, the same as mentioned in the preceding note.

"Here Lyes y^e Body of Mr Nathaniel Holmes who Dec^d July y^e 25th 1727 in y^e 84th year of his Age."

NOTE. — He was the son of John Holmes, who, as early as 1634, was messenger of the General Court, &c., from whom most of the name in Plymouth are descended.

"Here Lyes ye Body of Mrs Marcy Holmes wife of Mr Nathl Holmes who Dec^d Feb^{ry} 11th 1731|^2 in ye 81st year of Her Age."

NOTE. — She was the daughter of John Faunce, who came over in the ship Ann, in 1623, and died November 29, 1653, and sister of Elder Thomas Faunce.

"Here Lyes ye Body of Capt William Shurtleff, who Dec^d Feb^{ry} The 4th 1729|^{30} In The 72^d year Of His Age."

NOTE. — He was the son of William Shurtleff, whose name first appears on record September 2d, 1634, and who, in about the year 1660, removed to Marshfield, and was killed, with two others, during a terrific thunderstorm, June 23, 1666. William, the son, was for some years a selectman of Plymouth, a delegate to the provincial assembly in 1694, and held several other important stations.

"In memory of Mr Gideon White who departed this life March ye 6th 1779 Aged 62 years. Also in memory of Capt Cornelius White his son who founder'd at sea Sepr ye 22d 1779 Aged 35 years."

NOTE. — He was the son of Cornelius White, and the third in descent from William White, who came in the Mayflower, and died the first winter.

"To the memory of Mrs Joanna White wife of Captain Gideon White who died September 23ᵈ 1810 in the 95ᵗʰ year of her age."

NOTE. — She was the daughter of Thomas Howland, the son of Joseph, the son of John Howland, who came in the Mayflower. She was well acquainted with, and visited the family of Elder Faunce, and from her and her children, so remarkable for their longevity, is derived much of the valuable traditionary lore connected with early times, which she received from the frequent communications of the Elder himself.

"This stone is erected by her surviving connexions, to perpetuate the memory of Hannah White, daughter of Gideon and Joanna White, who died January 3d, 1841, aged 93 years. Her long pilgrimage on earth was ennobled by the practice of the duties of Christianity, cheered by its hopes and sustained by its faith."

We subjoin the following extracts from Mr. Bartlett's Pilgrim Fathers, as showing the impressions of an intelligent traveller, respecting a spot universally interesting to visitors :

"The 'Burying' Hill is the most remarkable spot in Plymouth. From whatever side we approach the town, it rises conspicuously, above all its buildings; a lofty green mound, covered with dark gray tombstones, the first place to receive the rays of the sun, and the last upon which they linger.

"Let us ascend to it by the narrow foot-path from the head of Leyden-street, worn deeply in the thick and mossy turf, and, seated on one of the tombstones, look out upon the surrounding scene. What a Sabbath stillness reigns around ! Scarcely a sound arises from the town below, half

buried among its leafy groves; though the curling smoke tells of many a cheerful home concealed amidst the foliage. It is morning, the tide is in, the wide expanse of the bay glitters with light, and a fresh and bracing sea-breeze pleasantly salutes us. The robin redbreast, a much larger bird than his elder brother in England, hopping from stone to stone, seems to haunt this fresh and breezy eminence. The view that it commands is pleasing from its wide expanse of sea and shore. But the spot whereon we stand, the cemetery, is itself the most striking feature of the scene.

"In wandering about this venerable place of sepulture, I was particularly struck with the longevity attained by a large proportion of its tenants. It is remarkable that many of those who survived the first winter, fatal to half their companions, and became accustomed to the climate, which, if keen and cutting, is remarkably pure and salubrious, should, with their immediate descendants, have lived to eighty, ninety, and, in some few instances, above even a hundred years of age.

"Such, in its main features, is the Burying Hill, the most venerable, if not the most beautiful, necropolis to be met with on the soil of America."

On a bright summer's day, at full tide, let some thoughtful observer come

> "To the hill of hallowed brow,
> Where the Pilgrim sleepeth now."

Let him come when no cloud obscures the heavens, and the hushed air breathes no whisper; when the unruffled ocean holds mirrored on its tranquil bosom the varied forms of surrounding objects, and the chastened feelings of the hour court the sympathy of nature's repose, symbol of that

deeper repose brooding over the sleep of many generations.
Facing the beautiful expanse of waters before him, the green
ridge of Manomet is seen, rising nearly four hundred feet
above the ocean, having the beach stretching its slender
form from its northerly side three miles in extent, reposing
quietly beneath its misty veil of blue, as if to gain fresh
vigor to encounter the furious congregation of billows, that
often beat and foam against the huge rocks that encircle its
base.   Extending his vision across the bay, a distance of
twenty-five miles, the white cliffs of Cape Cod appear as if
suspended in mid-air by some secret enchantment of nature.
Contracting his vision within a narrower compass, it rests
on the white towers of the Gurnet light-house, reflected in
the depths below, occupying the extreme point of Marshfield beach, seven miles from the main land, from whence
the gleaming messenger of hope may sooner penetrate the
darkness of night, and guide the lost mariner to some haven
of safety.   Protected by Saquish head, stands Clark's
Island, where the wrecked shallop of the Mayflower,
shrouded in darkness, and just escaping destruction from the
foaming breakers of the neighboring cove, at last found
shelter ; and the weather-beaten Pilgrim, in his joyous hour
of safety from peril, "thanked God and took courage."
Beyond lies the extended village of Duxbury, sparkling in
sunlight, reaching to the Hill of Standish, full of interesting associations ; and Kingston, with its neat dwellings,
scattered along between pleasant groves and teeming flood,
terminating the survey of hills, and plains, and waters,
which once formed the active scene of intense labor, perilous
enterprise and enduring power, to men whose ashes now
mingle with the ground on which the rapt observer stands.

COLE'S HILL.

" How sadly winds the funeral train
  With feeble step across the plain !
  What anguish wrings affection's breast,
  That laid the *Pilgrim* to his rest !
  No requiem his, but ocean's roar,
  That broke in moans along the shore ;
  Or storms and waves that raging sweep,
  While gushing hearts are left to weep.''

COLE'S HILL is an open green spot fronting the harbor, a short distance above Forefather's Rock, commanding a beautiful view of the ocean and highlands by which the bay is encircled. It was the first burial-ground of the Pilgrims. On inspection it will be found to have undergone considerable changes since its first consecration as a temporary receptacle of the dead. In the year 1735, a large current of water, rushing through Middle-street, washed away some portions of the banks, displacing the remains of several bodies, deposited there in the winter of 1620 and spring of 1621. In the year 1809, a human skull was disinterred, the teeth of which were in a perfect state of preservation. The traditions respecting this place, and its consecrated uses by the Pilgrims, were received from the same unquestionable sources as are mentioned in the account of Forefather's Rock, on page nineteenth of this work, and are stated by Dr. Holmes, in his American Annals, and by the venerable Judge Davis, in a note to his edition of the New England Memorial, to have been received by them many years ago.

About fifty of those who came in the Mayflower were buried on this spot, near the foot of Middle-street. Among them were Gov. Carver, William White, Rose Standish, the wife of Captain Standish; Elizabeth, the wife of Edward Winslow, Christopher Martin, William Mullins, John and Edward Tilley, Thomas Rogers, Mary, the wife of Isaac Allerton.

On the twenty-third day of May, 1855, some workmen, while excavating a trench for the pipes of the water-works, exhumed parts of five skeletons. The exact spot of their discovery was the space in the middle of the road upon Cole's Hill lying between the two points, five rods south, and two rods north, of the foot of Middle-street. Some of the bones laid bare by the workmen were replaced in the trench, and the remainder collected by the town authorities for the purpose of verifying their identity as bones of the Pilgrims, and giving them a proper interment. One of the skulls was placed in the hands of Professor Oliver W. Holmes, of Boston, for examination, who, after a critical comparison with specimens in the cabinet of the Massachusetts Medical College, pronounced it a Caucasian skull, and thus, without doubt, the skull of one of the earliest settlers of Plymouth. History informs us that the place of interment was sown, and carefully levelled, in order to conceal their bones from the knowledge of the natives.

One skull, as demonstrated by the upper jaw, which displayed a beautiful set of teeth, and the wisdom-teeth just emerging from the bone, was that of a young person between seventeen and twenty-five, and of a young man, as other characteristics, the size of the teeth, the width of the ankle, &c., indicated.

The spot where the remains were found is now level, but was originally a slope, which was filled up for the purpose of a road. A foot and a half beneath the surface a stratum of black soil was exposed overlying the bones, and confirming the tradition that the place had been cultivated by the Pilgrims. The bodies had been buried in a horizontal position, with the heads to the west, and lying upon their backs. No traces of coffins were found,— a circumstance, considering the period of the interment, casting no doubt upon the identity of the remains, as the absence of beads, pipes, arrow-heads, &c., rendered it certain that they were not those of Indians.

The suffering, death, and funeral solemnities, of which this spot was once the trying scene, have been the subject of a description so consonant to the most elevated principles of our nature, that no better service can be rendered to every thoughtful observer, than its transcription into these pages :

" In a late undesigned visit to Plymouth, I sought the spot where their earlier dead were buried. It was a bank, you remember, somewhat elevated, below the town, and between it and the water, near and looking forth upon the waves, symbol of what life had been to them ; ascending inland, behind and above the rock, a symbol of that rock of ages, on which the dying had rested in the final hour. As the Pilgrim found these localities, you might stand on that bank and hear the restless waters chafe and melt against its steadfast bank ; — the unquiet of the world composed itself at the portals of the grave. On that spot have aid to rest together, the earth carefully smoothed down, that the Indian might not count the number, the true, the pious, the beautiful, and the brave, till the heavens be no more. There, certainly, was buried the first governor (Carver), ' with three volleys of shot fired over him ; ' and there was buried Rose, the wife of Miles Standish.

8

" ' You shall go to them,' wrote Robinson, in the same
letter from which I have read; ' but they shall not return
to you.'

" I can seem to see, on a day quite towards the close of
their first month of March, a diminished procession of the
Pilgrims, following another dearly loved and newly dead, to
that brink of graves; and pausing sadly there before they
shall turn away to see that face no more. In full view from
that spot is the Mayflower, still riding at her anchor, but to
sail in a few days more for England, leaving them alone,
the living and the dead, to the weal or woe of their new
home. I cannot say what was the entire emotion of that
moment and that scene, but the tones of the venerated elder's
voice, as they gathered round him, were full of cheerful
trust; and they went to hearts as noble as his own ! This
spot, he might say, ' this line of shore, yea, this whole
land grows dearer, daily, were it only for the precious dust
which we have committed to its bosom. I would sleep here,
when my own hour comes, rather than elsewhere, with those
who have shared with us in our exceeding labors, and whose
burdens are now unloosed forever. I would be near them
in the last day, and have a part in their resurrection. And
now,' he proceeded, ' let us go from the side of the grave,
to work with all our might what we have to do. It is in
my mind that our night of sorrow is well-nigh ended, and
that the joy of our morning is at hand. The breath of the
pleasant south-west is here, and the singing of birds. The
sore sickness is stayed, somewhat more than half our number remain, and among them some of our best and wisest,
though others have fallen asleep. Matter of joy and thanks-
giving to Almighty God it is, that among you all, the living and the dead, I know not one, — even when disease had

touched him, and sharp grief had made his heart as a little child's, — who desired, yea, who could have been entreated to go back to England by yonder ship. Plainly it is his will that we stand or fall here. All his providences, these three hundred years, declare it, as with beams of the sun. Did he not set his bow in the clouds, in that bitter hour of embarking, and build his glorious arch upon the sea for us to sail through hitherward? Wherefore let us stand to our lot! If he prosper us, we shall found a church, against which the gates of hell shall not prevail; and a colony, a nation, by which all the nations shall be healed, and shall be saved. Millions shall spring from our loins, and trace back, with lineal love, their blood to ours. Centuries hereafter, in great cities, the capitals of mighty states, and from the tribes of a common and happy Israel, shall come together, the good, the distinguished, the wise, to remember our dark day of small things; yea, generations shall call us blessed.'

" Without a sign, calmly, with triumph, they turned away from the grave. They sent the Mayflower away, and went back, those stern, strong men, to their imperial labors." *

CLARK'S ISLAND.

" *The modest isle of yonder bay,*
. Screened from the rougher blasts and spray,
There, long by storm and billow driven,
With mast and sail to fragments riven,
The wanderers sought its welcome shore,
And safe their struggling shallop moor ;

* Choate's Oration, delivered before the New England Society, at New York, Dec. 22d, 1843.

There watchful met the earliest dawn,
Which first revealed the Sabbath morn,
That prayer and praise might o'er the deep
Their swelling strains harmonious keep.
New England's first-born Sabbath day
On time's dark flood has passed away,
The Pilgrim chant is heard no more,
That echoed once upon that shore,
And hushed the lips whose accents gave
Their grateful notes to wind and wave ;
But still the hours of peaceful rest
From earthly cares are ever blest,
And wing our thought to scenes divine,
Where faith and hope no more decline."

THIS island received its name from Clark, the master's
mate of the ship Mayflower. It is in some measure sheltered from the ocean by Saquish on the south, and Marshfield beach on the east. It presents a beautiful feature in
the scenery of Plymouth harbor, distant three miles from
town, but is chiefly interesting in connection with the Pilgrims, who providentially found a shelter by its side on the
night of December 8th, 1620. Having taken their departure from Eastham, and coasted along Barnstable Bay about
forty-five miles, and being overtaken by a storm on entering
Plymouth harbor, they narrowly escaped running the shallop into a cove full of breakers, which is formed between the
Gurnet light-house and Saquish head, — a distance of about
two miles. On approaching the breakers, a resolute seaman
at the helm cried out to the oarsmen, "if they were men,
about with her, or they were all cast away ;" which call
was promptly executed, and, favored by the flood-tide, they
weathered Saquish head, and secured a shelter. Here they
kindled a fire and spent the night. In the morning they
explored the island, without finding either dwellings or

inhabitants. The weather being extremely cold, Saturday, the ninth, was spent in recruiting their strength, drying their arms, and repairing the shallop. The next day being Sunday, "they rested," and kept the first New England Sabbath, notwithstanding the urgent necessity then existing to hasten their explorations for some place of permanent settlement.

On Monday, the 11th of December, they sounded the harbor, and landed on the Rock of Plymouth, which date corresponds with the 21st of December, new style, according to the decision of our best astronomers, though the 22d has usually been the day of anniversary celebrations.

In the year 1637, "The court granted that Clark's Island, the Eel river Beach, Saquish and the Gurnet's Nose shall be and remain unto the town of Plymouth." The island was originally well wooded, principally with red cedar, which in after times was frequently converted into gate-posts for the supply of Boston market. Four or five weather-beaten tenants of this spot still remain, and might in their days of youthful vigor have formed part of the forest which poetry has delightfully personified in connection with the fathers,

> " When the leafless woods repeated
> The music of their psalm,
> When they shook the depths of the desert gloom
> With their song of lofty cheer."

This island contains eighty-six and a quarter acres, according to a survey ordered by Sir Edmund Andros, Feb. 23d, 1687, executed by Phillip Wells, and was pronounced by Gov. Hutchinson one of the best in Massachusetts. It was sold by the town, in 1690, to Samuel Lucas, Elkanah

8*

Watson, and George Morton. The late John Watson, Esq.,
was the proprietor of the island, where he resided about
forty years, and died Feb. 1, 1826, in the seventy-eighth
year of his age. He was one of the founders of the Old
Colony Club, in 1769, and President of the Pilgrim Society
after the year 1820 till his death. The place is now under
good cultivation by his son, Mr. Edward Watson. On a
very accurate map of Plymouth, drawn by James Blasco-
with, Esq., a naval engineer, by order of the British government, in the year 1774, a large rock on the island is
named *Election Rock*, which, according to information
obtained from elderly persons now living, probably derived
its name from the fact that parties of pleasure in early
times resorted there to spend election holidays.

It ought, perhaps, to be stated here that history has not
preserved the Christian names of either Jones or Clark, the
master and mate of the Mayflower, or of Reynolds, master
of the Speedwell.

BILLINGTON SEA.

THIS beautiful expanse of water, though it may not justly
aspire to all the dignity which its name would seem to
import, and which, soon after its discovery, received from
the planters themselves the more unassuming and appropriate appellation of Fresh Lake, still possesses strong
attractions to the lovers of nature in her more secluded but
not less interesting manifestations of beauty.

It was discovered by " Francis Billington," in 1621,
who, " having the week before (on the eighth of January)
seen from the top of a tree on a high hill a great sea, as
he thought, went with the master's mate to see it." They

found seven or eight wigwams, but no inhabitants. Whether these dwellings served for occasional accommodation to the Namasket Indians, when visiting the sea-shore for shell-fish, or had been deserted in consequence of the destructive plague of 1616, must remain the subject of conjecture only. It is quite probable, however, that the Indian path from Namasket wound its way along this woodland region, and so continued on the south side of Town Brook. It is about one and a half miles long, and half a mile in width at its extreme points, and six miles in compass along its winding shores. It embosoms an island containing two acres of land, formerly covered with every variety of forest-trees, and now mostly replaced by an orchard and dwelling-house. Some thirty years ago it was the usual and favorite resort of social parties from town, since which it has in some measure experienced the rivalship peculiar to all human concerns; while South, Long and Herring Ponds, having deeper water and greater abundance of fish, often divert the votaries of innocent amusement to their attractive shores.

During the last summer, this ancient and agreeable resort seems to have acquired new favor in public estimation; and among the throng of visitors to Plymouth, in quest of antiquity and to seek relaxation from the cares of city life, many have found its shady groves a source of refreshment and delight.

The water-power afforded by this spacious fountain, from whence Town Brook proceeds in its course of two miles to the harbor, is not liable to the many fluctuations incident to most of our streams. It has, from time immemorial, been of great importance to our citizens, and might, with skilful improvements, increase the productive power of our manufactures to a very large extent.

In this comparatively sequestered region the eagle still maintains his ancient dominion, majestically soaring above his native hills, the abode of many generations. Here the beautiful wood-duck still roams, though with diminished chances of success, in quest of a secluded retreat, and the bounding deer, sportively ranging through forest and glade, finds refreshment on the margin of its pure waters; or, when heated in the chase from some perilous onset of the reckless hunter, with hurried flight venturously braves the welcome flood, his only chance of security from unrelenting pursuit.

SAMOSET, THE INDIAN SAGAMORE.

HIS INTERVIEW WITH THE PILGRIMS.

" *The path through which Samoset came,*
And boldly welcomed them by name,
Whose practised skill and counsel sage
Inscribed appear on history's page,
That tells his worth and friendship true,
And yields the praise so justly due —
His comely form and features stand,
Portrayed by Sargent's tasteful hand,
Beside the group of exiled name
Who pressed the *Rock* of endless fame."

THE interview of Samoset with the Pilgrims was an important event in their early history, and the reader will doubtless desire an account of it. The following description of this novel scene, by one present on the interesting occasion, is therefore offered :

" Friday, the 16th, a fair, warm day towards. This

morning we determined to conclude of the military orders, which we had begun to consider of before, but were interrupted by the savages, as we mentioned formerly. And whilst we were busied hereabout, we were interrupted again; for there presented himself a savage, which caused an alarm. He very boldly came all alone, and along the houses, straight to the rendezvous, where we intercepted him, not suffering him to go in, as undoubtedly he would out of his boldness. He saluted us in English, and bade us 'Welcome ;' for he had learned some broken English among the Englishmen that came to fish at Monhiggon, and knew by name most of the captains, commanders and masters, that usually come. He was a man free in speech, so far as he could express his mind, and of a seemly carriage. We questioned him of many things; he was the first savage we could meet withal. He said he was not of these parts, but of Morattiggon,* and one of the sagamores or lords thereof; and had been eight months in these parts, it lying hence a day's sail with a great wind, and five days by land. He discoursed of the whole country, and of every province, and of their sagamores, and their number of men and strength. The wind beginning to rise a little, we cast a horseman's coat about him; for he was stark naked, only a leather about his waist, with a fringe about a span long, or little more. He had a bow and two arrows; the one headed, and the other unheaded. He was a tall, straight man, the hair of his head black, long behind, only short before, none on his face at all. He asked some beer, but we gave him strong water, and biscuit, and butter, and cheese, and pudding, and a piece of mallard; all of which he liked well,

* Probably the Island of Monhegan, in the State of Maine.

and had been acquainted with such amongst the English. He told us the place where we now lived is called Patuxet, and that about four years ago all the inhabitants died of an extraordinary plague, and there is neither man, woman, nor child remaining, as, indeed, we have found none; so as there is none to hinder our possession, or to lay claim unto it. All the afternoon we spent in communication with him. We would gladly have been rid of him at night, but he was not willing to go this night. Then we thought to carry him on shipboard, wherewith he was well content, and went into the shallop; but the wind was high and the water scant, that it could not return back. We lodged him that night at Stephen Hopkins'* house, and watched him."

The uncertainty of the Indians as to the numbers and strength of the Pilgrims, and the dread inspired by the use of fire-arms, probably induced them to preserve a cautious reserve for more than three months. During this time the Pilgrims were struggling, through every variety of difficulty and suffering, to provide a shelter for themselves and their families, and might have become an easy prey to any hostile effort against them. Before their habitations had been sufficiently secured against the inclemency of winter, many from previous exposure were seized with sickness and died. In their feeble state, ignorant of the power, fearful of renewed hostility from the Indians, who shall attempt to describe their hour of agony?

At this moment of painful suspense and apprehension of thick-coming dangers, with what indescribable emotions of joy did the Pilgrim, as he walked forth in the morning of that day, to resume the labor of defensive preparation, hear

---

* Probably the house then building at the corner of Leyden and Main sts.

the first sounds of friendly salutation, when Samoset, boldly approaching the humble dwellings, called aloud, "Welcome! welcome Englishmen!" It little mattered that Indian proficiency had mastered only some broken fragments of the English tongue; the tones of welcome were those of rapture, and needed no medium of polished phrase to reach the heart. The interview was full of interest, and its consequences proved highly beneficial.

Samoset is not mentioned in history after the interview with Massasoit, which occurred a few days after the occurrences above narrated. It is, therefore, probable that he soon returned to his native home in the eastern country, from whence it is generally supposed he came, and that no opportunity was afterwards presented to renew the friendly salutations with which he first met the Pilgrims.

WATSON'S HILL.

MASSASOIT.

" *The rising hill*, upon whose brow
Was first exchanged the solemn vow,
Where Massasoit, the Indian Chief,
So freely tendered kind relief,
And by whose early proffered aid
A lasting peace was firmly made.
While Carver, Winslow, Bradford, stand,
Time-honored Fathers of our land,
This chieftain, too, shall homage claim
Of praise far more than princely fame ;
True-hearted, gentle, kind and brave,
Unfading honors crown his grave."

THIS hill * rises to an elevated height on the south side

* Indicated by the wind-mill now on its summit.

of Town Brook, and was called Strawberry Hill by the first planters. It was early owned by George Watson, an ancient and valuable settler. Its Indian name was Cantauganteest; the signification of which has not been ascertained, though diligent inquiry has been made for that purpose. Since the days of Eliot, Mayo, Cotton, and Treat, the language and the race of Indians seem to have shared one common fate. It might become an interesting subject of speculation to consider what effect would be produced on the minds of those devoted missionaries, were they permitted to visit the earth and witness the desolation which has spared hardly a solitary descendant of the numerous converts they once gathered into the fold of Christian hope.

On the summit of this hill Massasoit appeared with his train of sixty men, where hostages were exchanged between him and the Pilgrims, as a preliminary step to the treaty of peace which immediately followed. And the interview is thus described by one present at the time of its occurrence :

"Thursday, the 22d of March, was a very fair, warm day. About noon we met again about our public business. But we had scarce been an hour together, but Samoset, came again, and Squanto, the only native of Patuxet, where we now inhabit, who was one of the twenty captives that by Hunt were carried away, and had been in England, and dwelt in Cornhill with Master John Slanie, a merchant, and could speak a little English, with three others; and they brought with them some few skins to truck, and some red herrings, newly taken and dried, but not salted ; and signified unto us that their great sagamore, Massasoyt, was hard by, with Quadequina, his brother, and all their men. They could not well express in English what they would;

but after an hour the king came to the top of a hill over against us, and had in his train sixty men, that we could well behold them, and they us. We were not willing to send our governor to them, and they were unwilling to come to us. So Squanto went again unto him, who brought word that we should send one to parley with him, which we did, which was Edward Winsloe, to know his mind, and to signify the mind and will of our governor, which was to have trading and peace with him. We sent to the king a pair of knives, and a copper chain with a jewel at it. To Quadequina we sent likewise a knife, and a jewel to hang in his ear, and withal a pot of strong water, a good quantity of biscuit, and some butter; which were all willingly accepted.

"Our messenger made a speech unto him, that King James saluted him with words of love and peace, and did accept of him as his friend and ally; and that our governor desired to see him and to truck with him, and to confirm a peace with him, as his next neighbor. He liked well of the speech, and heard it attentively, though the interpreters did not well express it. After he had eaten and drunk himself, and given the rest to his company, he looked upon our messenger's sword and armor, which he had on, with intimation of his desire to buy it; but, on the other side, our messenger showed his unwillingness to part with it. In the end, he left him in the custody of Quadequina, his brother, and came over the brook, and some twenty men followed him, leaving all their bows and arrows behind them. We kept six or seven as hostages for our messenger. Captain Standish and Master Williamson met the king at the brook, with half a dozen musketeers. They saluted him, and he them; so one going over, the one on the one side, and the other on the other, conducted him to a house then in build-

9

ing, where we placed a green rug and three or four cush-
ions. Then instantly came our governor, with drum and
trumpet after him, and some few musketeers. After salutations, our governor kissing his hand, the king kissed him;
and so they sat down. The governor called for some strong
water, and drunk to him; and he drunk a great draught
that made him sweat all the while after. He called for a
little fresh meat, which the king did eat willingly, and did
give his followers. Then they treated of peace, which was:

"1. That neither he nor any of his should injure or do
hurt to any of our people.

"2. And if any of his did hurt to any of ours, he
should send the offender, that we might punish him.

"3. That if any of our tools were taken away, when
our people were at work, he should cause them to be restored; and if ours did any harm to any of his, we would
do the like to them.

"4. If any did unjustly war against him, we would aid
him; if any did war against us, he should aid us.

"5. He should send to his neighbor confederates to certify them of this, that they might not wrong us, but might
be likewise comprised in the conditions of peace.

"6. That when their men came to us, they should leave
their bows and arrows behind them, as we should do our
pieces when we came to them.

"Lastly, that doing thus, King James would esteem of
him as his friend and ally.

"All which the king seemed to like well, and it was
applauded of his followers. All the while he sat by the
governor he trembled for fear. In his person he is a very
lusty man, in his best years, an able body, grave of countenance, and spare of speech; in his attire little or nothing

differing from the rest of his followers, only in a great chain of white bone beads about his neck ; and at it, behind his neck, hangs a little bag of tobacco, which he drank,* and gave us to drink. His face was painted with a sad red, like murrey, and oiled both head and face, that he looked greasily. All his followers likewise were in their faces, in part or in whole, painted, some black, some red, some yellow, and some white, some with crosses, and other antic works ; some had skins on them, and some naked ; all strong, tall men in appearance.

" So, after all was done, the governor conducted him to the brook, and there they embraced each other, and he departed ; we diligently keeping our hostages."

This place was probably a favorite resort of the natives prior to the landing. Excavations have been made at various times, and Indian remains have been found there within a few years. On the west side shells are found in large quantities, evidently the remnant of many a simple *Indian feast*, for which the situation possessd every advantage, having the best springs close at hand, of which none were better judges than the natives, till their taste became perverted by the immoderate use of the *strong water* supplied them by the reckless white men, who have so often unscrupulously employed the article, both to their own destruction and the oppression of that injured race.

The treaty of peace, made on the occasion above stated, having been concluded, under the influence of upright intentions, by both of the parties concerned, proved mutually advantageous, and continued, without any serious disturbance on either side, for more than fifty years.

* Or the same as smoking tobacco.

CAPTAIN'S HILL.

" We trace the *mount*, which gently soars
Above the sea and circling shores,
Where Standish, first of martial name,
Who dauntless won heroic fame,
Skilful and brave to guide the band
Which firm achieved this chosen land,
Was wont to gaze on every side,
And scan the sail of every tide."

THIS beautiful mount is situated in the south-easterly
part of Duxbury, and was at an early period assigned, with
land adjacent, to Miles Standish, the intrepid military
leader of the Pilgrims. Its summit, in a gradual ascent, is
about four hundred yards from the water, and about one
hundred and eighty feet above the ocean, by which it is
washed, on its west, south, and easterly sides. It affords
an extensive and delightful view of the surrounding country,
the harbor, Bay of Cape Cod, and Manomet. The dwelling-
house and spring of Standish were on the southerly part of
the mount, and but a short distance from the water. The
house was burnt, as we have learned from good authority,
while occupied by Alexander, the oldest son of Captain
Standish. In a communication from Lewis Bradford, Esq.,
the aged and venerable Town Clerk of Plympton, he observes, " I have found that Alexander Standish was Town
Clerk, and also a deacon of the church, in Duxbury, and
that he lived in the house where his father lived, which was
burnt, and the Town Records of Duxbury up to that time
burnt in it." The ruins of this house still remain and
frequently attract antiquarian curiosity. Implements of
household use, and parcels of coin partially scorched by fire,

found in these ruins, have been deemed as trophies amply rewarding the labor expended in procuring them.

The burial-place of Standish is not certainly ascertained; but was probably in the old burying-ground in Duxbury, not far from his house.

The will of Captain Miles Standish is dated March 7, 1655, and the following clause relates to property in England: "I give unto my son and heir apparent Alexander Standish all my lands as heir apparent by lawful descent in Ormistic Bousconge Wrightington Maudsley Newburrow Cranston and in the Isle of Man and given to mee as right heire by lawful descent, but surreptitiously detained from mee my great-grandfather being a second or younger brother from the house of Standish of Standish." It appears that Miles, the oldest son of Alexander, inherited the homestead at Duxbury, and died there, leaving a will, dated August 31, 1739, in which he gives his homestead, one hundred and twenty acres, to Miles, his son, his wife, Experience, to have half the income, and legacies to the following named daughters: Sarah, wife of Abner Weston, Patience, wife of Caleb Jenney, Priscilla and Penelope Standish. Penelope died in 1740. Miles Standish, above named, lived in Duxbury, and July 3, 1763, by deed, in which his wife Mehitable joined, sold his remaining homestead to Samuel and Sylvanus Drew, who about the same time sold it to Wait Wadsworth. He probably soon moved to Bridgewater, and July 1, 1765, purchased a farm (at Teticut), costing two hundred and fifty-three pounds six shillings and eight pence, of Elijah Leach. He sold, his wife Mehitable joining in the deed, to his son Miles, the same farm, April 28, 1779. Judge Mitchell states that he died in 1785, aged eighty, and that his son removed to Pennsyl-

9*

vania, and that he also had a son Miles ; from all which it
seems probable that the son of the last named Miles is the
rightful heir to the Standish property in England, if any
such there be.

PILGRIM HALL.

THE corner-stone, containing historical inscriptions, was
laid September 1, 1824, with religious ceremonies. This
monumental edifice is situated on Court-street; it is seventy
by forty feet, constructed of unwrought split granite, in a
plain and substantial mode of architecture, contains a dining-
room on the basement, and a spacious hall above. The
ground on which it stands was a part of the extensive estate
of Mr. Thomas Southworth, in 1668, and is probably comprised within the "four acres given him by his mother, Mrs.
Alice Bradford," relict of Governor Bradford. When Plymouth was first planted, there was a north and a south
common field, for tillage, for several years, on either side
of the town, near the shore. This falls within the "north
field," and probably within the stockade and palisadoes of
nearly half a mile in compass. Just below it, abutting on
" the shore, were the six-acre brick-kiln field," of the first
planters. The eastern prospect from it is interesting, bring-
ing into view the harbor, the near shores of Duxbury and
Marshfield, the highlands of Manomet, the ocean, and occasionally in the summer, the looming cliffs of Cape Cod —
the first resting-place of the Pilgrims.

The Pilgrim Hall, which is now fitted up in a manner
convenient and appropriate, for the reception of interesting
memorials connected with the Pilgrims, contains the following, among other attractions to the antiquarian visitor :

The Landing of the Fathers in 1620, painted by the late Henry Sargent, Esq., of Boston, and generously presented by him to the Pilgrim Society. It was valued at three thousand dollars. The gilt frame was purchased by the Pilgrim Society, with funds raised by subscription, and cost about four hundred dollars. It is thirteen by sixteen feet.

The following individuals are represented in the painting, attired in the costume of their time :

1st. Governor Carver and his wife and children. 2d. Governor Bradford 3d. Governor Winslow. 4th. Wife of Governor Winslow. 5th. Mr. William Brewster, the Elder of Leyden Church. 6th. Captain Miles Standish. 7th. Mr. William White, and his child Peregrine. 8th. Mr. Isaac Allerton and his wife. 9th. Mr. John Alden. 10th. Mr. John Turner. 11th. Mr. Stephen Hopkins, his wife and children. 12th. Mr. Richard Warren. 13th. Mr. Edward Tilley. 14th. Mr. Samuel Fuller. 15th. Wife of Captain Standish. 16th. Samoset, an Indian Sagamore or Lord. 17th. Mr. John Howland, son-in-law of Governor Carver.

PORTRAITS. — 1st. Edward Winslow, painted in London, in 1651, copied from the original, by C. A. Foster. 2d. Josiah Winslow, the first native Governor of the Old Colony, painted in London, in 1651; copied from the original, by C. A. Foster. 3d. Governor Josiah Winslow's wife, Penelope Pelham; copied from the original, by C. A. Foster. 4th. General John Winslow; copied from the original, by C. A. Foster. The portrait of Governor Edward Winsh w is the only one preserved of those who came in the Mayflower The originals of these paintings belong to Isaac Winslow, Esq., of Boston, and are now in the rooms of the Massachusetts Historical Society. 5th. A portrait of the

Hon. Ephraim Spooner, presented by Thomas Davis, Esq.; of Boston. 6th. A portrait of John Alden, Esq., of Middleborough, who died in 1821, aged one hundred and two years. He was the great grandson of John Alden, who came in the Mayflower; painted and presented by Cephas Thomson, Esq. '.th. A portrait of Hon. John Trumbull, presented by Colonel John Trumbull. This portrait was painted in 1781. The face was executed by Mr. Stewart, and the other parts by Mr. Trumbull himself while a student with him. 8th. A portrait of James Thacher, M.D., late Librarian and Cabinet-keeper of the Pilgrim Society. It was painted by Mr. Frothingham, in January, 1841, by order of the Pilgrim Society, pursuant to a vote expressing their sense of the valuable services he had rendered, in promoting the objects of said society.*

A portrait of James Kendall, D.D., Senior Pastor of the first church.

The bust of Hon. Daniel Webster, presented by James T. Hayward, Esq., of Boston. The bust of Hon. John Adams, presented by Samuel Nicolson, Esq.

The addition of Weir's painting, copied from the original at Washington, representing the memorable scene of the

---

* Dr. Thacher was appointed Librarian and Cabinet-keeper of the Pilgrim Society, at its first organization, and his indefatigable efforts contributed largely to the promotion of its objects. The following extract from the report of a Committee of the Society indicates the sense entertained of his services : " The undersigned, to whom was referred the report of Dr. James Thacher, respecting the Iron Railing around the Forefather's Rock, report, that the Society are indebted to Dr. Thacher for this beautiful and costly monument, which, while it secures the Pilgrim Rock from further depredation, records, for the benefit of posterity, the names of our fathers, and affords a pleasing subject of contemplation to many strangers who visit us." — Dr. Thacher died May 23, 1844, aged ninety

embarkation of the Pilgrims at Delft-haven, would afford a valuable addition to the attractions of Pilgrim Hall, which it is hoped will be made, when the requisite means can be obtained for accomplishing so desirable an object.

Among the antiquities in the Cabinet of the Pilgrim Society, are the following :

A chair which belonged to Governor Carver. The sword of Miles Standish, presented by William S. Williams, Esq. A pewter dish which belonged to Miles Standish, presented by the late Joseph Head, Esq. An iron pot which belonged to Miles Standish, presented by the late John Watson, Esq. A brass steelyard, owned by Thomas Southworth. A cane which belonged to William White, presented by Hon. John Reed. A dressing-case which belonged to William White. The gun-barrel with which King Philip was killed, presented by Mr. John Cook, of Kingston. The original letter of King Philip to Governor Prince, written in 1662. A china mug and leather pocket-book which belonged to Thomas Clark. A piece of ingenious embroidery, in a frame, executed by Lorea Standish, a daughter of Miles Standish, presented by Rev. Lucius Alden, of East Bridgewater.

An ancient deed, having the signature of Peregrine White, the first Englishman born in New England, and acknowledged before Governor Josiah Winslow, June 9, 1678, presented by Mr. Sherman, of Marshfield.

An ancient bond, dated the last day of June, 1688, having the signature of Peregrine White, presented by Mr. William S. Russell, of Plymouth.

An ancient deed, written and acknowledged before Miles Standish, August 28, 1655, presented by Joseph F. Wadsworth Esq., of Duxbury.

An ancient instrument, the receipt of heirs of Governor
Thomas Prince, containing the signatures of Governor Josiah
Winslow and Resolved White, the brother of Peregrine
White.   Also the signatures of Wm. Crow, John Freeman,
Jonathan Sparrow, John Trasie, Jeremiah Howe, Arthur
Howland, Isaac Barcar, Mark Snow, dated July 4, 1674,
presented by Amos Otis, Esq., of Yarmouth.

An ancient deed, written by John Alden, with his signature as magistrate, July 2, 1653, presented by Isaac Fobes,
Esq., of Bridgewater.

A commission from Oliver Cromwell to Governor Edward
Winslow, dated April, 1654, presented by Pelham Winslow,
Esq., of Boston.

A bust of Henry Sargent, Esq., presented by his sons.

A chair, which belonged to Elder William Brewster, presented by Mr. —— Brewster, of Duxbury.

An ancient couch, which belonged to Governor John
Hancock, presented by Captain Josiah Sturgess.

A pewter dish, which belonged to Mr. John Atwood,
bearing date 1642, presented by the late Rosseter Cotton,
Esq., of Plymouth.

A portrait of Major General Benjamin Lincoln.

An antique clock, which belonged to Governor John
Hancock, which was taken to West Bridgewater from Bos-
ton, at the time of the siege, presented by Mrs. Mary
Whitman.

A cane, made from the pear-tree, set out by Governor
Thomas Prince, at Eastham, Cape Cod, about the year
1644, presented by Amos Otis, Esq., of Yarmouth.

A gourd-shell, which belonged to Mr. George Soule, presented by Mrs. Faith Fuller, of Halifax, Mass.

A foot-wheel, presented by Mrs. Priscilla Lucas, of

Kingston; the said wheel belonged to her grandmother, who was the third in descent from Governor William Bradford.

A coat of arms of England, formerly in the old court-house in Plymouth, and hung over the judge's seat, presented by Cornelius White, Esq , of Shelburn, Nova Scotia

An ancient platter, which belonged to the first Waterman, who came over to this country at a very early date, presented by Mrs. Bethiah Ford, of Worcester, Mass.

A tea-pot, which belonged to the widow Foord, who came over in the ship Fortune, presented by Mrs. Bethiah Ford, of Worcester, Mass.

An instrument, purporting to be an agreement between John Alden and an Indian Sachem, dated May 17th, 1661, presented by Dr. John Batchelder, of Sandwich.

Fac simile of a certificate of Lord Nelson, dated on board his majesty's ship, 17th August, 1782, in Boston Bay, presented by the late Isaac P. Davis, Esq., of Boston.

The trunk of a pear-tree, which was planted by Governor Prince, in Eastham, Cape Cod, presented by Amos Otis, Esq., of Eastham.

A large painting of the Landing of the Pilgrims, presented by the late Robert G. Shaw, Esq., of Boston.

A gunspring and nails, dug from the ruins of Captain Miles Standish's house, in Duxbury, presented by Mr. George Sears, of Duxbury.

An old hoe, dug from the cellar where once stood the Old Colony trading-house, on the Manomet river; as early as the year 1627, presented by Dr. John Batchelder, of Manomet.

A copy of the compact of the Pilgrim Fathers, signed on board of the Mayflower, November, 1620. Also a copy of Rev. John Robinson's parting advice to the Pilgrim Fathers, and a copy of his letter, presented by N. D. Gould, Esq., of Boston.

An ancient commission, from Jonathan Belcher, Esq., to Isaac Lothrop, Esq., given in the year 1732, presented by Leander Lovell, Esq., of Plymouth.

An ancient plate, which belonged to Governor Bradford, presented by Mrs. Abigail Willis, of Kingston.

A sword, which belonged to Peregrine White's grandson, presented by Miss Sybil White, of Marshfield.

A pair of spectacles, which belonged to Colonel Benjamin Church, presented by Mr. Joseph Church, of Rochester.

A piece of timber, from the house of Elder Thomas Faunce, who was the last ruling elder in the first church of Plymouth, and who died in the year 1745, at the advanced age of ninety-nine years, presented by Mr. Ezekiel Morton, of Plymouth.

Besides the above, many valuable relics of the Pilgrims are scattered abroad in various quarters, and among others the large arm-chair which came over in the Mayflower, with staples attached to it, by which the same was fastened to the floor or deck, owned by Madam Warren, of Plymouth.

A bead purse, wrought by Mrs. Penelope Pelham Winslow, wife of Gov. Josiah Winslow, while on her voyage to America; and a gold ring, worn by the Governor, and containing his hair, owned by Mrs. Anna Hayward, widow of the late Nathan Hayward, M.D. Both of the ladies above named were daughters of Pelham, the son of Gen. John Winslow.

The silver canteen, and several pewter platters, marked E. W., which belonged to Gov. Edward Winslow, and several other articles, owned by the Misses Jane R. and Elizabeth P. Sever, of Kingston. The Fuller cradle, owned by Jacob Noyes, Esq., of Abington.

A gun, measuring seven feet, four and a half nches, including the stock, the length of the barrel six feet one and a half inches, the calibre will carry twelve balls to the pound, the face of the lock ten inches long, the whole weight of the gun twenty pounds twelve ounces; a sword, three feet, five and a half inches long, which belonged to John Thompson, of Middleborough, one of the early comers, who died in 1696, aged eighty years; now owned by Capt. Zadock Thompson, of Halifax.

A brass pistol, which belonged to the same individual, and a halberd, having the date, 1623, cut on its face, are owned by the descendants of the late Adam Thompson, deceased.

An arm-chair, which belonged to Gov. William Bradford, used at the first celebration of the Old Colony Club, in 1769, formerly owned by Dr. Lazarus Le Baron, and now by Nathaniel Russell, Esq., of Plymouth.

Several valuable articles are deposited in the rooms of the Massachusetts Historical Society in Boston, namely, the swords of Gov. Carver, and Col. Benjamin Church; the gun-lock attached to the gun with which King Philip was killed. A Bible which belonged to Isaac Allerton, and some other antiquities connected with Old Colony men and times.

One important object with the founders of the Pilgrim Society was, to collect a library illustrative of our early history, which, it is hoped, will be kept in mind, to the better promotion of so desirable an end.

There is also a library, consisting of miscellaneous works, presented by various individuals since the formation of the Pilgrim Society, in 1820. The iron railing in front of Pilgrim Hall, enclosing a part of Forefathers' Rock, was designed by the late George W. Brimmer, Esq., of Boston. The names inscribed upon it — forty-one in number — are those who signed the compact on board the Mayflower, in Cape Cod harbor, Nov. 11th, 1620. This railing cost four hundred and ten dollars, and the funds were obtained by subscription.

The records of the late librarian and cabinet-keeper abound with evidences of great efforts on the part of the Plymouth ladies, at various times, in procuring means to aid the society in promoting its objects. Besides the subscriptions obtained in Plymouth, Boston, and other places, by means of which the hall was originally built, donations have been received from the heirs of the late Samuel Davis, Esq., of the lot on which the hall stands; from the late Dr. Nathaniel Lothrop the sum of five hundred dollars, and the late Miss Rebecca Frazier, of Duxbury, five hundred dollars, which last bequest was specially to be applied for the purpose of procuring appropriate paintings.

THE EMBARKATION OF THE PILGRIMS AT DELFT-HAVEN, JULY 22d, 1620, AND A DESCRIPTION OF WEIR'S PAINTING.

" O, 't was no earth-born passion
That bade the adventurers stray ;
The earth with all its fashion
With them had passed away."   FLINT.

THE embarkation from Delft-haven designates a point of exciting interest in the history of the Pilgrims; and, whether we regard it as a striking development of the purest affections and higher principles of our nature, or with reference to its general results on human affairs, possesses the strongest claims to attention from the orator, poet and painter.

Holland, at this point of time, engrossed a large share of the tonnage owned by all Europe, and the preparations, for even a remote voyage, of a vessel sixty tons burthen only, were not of unfrequent occurrence. Truth requires us not to confound the individuals concerned in this event among the ordinary adventurers of that time ; but as influenced by motives of the highest order, as the honored instruments of opening a new theatre of human action, where freedom, exhausted in her conflicts with the corruption of accumulated ages, might break from the Old World, and breathe the invigorating atmosphere of the New.

The parting scene at Leyden is thus described in Gov. Bradford's History, from which extracts have previously been made : " So, being ready to depart, they had a day of solemn humiliation, their pastor taking his text from Ezra the 8th, 21, upon which he spent a part of the day very profitably, and very suitably to their present occasion. The rest of the time was spent in pouring out prayers to the Lord, with great fervency, mixed with abundance of tears. And the time being come when they must depart, they were accompanied with most of their brethren out of the city, unto a town, sundry miles off, called Delft-haven, where the ship lay ready to receive them. So they left that good and pleasant city, which had been their resting-place near twelve years. But they knew they were PILGRIMS, and looked not much on those things, but lifted up their eyes to heaven, their dearest country, and so quieted their spirits.*

---

* " I think I may, with singular propriety, call their lives a *pilgrimage*. Most of them left England about the year 1609, after the truce with the Spaniards, young men between twenty and thirty years of age. They

When they came to the place they found the ship and all things ready, and such of their friends as could not come with them, followed after them, and sundry also came from Amsterdam,* to see them shipped, and to take their leave of them. That night was spent with little sleep by the most, but with friendly entertainment and Christian discourse, and other real expressions of true Christian love. The next day (July 22d), the wind being fair, they went on board, and their friends with them; when truly doleful was the sight of that sad and mournful parting. To see what sighs, and sobs, and prayers, did sound amongst them; what tears did gush from every eye, and pithy speeches pierced each other's heart; that sundry of the Dutch strangers, that stood on the quay as spectators, could not refrain from tears. Yet comfortable and sweet it was, to see such lively and true expressions of dear and unfeigned love. But the tide, which stays for no man, calling them away that were thus loth to depart, their reverend pastor, falling down upon his knees, and they all with him, with watery cheeks commended them, with most fervent prayers, to the Lord, and his blessing; and then, with mutual embraces and many tears, they took their leaves of one another, which proved their last leave to many of them. Thus hoisting, with a prosperous wind we came in a short time to Southampton, where they found the bigger ship come from London, lying ready with all the rest of their company."

" The embarkation at Delft-haven, that scene of interest

spent near twelve years among the Dutch, first at Amsterdam, afterwards at Leyden. After having arrived to the meridian of life, the declining part was to be spent in another world, among savages, of whom every European must have received a most unfavorable, if not formidable idea."
— *Hutchinson, History Mass.*, II., 452.

     * About fifty miles from Delft-haven.

unparalleled, on which a pencil of your own has just enabled us to look back with tears, and praise, and sympathy, and the fond pride of children; that scene of few and simple incidents; just the setting out of a handful of not then very famous persons on a voyage; but which, as we gaze on it, begins to speak to you as with the voices and melodies of an immortal hymn, which dilates and becomes idolized into the auspicious going forth of a colony, whose planting has changed the history of the world; a noble colony of de-voted Christians, — educated, firm men, valiant soldiers, and honorable women; a colony, on the commencement of whose heroic enterprise the selectest influences of religion seemed to be descending visibly, and beyond whose perilous path are hung the rainbow and the western star of empire." *

An obliging correspondent, — Mr. W. A. Gay, of Hing-ham, — has furnished the following description of Weir's painting of the embarkation.

" The scene is laid on the deck of the vessel. Mr. Rob-inson, their pastor, is making the parting prayer, just before her departure.

" Elder Brewster holds the open Bible; Gov. Carver, Mr. Bradford, with their wives, form the centre group of the picture.

" On the right, Miles Standish, the soldier, with his wife Rose, who found an early grave in the new country.

" Mr. and Mrs. White, the parents of Peregrine, the first child born in the colony, on the left.

" Beyond the centre group, Mr. Fuller is seen parting with his wife, who remains behind.

" Mr. and Mrs. Winslow, a newly-married couple, were travelling on the continent at the time Mr. Robinson was

* Hon Rufus Choate's Oration at New York, Dec. 22d, 1843.

10*

preaching in Holland; and were so much pleased with him, that they joined the company and came out with them.

"A boy leaning over the side of the vessel, belonging to Mr. Winslow's family, wears a silver canteen, which bears the initials E. W., now in existence.

"Captain Reynolds, in the background, orders a sailor on board with the cradle in which Peregrine was rocked. His face expressive of double meaning, as it is said he had been bribed not to bring the company out.

"The screw, which probably saved the vessel, lies in the foreground, with a group of armor, matchlocks, &c.

"Various figures, members of the different families, fill up the picture. Mr. Robinson remained behind."

Spectators on the wharf could not refrain from tears at the "sad and mournful parting."

The picture is true to the minutest particular, in costume and in color, to the "sad colors" of the time, and taste of the Pilgrims; with some exception for Mrs. Winslow, who, being a bride, and of the wealthier class, was dressed accordingly.

The whole picture is true to nature and the character of the scene.

It was on board the Speedwell, and that small vessel held the germ of a republic.

This painting is now in one of the panels in the Rotunda of the Capitol at Washington.

PILGRIM SOCIETY.

THE Pilgrim Society was formed in 1820, by the citizens of Plymouth and others in New England, to commemorate the landing, and to honor the memory of those intrepid men who first stepped on Plymouth Rock. The Constitution was adopted May 29th, 1820, and the following extract from the concluding part of its preamble, shows the purpose of its organization :

" That these historical events should be perpetuated by durable monuments to be erected at Plymouth, is a desirable object, in which public feeling very laudably concurs, and which has led to the institution and incorporation of the Pilgrim Society. We, therefore, many of us the lineal descendants, and all of us holding their memory in respect and honor, approve, adopt and subscribe to the rules and regulations of the Pilgrim Society, as members of the same."

The condition of membership was formerly the payment of ten dollars ; now reduced to the sum of five dollars. An appropriate diploma has been prepared for distribution to those who join the Society. The first Presidents of the Society were Hon. Joshua Thomas, John Watson, Alden Bradford, Nathaniel M. Davis, and Charles H. Warren, Esqs.*

The officers for 1855, are Richard Warren, of New York, President; Samuel Nicolson, of Boston, Vice-President; Elliot Russell, Recording Secretary; Benjamin M. Watson, Corresponding Secretary; Lemuel D. Holmes, Librarian and Cabinet-Keeper; Isaac N. Stodderd, Treasurer. Isaac L. Hedge, Abraham Jackson, Winslow Warren, Andrew L. Russell, Timothy Gordon, William S. Russell, James T. Hayward, Samuel H. Doten, Eleazer C. Sherman, Charles G. Davis, Thomas Loring, of Plymouth, John H. Clifford. of New Bedford, Samuel T. Tisdale, of New York, Wil-

* Only one officer of the Society appointed at its first organization in 1820, now survives, viz., the Hon. William Sturgis, of Boston, who was a Trustee.

liam Thomas, Nathaniel B. Shurtleff, Frederick Gleason, of Boston, Trustees. Charles G. Davis, Secretary of the Board of Trustees.

The following is a list of those who have delivered public addresses in commemoration of the landing of the fathers in 1620. The asterisk affixed to some of the names designates those whose discourses have not been published.

1769, First celebration by Old Colony Club.

1770, Second celebration by Old Colony Club.

1771, Third celebration by Old Colony Club.

1772, Rev. Chandler Robbins, for Old Colony Club.

1773, Rev. Charles Turner, for Old Colony Club. By the town and by the First Parish.

1774, Rev. Gad Hitchcock, Pembroke.

1775, Rev. Samuel Baldwin, Hanover.

1776, Rev. Sylvanus Conant, Middleborough.

1777, Rev. Samuel West, Dartmouth.

1778, Rev. Timothy Hilliard, Barnstable.*

1779, Rev. William Shaw, Marshfield.*

1780, Rev. Jonathan Moor, Rochester.*

From this time the public observances of the day were suspended, till

1794, Rev. Chandler Robbins, D. D., of Plymouth.

1795, ⎫
1796, ⎬ Private celebration.
1797, ⎭

1798, Dr. Zaccheus Bartlett, Plymouth, Oration.*

1799, The day came so near that appointed for the ordination of Rev. Mr. Kendall, that it was not celebrated by a public discourse.

1800, John Davis, Esq., Boston, Oration.*
1801, Rev. John Allyn, D. D., Duxbury.
1802, John Quincy Adams, Esq., Quincy, Oration.
1803, Rev. John T. Kirkland, D. D., Boston.*
1804, (Lord's Day) Rev. James Kendall, Plymouth.*
1805, Alden Bradford, Esq., Boston.
1806, Rev. Abiel Holmes, D. D., Cambridge.
1807, Rev. James Freeman, D. D., Boston.*
1808, Rev. Thaddeus M. Harris, Dorchester.
1809, Rev. Abiel Abbot, Beverly.
1811, Rev. John Elliot, D. D., Boston.
1815, Rev. James Flint, Bridgewater.
1817, Rev. Horace Holley, Boston.*
1818, Wendell Davis, Esq., Sandwich.*
1819, Francis C. Gray, Esq., Boston.
1820, Daniel Webster, Esq., Boston, by Pilgrim Society.
1824, Professor Edward Everett, Cambridge, by Pilgrim Society.
1831, Rev. John Brazer, Salem, by First Parish in Plymouth.*

The following Anniversaries were commemorated by the Third Parish in Plymouth :

1826, Rev. Richard S. Storrs, Braintree.
1827, Rev. Lyman Beecher, D. D., Boston.
1828, Rev. Samuel Green, Boston.
1829, Rev. Daniel Huntington, Bridgewater.
1830, Rev. Benjamin Wisner, D. D., Boston.
1831, Rev. John Codman, D. D., Dorchester.
1832, Rev. Convers Francis, of Watertown, for the First Parish.

1832, Rev. Mr. Bigelow, of Rochester, for the Third Parish.

1833, Rev. Mr. Barrett, of Boston, for the First Parish.

1834, Rev. G. W. Blagden, of Boston, for the Pilgrim Society.

1835, Hon. Peleg Sprague, by Pilgrim Society.

1837, Rev. Robert B. Hall, by Pilgrim Society.*

1838, Rev. Thomas Robbins, by Pilgrim Society.*

1841, Joseph R. Chandler, Esq., of Philadelphia, by Pilgrim Society.*

1845, A public celebration, religious services in the First Church, a public dinner and addresses.

1846, Rev. Mark Hopkins, D. D., President of Williams College.

1848, Rev. Samuel M. Worcester, D. D., of Salem, for the Robinson Society.

The following resolution was unanimously adopted at a meeting of the society in May, 1850:

" *Resolved*, That it is expedient to erect a monument on or near the Rock on which the Pilgrims landed, and to make other improvements in the vicinity, and that the Trustees have full power to take such measures as they may deem expedient to carry these objects into effect."

Judging from the opinions expressed by intelligent visitors from almost every part of the Union, the objects proposed in the foregoing resolution may be fully accomplished, whenever the requisite measures are adopted, and a suitable appeal is made to the public for its countenance and aid in so desirable a work.

On the 27th day of May, 1850, a committee, consisting of James Savage, Charles H. Warren, Nathaniel B. Shurtleff, Boston, Abraham Jackson and Timothy Gordon, of Plymouth, presented a Report, recommending the following : "That the celebration in future of the landing of the Pilgrims at Plymouth, be held on the *twenty-first* day of December; but when that day falls on Sunday, then to be held on the twenty-second." This report was unanimously accepted, and the following vote was passed : "That this Society will hereafter regard the *twenty-first* day of December as the true anniversary of the landing of the Pilgrims."

Truth is desirable at all times, and on all subjects; and we trust the true day will, at no distant period, be adopted as that of celebration, though present feelings and associations may cling to the twenty-second in preference.

The first day of August, 1853, being the two hundred and thirty-third anniversary of the embarkation of the Pilgrims at Delft-Haven, in Holland, may well be regarded as one of the most interesting and memorable occasions which have occurred since the organization of the Pilgrim Society. It was celebrated, for the first time since the landing, in a manner evincing the deep interest with which not only the Pilgrim Society and town, but all New England, regard the memory of the venerable men, the devoted Christian heroes, who landed on the Rock of Plymouth, and laid the foundation of New England empire, based upon the laws of God and the rights of man. The celebration of the embarkation, for more than a year previous to its occurrence, engaged the earnest attention of the Pilgrim Society, and was considered not only as the just recognition of an event second, in its moral, religious and political results, to none other recorded in history, but which might afford a proper occasion to present, for public consideration, the long-cherished purpose of the Society, to erect an appropriate monument in honor of the Pilgrims and the great principles which they first promulgated, and successfully established. At a meeting of the Society, held on March 10th, 1853, expressly called for the purpose, the trustees were authorized and requested to make suitable arrangements "to celebrate the event." It may safely be assumed that no occasion of a similar nature has excited a deeper interest in the public mind, none has enlisted more ardent feelings of mutual coöperation among all concerned in this great celebration, or has imparted more general satisfaction to the animated throng of visitors from every quarter of our country; as will more fully appear on reference to the detailed proceedings of the day, published by the trustees, and filed among the Records of the Pilgrim Society.*

THE OLD COLONY CLUB.

As our public anniversary celebrations originated with this association, some account of its origin will doubtless be interesting to the reader. It was formed in 1769, as will be seen from the following extracts, copied from the records which are now in existence.

"*January* 16*th*, 1769. — We whose names are underwritten, having maturely weighed and seriously considered the many disadvantages and inconveniences that arise from intermixing with the company at the taverns in this town, and apprehending that a well-regulated club will have a tendency to prevent the same, and to increase not only the

---

* For a description of the proposed new Monument, see p. 193.

pleasure and happiness of the respective members, but, also, will conduce to their edification and instruction, do hereby incorporate ourselves into a society, by the name of the *Old Colony Club.* For the better regulation of which we do consent and agree to observe all such rules and laws as shall from time to time be made by the Club. Dated at our Hall, in Plymouth, the day and year above written.

ISAAC LOTHROP,	EDWARD WINSLOW, JR.,
PELHAM WINSLOW,	JOHN WATSON,
THOMAS LOTHROP,	ELKANAH CUSHMAN.
JOHN THOMAS,	

" *December* 18*th.* — At a meeting of the Club, voted, that Friday next be kept by this Club in commemoration of the landing of our worthy ancestors in this place; that the Club dine together at Mr. Howland's and that a number of gentlemen be invited to spend the evening with us at the Old Colony Hall.

" *Old Colony Day. First Celebration of the Landing of our Forefathers.* — Friday, December 22. The Old Colony Club, agreeably to a vote passed the 18th instant, met in commemoration of the landing of their worthy ancestors in this place. On the morning of the said day, after discharging a cannon, was hoisted upon the hall an elegant silk flag, with the following inscription, ' *Old Colony,*' 1620. At eleven o'clock, A. M., the members of the club appeared at the hall, and from thence proceeded to the house of Mr. Howland, inn-holder, which is erected upon the spot where the first licensed house in the Old Colony formerly stood; at half after two a decent repast was served, which consisted of the following dishes, viz. :

" 1, a large baked Indian whortleberry pudding; 2, a dish

11

of sauquetach (succatach, corn and beans boiled together);
3, a dish of clams; 4, a dish of oysters and a dish of codfish; 5, a haunch of venison, roasted by the first jack
brought to the colony; 6, a dish of sea-fowl; 7, a dish of
frost-fish and eels; 8, an apple pie; 9, a course of cran-
berry tarts, and cheese made in the Old Colony.

"These articles were dressed in the plainest manner (all
appearance of luxury and extravagance• being avoided, in
imitation of our ancestors, whose memory we shall ever
respect).   At four o'clock, P. M., the members of our club,
headed by the steward, carrying a folio volume of the laws
of the Old Colony, hand in hand, marched in procession to
the hall.   Upon the appearance of the procession in front
of the hall, a number of descendants from the first settlers
in the Old Colony drew up in a regular file, and discharged
a volley of small arms, succeeded by three cheers, which
were returned by the Club, and the gentlemen generously
treated.   After this, appeared at the private grammar-
school, opposite the hall, a number of young gentlemen,
pupils of Mr. Wadsworth, who, to express their joy upon
this occasion, and their respect for the memory of their
ancestors, in the most agreeable manner joined in singing a
song very applicable to the day.   At sunsetting a cannon
was discharged, and the flag struck.   In the evening the
hall was illuminated, and the following gentlemen, being
previously invited, joined the Club, viz.:

Col. George Watson,	Capt. Elkanah Watson,
Col. James Warren,	Capt. Thomas Davis,
James Hovey, Esq.,	Dr. Nathaniel Lothrop,
Thomas Mayhew, Esq.,	Mr. John Russell,
William Watson, Esq.,	Mr. Edward Clark,
Capt. Gideon White,	Mr. Alexander Scammell,

Mr. PELEG WADSWORTH,

Mr. THOMAS SOUTHWORTH HOWLAND.

" The President, being seated in a large and venerable chair,* which was formerly possessed by William Bradford, the second worthy governor of the Old Colony, and presented to the club by our friend Dr. Lazarus Le Baron, of this town, delivered several appropriate toasts.† After spending the evening, in an agreeable manner, in recapitulating and conversing upon the many and various advantages of our forefathers in the first settlement of this country, and the growth and increase of the same, at eleven o'clock in the evening a cannon was again fired, three cheers given, and the Club and company withdrew."

In 1770, the anniversary of the landing was celebrated

---

* This ancient chair is now in the family of Nathaniel Russell, Esq.

† 1. To the memory of our brave and pious ancestors, the first settlers of the Old Colony.

2. To the memory of John Carver, and all the other worthy Governors of the Old Colony.

3. To the memory of that pious man and faithful historian, Mr. Secretary Morton.

4. To the memory of that brave man and good officer, Captain Miles Standish.

5. To the memory of Massasoit, our first and best friend, and ally of the Natives.

6. To the memory of Mr. Robert Cushman, who preached the first sermon in New England.

7. The union of the Old Colony and Massachusetts.

8. May every person be possessed of the same noble sentiments against arbitrary power that our worthy ancestors were endowed with.

9. May every enemy to civil or religious liberty meet the same or a worse fate than Archbishop Laud.

10. May the Colonies be speedily delivered from all the burdens and oppressions they now labor under.

11. A speedy and lasting union between Great Britain and her Colonies.

12. Unanimity, prosperity, and happiness to the Colonies.

much in the same manner as in the preceding year, with the addition of an address by Edward Winslow, Jun., Esq.,* the first ever delivered on any similar occasion.

CAPE COD.

CAPE COD was discovered by Bartholomew Gosnold, on the 15th of May, 1602, and was visited by Henry Hudson, in August, 1609, and by Captain John Smith, in 1614. It was named by Gosnold, from the abundance of codfish taken in its neighborhood. Its harbor is considered one of the best on the New England coast for vessels of every size. The infamous conduct of Captain Hunt (so indignantly condemned by Smith), in kidnapping twenty-seven of the natives, in 1614, had justly incensed the tribe of Nauset, to which place five of them belonged. To this cause their hostile conduct towards the Pilgrims may properly be ascribed; for it appears that afterwards, when explanations were made, disclaiming any participation in the conduct of Hunt, friendly relations existed, which were rarely interrupted. Cape Cod, Nantucket and New Bedford, have been distinguished for the nautical skill and enterprise of their citizens, unsurpassed by any equal population in the world, and by our wisest statesmen have been regarded as the main supports of our naval strength. On this subject, Edmund Burke, in 1774, addressing the House of Commons on American affairs, pronounced an eulogy deserving of grateful remembrance : " No sea, but what is

---

* A son of the above, John F. Wentworth Winslow, Esq., now resides at Woodstock, in New Brunswick, is Sheriff of Carlton Co., and the oldest male descendant of Governor Edward Winslow, who came in the Mayflower.

vexed by their fisheries. No climate, that is not witness of their toils. Neither the perseverance of Holland, nor the activity of France, nor the dexterous and firm sagacity of English enterprise, ever carried their most perilous mode of hardy industry to the extent to which it has been pursued by this recent people; a people who are still in the gristle, and not hardened into manhood."

The population of Cape Cod is thirty-five thousand two hundred and seventy-nine; Nantucket, eight thousand five hundred and forty-two; Dukes County, four thousand five hundred and forty; New Bedford, sixteen thousand four hundred and sixty-four. Aggregate, sixty-four thousand eight hundred and twenty-five.

PLYMOUTH COLONY RECORDS.

In the year 1818, three Commissioners, viz., James Freeman, Samuel Davis, and Benjamin R. Nichols, "were appointed by the Legislature of the State, and were authorized to cause the records to be transcribed, and afterwards to return the originals to the Register of Deeds' Office in Plymouth, and to deposit the copies in the office of the Secretary of the Commonwealth." Full Indexes were made to them, and the volumes were interleaved and new bound. The original charter of the Colony being considerably defaced, it was repaired and placed in a port-folio, with the seal of the Plymouth Company in England annexed to it. The seal is about four inches in diameter. It was much broken, but the parts were carefully cemented and secured together, and inclosed in a case, so that the original impression may be seen.

The records are now arranged chronologically, and in
11*

such a manner that the legislative proceedings or court orders form six separate volumes; the wills and inventories, four; deeds, six; laws, one; acts of Commissioners of United Colonies, two. There is also an imperfect volume of the records of these Commissioners, being, as is supposed, their original minutes. There is also one volume of Indian deeds, bound up with the Treasurer's accounts, and lists of freemen, and one volume of actions, marriages, births and deaths, making, in the whole, twenty-two volumes of original records.

The copies made from the above (deposited in the office of the Secretary of State) form eleven folio volumes, and are indexed like the originals. The records of the Commissioners of the United Colonies were formerly transcribed and published by Ebenezer Hazard, Esq. They compose nearly the whole of his second volume. This volume was compared by Mr. Nichols with the original records, and corrected by him; and the volume so corrected is deposited, with the copies above mentioned, in the office of the Secretary of the Commonwealth. They are kept in a separate case from the other records of the Commonwealth.

All the laws and legislative proceedings are copied, with such parts of the other records as were thought to be useful. The parts not copied are most of the private deeds, wills, and inventories. Care was taken to preserve in the copies the original paging and orthography.

The following statement will give a general view of the contents of the records:

There is nothing recorded in 1620, except a plan of the lots laid out at Plymouth.*

The next records are the allotments of land in 1623,† to

---

* See page 56.　† One acre, near the town, to each one in every family.

the passengers in the Mayflower, Fortune, and Ann, and a law establishing the trial by jury.

In 1627 there was a division of the cattle among the inhabitants.

There are but few other records previous to 1632.

In that year the General Court of Plymouth began to keep a regular journal of their proceedings, which they continued to the close of the colony, excepting the years 1687, and 1688, during the government of Sir Edmund Andros.

In 1636, a code of laws was made, with a preamble containing an account of the settlement of the Colony. Other laws were added at subsequent periods, and when any of the former were altered or repealed, this was done by making erasures and interlineations, instead of passing original acts. In the copy now made all these erasures and interlineations are noticed. In 1658 the laws were revised and entered in another book. Most of them were transcribed from the former code, and the dates when they were first enacted inserted in the margin. Other laws were inserted afterward, till 1664, when they appear to have been again revised. A third book of laws was then made, similar to the former. This book contains all the laws passed from that time till 1682.

The laws of the colony thus existed in three separate parts. They are now bound together and indexed, and a complete copy made of them.

There was another code made in 1671, and printed. The manuscript of this code no longer exists. But one of the printed copies may be found in the library of the Historical Society, bound up with the laws of Massachusetts and Connecticut. This code is very different from the former. It contains some new laws, and omits most of those which before existed.

From these records a knowledge may be obtained of all the principal men who lived in the Colony, of the Governors, Assistants, Deputies, or Representatives, Selectmen of towns, and other civil officers, military officers and freemen. There are lists of all the freemen in the Colony at several periods, also records of marriages, births, and deaths. The latter records, however, are imperfect.

Marriages were never solemnized by ministers, but magistrates were especially appointed for that purpose.

The following extracts from the O. C. Records, 1st vol. of Deeds, being the first acts of legislation on *Record*, may interest the reader:

Trial by Jury. — "It was ordained 17 Desemb Anno 1623, by the court then held that all criminall facts; and also all matters of trespasses; and debts betweene man and man should be tried by the verdict of twelve honest men to be empanelled by authority in forme of a jurie upon their oath."

Exportation of Timber prohibited. — "It was decreed by the Court held the 29th of March, Anno 1626, that for the preventing of such inconveniences, as doe, and may befall the plantation by the want of timber, that no man of what condition soever sell or transport any manner of workes as frames for houses plankes board shiping shalops, boates, canoes, or whatsoever may tende to the destrucktion of timber aforesaid how little soever the quantitie be, without the consent approbation and likeing of the Governour and Counsell; and if any be found faulty herein and shall imbarke or any way convey to that end to make sale of any the goods aforesaid expressed or intended by this decrce the same to be forfited and a fine of twise the valew for all so sould to be duly taken by the Governour for the use and benefit of the Company."

Handicraftsmen forbidden to work for Strangers. — " It was further decreed the day and year above written for the preventing such abuses as doe & may arise amongst us that no handicraftsmen of what profession so ever as taylors shoemakers carpenters joyners smiths sawiers or whatsoever wch do or may reside or belong to this plantation of Plymouth shall use their science or trades at home or abroade for any strangers or foreigners till such time as the necessity of the colony be served without the consent of the Governo^r and councill, the breach thereof to be punished at their discretion."

No corn, beans or peas, to be exported. — " It was ordained the s^d 29 of March 1626; for the preventing scarsity as alsoe for the furthering of our trade that no corne beanes or peaes be transported, imbarked or sold to that end to be conveyed out of the colony without the leave and license of the Governour and counsell; The breach whereof to be punished with lose of the goods so taken or proved to be sold ; and the seller further find or punished or both at the discression of the Govr and councill."

Dwelling-houses to be covered with board or pale. — " It was agreed upon by the whole court held the sixth of January 1627, that from hence forward no dwelling house was to be covered with any kind of thache as straw reed &c. but with either board or pale and the like to wit of all that were to be new built in the towne."

Several fires had occurred before this period, and this

law was doubtless intended to prevent similar occurrences in future.

1627. "Edward Winslow hath sold unto Capt Myles Standish his six shares in the red Cow for and in consideration of five pounds ten shillings to be pd in corne at the rate of six shillings p. bushell freeing the sd Edward from all manner of charge belonging to the said shares during the terme of the nine yeares they are let out to halves and taking the benefit thereof."

The value of the Red Cow in 1627 is estimated at about one hundred and sixty dollars in our currency — reference being had to the comparative value of money between that time and the present.

The first importation of cattle was made under the direction of Edward Winslow, in 1624, and consisted of one bull and three heifers. In 1627, after the Pilgrims had bought out the interests of the Merchant Adventurers of London, for the sum of eighteen hundred pounds sterling, to be paid in annual instalments of two hundred pounds, the cattle on hand, which had increased to twelve in number, were divided in the following manner : Twelve equal lots were made, consisting of thirteen persons to each lot — the names of which are all recorded. These lots were drawn for, by the parties concerned, as was the usual Pilgrim practice, the whole number of share-holders being one hundred and fifty-six ; affording the first recorded *Cattle Show in New England.*

THE DUTCH EMBASSY FROM NEW NETHER-LAND TO PLYMOUTH COLONY, IN 1627.

The visit of Isaack De Rasieres, in behalf of the Dutch West India Company, established at Manhattan, now New York, to the Plymouth Colony, in the year 1627, appears to have proved not only highly beneficial in its results to the parties concerned, but may justly be regarded as a starting-point in the diplomatic relations of our country, which have since extended to every part of the civilized world ; while the curious observer of human affairs, in tracing our commercial progress through the lapse of more than two centuries, finds a rapidity and extent of growth probably unexampled in the annals of maritime enterprise. The correspondence between the parties of this early negotiation is fortunately preserved, and appears highly creditable to both. The whole affair acquires additional interest from the fact that De Rasieres, after his visit, addressed a letter to one of his employers, containing a minute description of Plymouth and other parts of the Old Colony, which has recently been rescued from oblivion, while nearly all other records pertaining to the celebrated West India Company are irretrievably lost. The following extracts,* which briefly describe the Dutch establishment above referred to, are here introduced for the benefit of the reader : " The territory bounding on the river discovered by Hudson in 1609, and explored by the Dutch between that date and 1614, together with the sea-coasts between the fortieth and forty-fifth degrees of north latitude, received, in the year last mentioned, from the charter of the States General, or the United Provinces,

* See the address of Hon. B. F. Butler, New York His. Colls., New Series, No. 2, page 13.

the name of New Netherlands. The exclusive right of trading with this extensive region was granted by the charter. for three years, from the first day of January, 1615, to Gerrit Jacob Witsen, of Amsterdam, and other merchants associated with him, who had been concerned in the previous voyages to the Island of Manhattan, and in the trading houses established there and on Hudson river, and who were now incorporated by the name of the United New Netherland Company. The Dutch rule, dating its commencement in 1614, lasted continuously but fifty years, ten of which had passed away before the settlements were placed under a regular local government. So slow was their after-growth, that, in 1664, when the colony was surrendered to the English, its population did not exceed ten thousand souls." "On the 3d of June, 1621, the States General established by law the famous 'Chartered West India Company.'"

From an article in the New York Historical Collections, vol. II., New Series, page 278, entitled "Early Colonization of New Netherland," it appears that the colony had, in 1625, increased to two hundred souls; and, in 1628, numbered two hundred and seventy souls, including men, women and children. In 1625, one hundred and three head of cattle were imported, of which some twenty were lost. It is quite remarkable that no interview occurred sooner between the Pilgrims and the Dutch. In the year 1623, intelligence arrived that Massasoit was suddenly seized with dangerous sickness, and that a Dutch ship had been driven on shore before his dwelling, and Governor Winslow was deputed to visit him. Among other reasons assigned for this measure, in Winslow's Relation, was the following: "And the rather because we desired to have some conference with the Dutch, not knowing when we should find so fit an occasion."

This is the only reference to the Dutch in our early history, after the landing, till the visit of De Rasieres, in 1627. The ship had sailed before Winslow arrived at the residence of Massasoit.

"[THIS* year we had letters sent us from the Dutch plantation, of whom we had heard much by the natives, but never could hear from them nor meet with them before themselves thus writ to us, and after sought us out; their letters were writ in a very fair hand, the one in French, and the other in Dutch, but were one verbatim, so far as the tongue would bear.

"Here follows a letter † in Low Dutch, from Isaac de Razier· at Manhatas, in Fort Amsterdam, March 9, 1627, N. S., to the Governour of New Plymouth.

"I will not trouble myself to translate this letter, seeing the effect of it will be understood by the answer which now follows in English, though writ to them in Dutch.]

"To the Honorable and Worshipful the Director and Council of New Netherland, our very loving and worthy friends and Christian neighbours.

THE Governour and Council of Plymouth in New England wish your Honrs Worships all happiness, and prosperity in this life, and eternal rest and glory with Christ Jesus our Lord in the world to come.

"We have received your letters, wherein appeareth your good will and friendship toward us, but is expressed with over high titles, and more than belongs to us, or than is

---

* See Mass. His. Collections, vol. III., first series, for the entire correspondence.

† A part only of this letter is here copied.

meet for us to receive: But for your good will and congratulation of our prosperity in this small beginning of our poor colony, we are much bound unto you, and with many thanks do acknowledge the same ; taking it both for a great honour done unto us, and for a certain testimony of your love, and good neighborhood. Now these are further to give your Honours, Worships, and Wisdoms to understand, that it is no small joy to hear, that it hath pleased God to move his Majesty's heart, not only to confirm that ancient amity, alliance, and friendship, and other contracts formerly made and ratified by his predecessors of famous memory; but hath himself (as you say) and we likewise have been informed, strengthened the same with a new union, the better to resist the pride of that common enemy the' Spaniards, from whose cruelty the Lord keep us both, and our native countries. Now for as much as this is sufficient to unite us together in love, and good' neighborhood in all our dealings ; yet are many of us further tied by the good and courteous entreaty which we have found in your country ; having lived there many years, with freedom and good content, as many of our friends do to this day ; for which we are bound to be thankful, and our children after us, and shall never forget the same, but shall heartily desire your good and prosperity, as our own forever. Likewise for your friendly proposition and offer, to accommodate and help us with any commodities or merchandize, which you have and we want, either for beaver, otters, or other wares, is to us very acceptable, and we doubt not but in short time we may have profitable commerce and trade together :

"By the Governour and Council, your Honours' and
Worships' very good friends and neighbours.

"New Plymouth, March 19th.

" [NEXT follows their reply to this our answer, very friendly, but maintaining their right and liberty to trade in these parts, which we had desired they would forbear ; alleging that as we had authority and commission from our king, so they had the like from the States of Holland, which they would defend.]

"August 7, 1627.

" Monsieur Monseignieur, William Bradford, Governeur in New Plernuen.

" [This will I put in English, and so will end with theirs, viz. :]

AFTER the wishing of all good unto you, this serves to let you understand, that we have received your (acceptable) letters, dated the 14th of the last month, by John Jacobson of Wiring, who besides, by word of mouth, hath reported unto us your kind and friendly entertainment of him ; for which cause (by the good liking and approbation of the Directors and Council) I am resolved to come myself, in friendship to visit you, that we may by word of mouth friendly communicate of things together; as also to report unto you the good will and favour that the Honourable Lords of the authorized West Indian Company bear towards you. And to show our willingness of your good accommodation, have brought with me some cloth of three sorts and colours, and a chest of white sugar, as also some seawan, &c., not doubting but, if any of them be serviceable unto you, we shall agree well enough about the prices thereof. Also John Jacobson aforesaid hath told me, that he came to you overland in six houres, but I have not gone so far this three or four years, wherefore I fear my feet will fail me; so I am constrained to entreat you to afford me the easiest means, that I may, with least weariness, come to congratulate with you. So leaving other things to the report of the bearer, shall herewith end; remembering my hearty salutations to yourself and friends, &c. from a-board the bark Nassaŭ, the 4th of October; before Frenchman's point.

" Your affectionate friend,

" Anno 1627.   "Isaac De Razier.

"[SO, according to his request, we sent our boat * for him, who came honorably attended with a noise of trumpeters; he was their upper *commis*, or chief merchant, and second to the Governour; a man of a fair and genteel behaviour, but soon after fell into disgrace amongst them, by reason of their factions; and thus at length we came to meet and deal together. We at this time bought sundry of their commodities, especially their *seawan* or *wampampeack*, which was the beginning of a profitable trade with us and the Indians. We further understood that their masters were willing to have friendship with us and to supply us with sundry commodities, and offered us assistance against the French, if need were. The which, though we know it was with an eye to their own profit, yet we had reason both kindly to accept it and make use of it: So after this sundry of them came often to us, and many letters passed between us, the which I will pass by, as being about particular dealings, and would not be here very pertinent; only upon this passage we wrote one to their Lords and masters; as followeth.] " †

---

* The boat was sent to Scusset Harbor, in Sandwich, from whence to Manomet River, on Buzzard's Bay, the distance by land is about six miles.

† The letter here alluded to is necessarily omitted.

LETTER OF ISAACK DE RASIERES.

The valuable and highly interesting letter of De Rasieres, written soon after visiting Plymouth in 1627, first appeared in the N. York Hist. Colls., vol. II., new series, and that part of it having special reference to the Old Colony is copied here by permission of John Romeyn Brodhead, Esq., late Secretary of Legation at the Court of London, by whose instrumentality it was recently obtained in Holland.* The introductory note of Mr. Brodhead affords valuable illustrations connected with the letter itself, which cannot fail to be highly appreciated by the reader.

"Note. — While engaged in making researches as Agent of the State of New York, in the Archives at the Hague, in 1841, it occurred to me that the MSS. Department of the Royal Library there might contain something relating to our history, and, with the assistance of Mr. Campbell, one of the Deputy Librarians, a careful examination was accordingly made in that Repository. But, with the exception of the fragment of one manuscript, a copy of which is now in the Secretary of State's Office, at Albany [Hol. Doc., vol. III., p. 90], nothing was then found. It seems, however, that a parcel of MSS. has recently been purchased for the Library, and among these Mr. Campbell's kind research has detected the letter, a copy of which he has made for the New York Historical Society. In the following translation I have endeavored to render, as *literally* as

---

* The indefatigable investigations of Mr. Brodhead in England, France and Holland, have resulted in the acquisition of many important documents connected with our colonial history, for an account of which see his Address before the New York Hist. Society, Nov., 1844.

possible, the original of a document, the high value of which
will be readily appreciated, when it is considered that it is
the *earliest description* we have of the Colony of New
Netherland and its neighborhood from an eye-witness.

" Wassenaer, it is true, in his ' Historiache Verhael,' — a
very rare work, which I have lately had the good fortune to
meet with in London, — gives several very interesting particulars respecting New Netherland, as early as 1623 and
1624 ; and we all know that De Laet published in 1625 an
account of the discoveries of Hudson and the other early
navigators to our coast, whose journals, he distinctly states,
he had before him when he wrote. But the earliest detailed
description of the Island of New York, by a person who
visited it himself in 1626, is now, for the first time, brought
to light. It will be remembered that among the documents
found in the Archives at the Hague, is a letter of Mr. P.
Schagen to the States General, dated at Amsterdam, November 5, 1626 [Hol. Doc., vol. I., p. 155), in which he
reports the arrival of the ship ' Arms of Amsterdam,'
which sailed from the North River on the 23d of September,
and brought the intelligence of the purchase of Manhatten
Island from the Indians, for the sum of about Twenty-four
Dollars. The writer of the following letter, Isaack de
Rasieres, went out passenger in this very ship, which arrived
in New Netherland, as he tells us, on the 27th of July,
1626 ; and as the purchase of the Island of Manhatten was
made before the 23d of September following, when the
' Arms of Amsterdam ' returned to Holland, it is quite
probable he was himself one of the witnesses of that interesting event. De Rasieres (whose name has been variously
and incorrectly spelled in our published documents), seems
to have been a French Protestant, whose ancestors, seeking

refuge from persecution, settled themselves on the River Waal, in Guelderland, and were hence called ' Walloons.' He was probably a protégé of Mr. Samuel Blommaert, one of the leading Directors of the West India Company, to whom, as a mark of his gratitude, he addressed his interesting letter. On his arrival at New Netherland, De Rasieres became ' Opper Koopman,' or Chief Commissary under Director Minuit, and also acted as Secretary of the Colony. In this capacity he conducted a correspondence with Governor Bradford, of New Plymouth, in March, 1627, and in the following October he was himself dispatched on an embassy to that Colony, where he was honorably received by Bradford, who speaks of him as the Dutch ' Upper Commies, or chief Merchant, and second to the Governor ; a man of fair and genteel behavior,'— adding that he 'soon after fell into disgrace among them by reason of their factions.' This is all we know of De Rasieres ; and without any precise information as to the cause of the seizure of his ' things and notes,' which he mentions in the beginning of his letter, we cannot but regret a circumstance but for which, as he himself tells us, we should have perhaps been gratified by a still more ample and detailed account than the one he has now left us, of the early days of New Netherland. De Rasieres' letter has no date, but it was evidently written from memory, and after his return to Holland,— probably about the close of 1627. Unfortunately, it is defective ; and, judging from the part immediately following the hiatus, we may reasonably infer that the missing portion would have been of the highest interest to us. It is quite probable that De Rasieres gave some particulars of the purchase of the island, as well as of the political and commercial situation of the infant colony, and of the topography of the country between Manhatten and Narraganset Bay. But still quite enough remains to us to induce lively congratulation that a happy chance has now placed so precious a fragment within our reach.

"J. ROMEYN BRODHEAD.

"London, 17th August, 1848."

"Coming out of the River Nassau,* you sail east and by north about fourteen miles along the coast, a half a mile from the shore, and you then come to 'Frenchman's Point,'† at a small river where those of Patucxet‡ have a house made of hewn oak planks, called Aptucxet, § where they keep two men, winter and summer, in order to maintain the trade and possession. Where, also, they have built a shallop, in order to go and look after the trade in sewan, in Sloup's Bay, ‖ and thereabouts, because they are afraid to pass Cape Malabaer, and in order to avoid the length of the way; which I have prevented for this year ¶ by selling them fifty fathoms of sewan, because the seeking after sewan by them is prejudicial to us, inasmuch as they would, by so doing, discover the trade in furs; which, if they were to find out, it would be a great trouble for us to maintain, for they already dare to threaten that if we will not leave off dealing with that people, they will be obliged to use

* Narraganset Bay.

† De Rasieres dates his letter to Governor Bradford, of 4th of October, 1627, from "aboard the barque Nassau," off this point. — See Coll. N. Y. Hist. Soc., vol. I., new series, p. 362.

‡ The Indian name for New Plymouth.

§ See Bradford's description of Manomet, in Prince, page 67 ; and see, also, Coll. N. Y. Hist. Soc., vol. I., new series, pp. 357, 358.

‖ The western entrance to Narraganset Bay.

¶ See, also, Bradford's account of this transaction, in Coll. N. Y. Hist. Soc., vol. I., new series, p. 357.

other means. If they do that now, while they are yet ignorant how the case stands, what will they do when they do
get a notion of it?

"From Aptucxet the English can come in six hours,
through the woods, passing several little rivulets of fresh
water, to New Plymouth, the principal place in the country
Patucxet, so called in their 'Octroye' from his Majesty in
England. New Plymouth lies in a large bay to the north
of Cape Cod, or Mallabaer, east and west from the said
[north] point of the cape, which can be easily seen in clear
weather. Directly before the commenced town lies a sand-
bank, about twenty paces broad, whereon the sea breaks
violently with an easterly and north-easterly wind. On the
north side there lies a small island, where one must run
close along, in order to come before the town; then the ships
run behind that bank and lie in a very good roadstead. The
bay is very full of fish, [chiefly] of cod, so that the Governor before named * has told me that when the people have
a desire for fish, they send out two or three persons in a
sloop, whom they remunerate for their trouble, and who
bring them, in three or four hours' time, as much fish as the
whole community require for a whole day,—and they muster
about fifty families.

" At the south side of the town there flows down a small
river of fresh water, very rapid, but shallow, which takes its
rise from several lakes in the land above, and there empties
into the sea; where in April and the beginning of May
there comes so many herring † from the sea which want to

* Probably in the portion of this letter which is unfortunately
missing.

† In the original Dutch, "ELFT" is generally translated shad; perhaps it would be more properly rendered *alewives*.   J. R. B.

ascend that river, that it is quite surprising. This river the
English have shut in with planks, and in the middle with a
little door, which slides up and down, and at the sides with
trellice-work, through which the water has its course, but
which they can also close with slides. At the mouth they
have constructed it with planks, like an eel-pot with wings,
where in the middle is also a sliding-door, and with trellice-
work at the sides, so that between the two [dams] there is a
square pool, into which the fish aforesaid come swimming in
such shoals, in order to get up above where they deposit
their spawn, . that at one tide there are ten thousand to
twelve thousand fish in it, which they shut off in the rear at
the ebb, and close up the trellices above so that no more
water comes in; then the water runs out through the lower
trellices and they draw out the fish with baskets, each
according to the land he cultivates, and carry them to it,
depositing in each hill three or four fishes, and in these they
plant their maize, which grows as luxuriantly therein as
though it were the best manure in the world ; and if they do
not lay this fish therein, the maize will not grow, so that such
is the nature of the soil.

" New Plymouth lies on the slope of a hill stretching
east towards the sea-coast, with a broad street about a cannon shot of eight hundred [yards] long, leading down the
hill, with a [street] crossing in the middle, northwards to
the rivulet, and southwards to the land. The houses are
constructed of hewn planks, with gardens also enclosed
behind and at the sides with hewn planks, so that their
houses and court-yards are arranged in very good order,
with a stockade against a sudden attack ; and at the ends
of the streets there are three wooden gates. In the centre,
on the cross-street, stands the Governor's house, before

which is a square enclosure, upon which four patereros [steen-stucken] are mounted, so as to flank along the streets. Upon the hill they have a large square house, with a flat roof, made of thick sawn planks, stayed with oak beams, upon the top of which they have six cannons, which shoot iron balls of four and five pounds, and command the surrounding country. The lower part they use for their church, where they preach on Sundays and the usual holidays. They assemble by beat of drum, each with his musket or firelock, in front of the captain's door; they have their cloaks on, and place themselves in order, three abreast, and are led by a sergeant without beat of drum. Behind comes the Governor, in a long robe; beside him, on the right hand, comes the preacher with his cloak on, and on the left hand the captain with his side-arms and cloak on, and with a small cane in his hand, and so they march in good order, and each sets his arms down near him. Thus they are constantly on their guard night and day.

" Their government is after the English form. The Governor has his council, which is chosen every year by the entire community by election or prolongation of term. In the inheritance they place all the children in one degree, only the eldest son has an acknowledgment for his seniority of birth.

" They have made stringent laws and ordinances upon the subject of fornication and adultery, which laws they maintain and enforce very strictly indeed, even among the tribes which live amongst them. They [the English] speak very angrily, when they hear from the savages that we should live so barbarously in these respects, and without punishment.

" Their farms are not so good as ours, because they are

more stony, and, consequently, not so suitable for the plough. They apportion their land according as each has means to contribute to the eighteen thousand guilders which they have promised to those who had sent them out; whereby they have their freedom without rendering an account to any one; only, if the king should choose to send a Governor-General, they would be obliged to acknowledge him as sovereign chief.

"The maize seed which they do not require for their own use is delivered over to the Governor, at three guilders the bushel, who, in his turn, sends it in sloops to the north for the trade in skins among the savages. They reckon one bushel of maize against one pound of beaver's skin; in the first place, a division is made according to what each has contributed, and they are credited for the amount in the account of what each has to contribute yearly towards the reduction of his obligation. Then with the remainder they purchase what next they require, and which the Governor takes care to provide every year.

"They have better means of living than ourselves, because they have the fish so abundant before their doors. There are also many birds, such as geese, herons, and cranes, and other small-legged birds, which are in great abundance there in the winter. The tribes in their neighborhood have all the same customs as already above described, only they are better con-ducted than ours, because the English give them the example of better ordinances and a better life; and who, also, to a cer-tain degree, give them laws, by means of the respect they from the very first have established amongst them.

"The savages [there] practice their youth in labor better than the savages round about us; the young girls in sowing maize, the young men in hunting. They teach them to endure privation in the field in a singular manner, to wit: when there is a youth who begins to approach manhood, he is taken by his father, uncle, or nearest friend, and is conducted blindfolded into a wilderness, in order that he may not know the way, and is left there, by night or otherwise, with a bow and arrows, and a hatchet and a knife. He must support himself there a whole winter with what the scanty earth furnishes at this season, and by hunting. Towards the spring they come again, and fetch him out of it, take him home, and feed him up again until May. He must then go out again every morning with the person who is ordered to take him in hand; he must go into the forest to seek wild herbs and roots which they know to be the most poisonous and bitter; these they bruise in water and press the juice out of them, which he must drink and immediately have ready such herbs as will preserve him from death or vomiting; and, if he cannot retain it, he must repeat the dose until he can support it, and until his constitution becomes accustomed to it so that he can retain it. Then he comes home, and is brought by the men and women, all singing and dancing, before the Sackima; and if he has been able to stand it all out well, and if he is fat and sleek, a wife is given to him.

" In that district there are no lions or bears, but there are the same kinds of other game, such as deers, hinds, beavers, otters, foxes, lynxes, seals, and fish, as in our district of country. The savages say that far in the interior there are certain beasts of the size of oxen, having but one horn, which are very fierce. The English have used great diligence in order to see them, but cannot succeed therein, although they have seen the flesh and hides of them which were brought to them by the savages. There are also very

13

large elks there which the English have indeed seen. The
lion skins, which we sometimes see our savages wear, are not
large, so that the animal itself must be small ; they are of
a mouse-gray color, short in the hair, and long in the claws.
The bears are some of them large and some small ; but the
largest are not as large as the middle-sized ones which come
from Greenland. Their fur is long and black, and their
claws large. The savages esteem the flesh and grease as a
great dainty. Of the birds, there is a kind like starlings,
which we call *maize-thieves*, because they do so much
damage to it. They fly in large flocks, so that they flatten
the corn in any place where they light, just as if cattle had
lain there. Sometimes we take them by surprise, and fire
amongst them with hail shot, immediately that we have made
them rise, so that sixty, seventy, and eighty fall all at once,
which is very pleasant to see. There are also very large
turkeys living wild ; they have very long legs, and can run
extraordinarily fast, so that we generally take savages with
us when we go to hunt them, for even when one has
deprived them of the power of flying, they yet run so
fast that we cannot catch them unless their legs are hit also.
In the autumn and in the spring there come a great many
geese, which are very good [to eat] and easy to shoot, inasmuch as they congregate together in such large flocks.
There are two kinds of partridges ; the one sort are quite
as small as quails, and the other like the ordinary kind here.
There are also hares, but few in number, and not larger than
a middle-sized rabbit ; and they principally frequent where
the land is rocky.

"This, sir, is what I have been able to communicate to
you from memory, respecting New Netherland and its neighborhood, in discharge of my bounden duty. I beg that the

same may be so favorably received by you, and I beg to recommend myself for such further service as you may be pleased to command me in, wherever you may find me.

" In everything your faithful servant,

" ISAACK DE RASIERES."

NOTE TO DE RASIERES' LETTER. — The letter of De Rasieres describes the town of Plymouth, its defensive array, and the manner of procedure observed by the church in attending public worship, with more minuteness of detail than is found in any of our early records or history. From the description of streets, it is evident that in 1627 Main-street ran at right angles with Leyden-street, which it crossed, continuing south partly over the lot now occupied by William R. Drew, and that of the late William Davis, Esq., and thence in a circular direction till it joined Summer-street. The words running " North towards the rivulet," doubtless refer to the first brook, near the dwelling-house of Mr. Ichabod Shaw. It seems probable, also, that Main-street, from its junction on the north side with Leyden-street, took a northerly course over the lot now owned and occupied by Josiah Robbins, Esq. The residence of Governor Bradford was probably that now occupied by Mr. Thomas Loring, at the corner of Main and Leyden streets, on the westerly side of said Main-street. This lot, it is inferred, was the homestead of Gov. Bradford, and it continued in possession of his descendants till the year 1695, when it was sold to John Murdock.

The reader will not fail to observe in this letter a reference to the high moral character of the Pilgrims, and its influence on the natives, contrasted with the prevailing practices in the Dutch settlement at the same time; a tribute the more valuable coming from so impartial, intelligent, and discriminating a source.

MANOMET. — This village forms a part of Sandwich, in Barnstable county, and is situated on the north-westerly part of Buzzard's Bay, about six and one-half miles by the road distant from Scusset harbor, in a north-easterly direction, and is thus described by the late Samuel Davis, Esq., of Plymouth. Manomet Bay is but a mile across, from a part of the Wareham shore to Manomet river, on the back shore of Sandwich. That rivulet was visited by Governor Bradford as early as 1622, to procure corn, and was the Pimesepoese of the natives. This compound phrase signifies " provision rivulet." What a remarkable coincidence in the aboriginal name and the colonial voyage! We do not assume this explanation without substantial and tenable grounds. The first part of the phrase, *pime*, is, in its uses, " food," " provision;" the latter, " little river." There too, it was, that a barque was built by the Plymouth Colonies in 1627, and a trade opened with the Dutch at New Netherlands (New York). It was, in fact, the Suez, while Plymouth was the Aleppo, of our ancestors. The traveller, therefore, as he passes on his way, may here make a pause, erect a pillar, and muse on the swift flight of ages. " How changeful and how brief ! "

The site of the Old Colony trading-house of the Pilgrims has been satisfactorily ascertained, as will appear from the following statement : In a grant of land made by the Colony to James Skiff, recorded, Book of Court Orders, vol. III., page 84, land is conveyed " which was formerly the Company's, where they had a trading-house." By means of this document and some other grants adjacent. which were placed in the hands of John Batchelder, M. D.,

of Manomet village, he has been able, after minute and careful investigation, to establish with certainty the fact above
stated; and the following particulars are extracted from
the account obligingly forwarded by him to the writer :

" The Old Colony trading-house stood on the south side
of. Manomet river, about one hundred and seventy rods from
the bridge, and about one and one-fourth miles from Agawam
Point, at the mouth of said river, where it enters Buzzard's
Bay. Its site is indicated by two remaining cellar-holes,
distinctly marked, so as to admit of measurement, and its
dimensions were about twenty by forty feet. It stood one
hundred yards from low-water mark, and an excellent
spring issues out near the water's edge, being the first that
appears from the mouth of the river upward. The village
was first settled by the English in 1685. The spots occupied by the first buildings erected there are all well known,
but no tradition exists as to the trading-house of the colony;
it having been generally a matter of conjecture only that
some kind of defence was erected there against the Indians,
though previous to the year 1685. The distance from the
trading-house to Sandwich village is, by the road, about six
and one-half miles, and an old cart-way is found of several
rods, strongly marked and much worn, near the site above
described, of which no account can be given by tradition or
history, except on the supposition that it was the travelled
approach to this interesting spot of Pilgrim commerce. The
width of the river at the above point is about fifteen rods.
Sagamore Hill, probably the residence of Cawnacome, the
Sachem visited by Gov. Bradford, is situated on the south
side of the river, on a bank about seventy-five feet in height,
which commands a fine view for several miles above and
below the stream. Upon the summit of this hill a large
13*

shell-heap is found, of considerable depth and extent, and others on its side and base. Tradition states that this hill was the residence of at least one sagamore."

Dr. Batchelder concludes, from careful investigations, that the river, called by De Rasieres Nassau, was the same that is now called the Weweantic, and that Frenchman's Point, from which his letter to Gov. Bradford was dated, in 1627, of which there is no trace in our history known to the writer, except in Morton's New England Memorial, page 61, was that now called Agawam Point. The population of Manomet village, so called, is now five hundred. The river still holds its claim to be called " provision rivulet ; " and in the summer season yields, in abundance, the bass (two species), blue fish, scapaug, tautaug, beside five species of edible shellfish,— oysters, quahogs, clams, winkles, and muscles. In the winter, besides the various kinds of shell-fish, we have the trout, frost-fish, and a rich, and, literally enough, an inexhaustible bed of eels. They form a continuous bed, occupying not only the bottom of the river, but nearly the whole extent of the marshes.

ALPHABETICAL LIST OF PASSENGERS

Who arrived at Plymouth in the Mayflower, one hundred and eighty tons burden, December 21st, 1620 ; the Fortune, of fifty-five tons, November 9th, 1621 ; the Ann, of one hundred and forty tons, and the Little James, of forty-four tons, the last of July, or the beginning of August, 1623.

THE letter attached to each name indicates the vessel in which the passenger came. M stands for the Mayflower, F for the Fortune, A for the Ann and Little James.

NAMES OF PASSENGERS.

A.

M Mr. Isaac Allerton,
M John Alden,
M John Allerton,
F John Adams,
A Anthony Annable.

B.

M Mr. William Bradford,
M Mr. William Brewster,
M John Billington,
M Peter Brown,
M Richard Britterige,
F William Bassite,
F William Beale,
F Edward Bompasse,
F Jonathan Brewster,
F Clement Brigges,
A Edward Bangs,
A Robert Bartlett,
A Fear Brewster,
A Patience Brewster,
A Mary Bucket,
A Edward Burcher.

C.

M Mr. John Carver,
M Francis Cook,
M James Chilton,

M John Crackston,
M Richard Clarke,
F John Cannon,
F William Coner,
F Robert Cushman,
F Thomas Cushman,
A Thomas Clarke,
A Cuthbert Cuthbertson,
A Christopher Conant.

D.

M Edward Dotey,
F Stephen Deane,
F Philip De La Noye,
A Anthony Dix.

E.

M Francis Eaton,
M Thomas English.

F.

M Mr. Samuel Fuller,
M Edward Fuller,
M Moses Fletcher,
F Thomas Flavell and son,
F Widow Foord,
A John Faunce,
A Goodwife Flavell,
A Edmund Flood,

A Bridget Fuller.

G.
M John Goodman,
M Richard Gardiner.

H.
M John Howland,
M Mr. Stephen Hopkins,
F Robert Hickes,
F William Hilton,
A Timothy Hatherly,
A William Heard,
A Margaret Hickes and her
    children,
A William Hilton's wife and
    children,
A Edward Holman.

J.
A John Jenny.

K.
A Manasses Kempton.

L.
M Edward Leister,
A Robert Long.

M.
M Mr. Christopher Martin,
M Mr. William Mullins,

M Edmund Margeson,
F Benet Morgan,
F Thomas Morton,
A Experience Mitchell,
A George Morton,
A Thomas Morton, Jr.

N.
F Austin Nicholas,
A Ellen Newton.

O.
A John Oldham.

P.
M Degory Priest,
F William Palmer,
F William Pitt,
F Thomas Prence,
A Frances Palmer,
A Mr. Perce's two servants,
A Joshua Pratt,
A Christian Penn.

R.
M Thomas Rogers,
M John Ridgdale,
A James Rand,
A Robert Rattliffe.

S.
M Capt. Miles Standish,
M George Soule,

F Moses Simonson,
F Hugh Statie,
F James Steward,
A Nicholas Snow,
A Alice Southworth,
A Francis Sprague,
A Barbura Standish.

T.

M Edward Tilly,
M John Tilly,
M Thomas Tinker,
M John Turner,

F William Tench,
A Thomas Tilden,
A Stephen Tracy.

W.

M Mr. Edward Winslow,
M Mr. William White,
M Mr. Richard Warren,
M Thomas Williams,
M Gilbert Winslow,.
F John Winslow,
F William Wright,
A Ralph Wallen.

Several names contained in the foregoing list are differently spelt in modern times, namely: Bassite is now spelt Bassett; Bompasse, Bumpas, sometimes Bump; Burcher is probably the same as Burchard, the name of an early settler in Connecticut; De La Noye, Delano; Dotey is on our records called Dote, Dotey, and now frequently written Doten; Simonson, sometimes written Symons, is now Simmons.

This list is copied from the allotment of lands, in 1623, found in the Old Colony Records, volume I., pages 4 to 11 inclusive.

CLOSING REMARKS ON THE PILGRIMS.

IN preparing the foregoing pages for publication, the writer has earnestly sought to present a just and true account of the motives, character and conduct of the

Pilgrims; not, however, without a consciousness that the estimate formed of their claims to the veneration and gratitude of the present age will, by many, be regarded as far exceeding the merits to which they are justly entitled.

The cry of intolerance, persecution, and injustice towards the natives, hastily assumed and framed into serious charges against them, is often deemed sufficient to outweigh other considerations challenging in their behalf our unqualified admiration. It is not difficult to trace the origin of these charges to the same spirit and source which originally drove them into banishment, which could not rest satisfied with this measure of punishment without the attempt to impugn their motives, detract from their worth, and misrepresent their conduct. The fearless spirits, who, at so early a period, dared to array themselves in open opposition to the unjust assumptions, both of the hierarchy and throne of England, could not fail to incur their unrelenting hostility.

But, whatever opinions may be entertained on these points,— whether the charges alleged rest upon any just grounds or not,— it will hardly be denied that the Pilgrims accomplished a vast work. While it would doubtless be unwise to claim for them an exemption from the common infirmities of our nature, the opposite extreme, which withholds a just recognition of their high achievements, is liable to far greater condemnation.

It may well deserve our attention to consider what might have been the condition of our country at the present moment, had their perilous enterprise failed of success. Nearly ten years had elapsed after the landing at Plymouth before any other colony, except the unsuccessful attempt of Weston, ventured to follow their example. Had their enterprise proved abortive, it appears reasonable to conclude that no similar purpose of colonization would have been renewed till many years had passed away, to soften the forbidding ·aspect of repeated failures, or to reconcile such a measure with the dictates of ordinary prudence.

France, at quite an early period, had, with laudable enterprise, explored our northern and western boundaries, and conceived the purpose of establishing a connected chain of fortified posts, designed eventually to control the destiny of North America. Who may not discern, in the *early* settlement of New England, the only effectual barrier to the execution of this magnificent project of the French nation? In point of fact, the contest for supremacy between England and France was long and earnest; and, at one time, it became extremely doubtful which of these great rivals of empire would ultimately prevail, notwithstanding the superiority of colonial strength possessed by the former power. New England enterprise and courage at last determined this doubtful, but all-important question; and history, faithful to its trust, in recording the chivalrous reduction of Louisbourg and other colonial achievements, will award the claims of justice, while it utters only the declarations of truth.

The intrepid pioneers, therefore, by whose instrumentality the great question was settled as to what nation of Europe should predominate in North America, justly deserve to be held in grateful remembrance on both sides of the Atlantic. Who does not rejoice that the English tongue has become the universal language of more than twenty millions of people, and that our institutions, which received their germ from

the best examples of Europe, moulded and improved by the
successive application of sound principles, aiming to promote
the general welfare, and grown into a wider expansion both
of civil and religious liberty, are the invaluable, undisputed
inheritance of our land? "By their fruits ye shall know
them. Not by the graceful foliage which dallies with the
summer's breeze; not by the flower which fades with the
perfume which it scatters on the gale; but by the golden,
perfect fruit, in which the mysterious life of the plant is
garnered up, which the genial earth and kindling sun have
ripened into the refreshment and food of man, and which,
even when it perishes, leaves behind it the germs of continued and multiplied existence." *

NOTE. — Without intending to justify intolerance in any form, whether
of ancient or modern date, it may be remarked that much of what is
charged upon the Fathers as such, resulted from their exposure to the
designs, often manifested by their enemies at home and abroad, to overthrow both their civil and religious institutions, which it had cost them
so much labor and hazard to establish, and which owed their final preservation to a wonderful prudence and persevering vigilance, defeating
not only the purposes of faction, but the assumptions of royal authority. The undue restriction of individual freedom seems to have been
the *incident* rather than the *aim* of their policy.

With respect to the charge of injustice towards the Indian race, we
quote the remarks of *James Otis* to Governor Barnard, in 1767 : "The
Indians had perfect confidence in our Fathers, and applied to them in
all their difficulties. Nothing has been omitted which *justice* or *humanity* required. We *glory* in their conduct ; we *boast* of it as unexampled."

This is not the place to discuss the question of the right of the aborigines to the entire soil of New England. It seems proper to state, however, that this right was recognized by the Pilgrims, and we are able to
trace on our records, the book and page where every tract of land was
duly conveyed by the Indians, according to the forms of law If it be said
that the consideration paid was merely nominal, it may be answered that

* Everett's Remarks at Plymouth, Dec. 22, 1845.

View of the Town and
Harbor of Plymouth

land, beyond the use of mere hunting, was estimated very differently by the natives, who esteemed it of small value except for that purpose, and the white man, who desired it for permanent cultivation. In reply to the superficial remarks sometimes made on this subject, the following is copied from the Address of the late Hon. John Quincy Adams, on the New England Confederacy: "The whole territory of New England was thus purchased, for valuable consideration, by the new-comers, and the Indian title was extinguished by compact fulfilling the law of justice between man and man. The most eminent writer on the law of nations, of modern times (Vattel), has paid a worthy tribute of respect to our forefathers, for their rigid observance, in this respect, of the natural right of the indigenous natives of the country. It is from the example of the New England Puritans that he draws the preceptive rule, and he awards to them merited honor for having established it.'

DESCRIPTION OF PLYMOUTH.

"They sounded the harbor and found it fit for shipping, and marched into the land and found divers corn-fields, and little running brooks, a place, as they supposed, fit for situation."—MORTON.

THE foregoing pages have occupied so much space, that only a brief account of Plymouth, as it now is, can here be presented to the reader.

PLYMOUTH is situated in north latitude (at the Court House), 41° 57' 6". Longitude from Greenwich, 70° 30' 54".

Its Indian name was Umpame, written Apaum in the Colony Records, and still so called by the natives of Massapee. It was also called *Patuxet*.

BOUNDS. — The bounds of Plymouth were determined by the Colony Court in the year 1640, of which the following is a description:

14

"It is enacted and concluded by the Court, that the bounds of Plymouth township shall extend southward to the bounds of Sandwich township; and northward to a little brook running from Stephen Tracy's to another little brook falling into Blackwater ; from the commons left to Duxbury, and the neighborhood thereabout; and westward eight miles up into the land, from any part of the bay or sea; always provided that the bounds shall extend so far up into the wood-lands as to include the south meadows towards Agawam, lately discovered, and the convenient uplands thereabout."

These bounds were quite extensive, comprising what have since become Plympton, in 1707, Kingston, in 1726, and part of Wareham, with Carver, taken from Plympton, and a part of Halifax, in 1734, also taken from Plympton. It is about sixteen miles in extent, from north to south, and varies from four and a half to nine in width.

Plymouth is built along the sea-shore, upon a moderate declivity descending from an extensive pine plain, about one-fourth of a mile broad, and one and a half miles in length.

FACE AND QUALITY OF THE SOIL. — The predominant growth of forest trees is *Pinus tæda*, designating a soil of third-rate quality, which covers much the greater part of the township.

A ridge of elevated pine hills commences at "Hither Manomet"* (so called in the records), within its limits on the sea, and terminates at Wood's Hole, twenty-seven miles, ranging north and south, through Sandwich, beyond which they assume a rocky and rugged form,

---

* Further Manomet Point, as seen from Sandwich, is a bold feature in prospective, from every part of the bay.

near Falmouth. The most elevated point in this ridge is about four miles from the Town-House in Plymouth, being three hundred and ninety-six feet in height, presenting an extensive and sublime prospect of ocean scenery.

- This elevated ridge separates Manomet Ponds, so called, from the more populous parts of the town. It is beautif situated, commanding a fine view of the bay, and is a rounded by elevated heights; and preserves, perhaps to this day, in its habits and character, as much of the sound prin ciple and primitive simplicity of ancient times as any part of our country.

GEOLOGY. — It is not a little curious that one loose rock on the shore of Plymouth Harbor should have become so famous as is that called the " Pilgrim Rock," where there is not known in the township a single ledge, save those the fisherman reaches with his lead at various points off the coast. All the rocks *in place* lie buried beneath an unknown thickness of sand, gravel, and clay, of the *Drift* formation. This, in many places, is at least two hundred feet thick, and is probably nowhere less than forty. The nearest ledges that appear are in Kingston, a mile or more over the line; and they are of granite, intersected by narrow trapdykes. So regular are some of these dykes, as exposed in the cutting of the railroad, that they were believed by many to be some ancient artificial structure. It is probable that this granitic formation extends further south beneath the drift; but from this point to Sandwich and round to the Cape the writer is not aware that any ledge is met with.

Spread over the country so extensively, the peculiarities of the drift formation are perhaps nowhere better developed

than in this neighborhood.   The broken surface of the little
hills is the counterpart, on the large scale, of the chopped
and troubled seas that break against their base.   No deep-
seated action has stirred up the mass, and thrown the surface
into the regular wave-like ridges of other regions.   The
power acting on the surface, that brought together and
spread these loose materials, has scooped out the hollows
between the hills, and made a thousand deep depressions,
now occupied by as many lakes and ponds.   These, of every
variety of form and size, lie scattered here and there, or
grouped together in the pitch-pine and scrubby oak woods.
Little brooks, flowing clearly over their sandy beds, connect
one with another, and then find their way to the sea-shore.
The barrenness of this geological formation is a surety that
the singular and romantic beauty it has given to the envi-
rons of Plymouth will not soon be impaired by the clearing
of the country.

BOTANICAL DESCRIPTION OF PLYMOUTH. — Plymouth
and its vicinity are somewhat remarkable for the diversity
of the plants indigenous to the soil; embracing both those
of a strictly botanical, and likewise those of a more general
interest.   It possesses hill, dale, meadow, swamp, marsh;
extended plains covered with a characteristic growth of the
pitch-pine, and likewise many sheets of fresh water, some
of which are of a picturesque character, some of considerable extent; others, again, of fairy size; and all embosomed
in its woods, interspersed among its ridges; or, perhaps,
connected with one another like chains of lakes, in miniature
proportions.   These various regions, though of the limited
extent of a few miles, are found to be stored with plants,
and have been repeatedly explored by botanists with that
success which prompts further inquiry.

The scenery in the immediate vicinity of the town is almost wholly maritime, and to its peculiar associations, as connected with Pilgrim history, owes its chief charms. A long extent of sea-beach stretches from the main land near Duxbury, known by the name of the Gurnet. To the westward rises Captain's Hill, an eminence of considerable height and of much interest, reminding us of that valiant Captain Miles Standish, whose house was situated near its foot. On the extreme east r se the bold blue heights of Manomet, and directly in front of the spectator as he stands on the hill of graves, is the narrow strip of sand which defends the harbor, and known as Plymouth beach. Nor will he fail to notice Clarke's Island, bearing a little to the north-east, with its few trees, which seem to cluster near the dwelling-houses of the farmstead. Washed up on these several beaches by the usual storms, may be found the various species of seaweeds (*Algæ*), which combine inimitable beauty in some of the more delicate forms with direct utility in the coarser kinds. The sands above high-water mark are covered with the useful beach-grass, the sea-pea, the maritime sandwort, etc. etc., and with the several other sorts of vegetation which usually thrive in such situations. The glancous-leaved seaside Gromwell (*Lithospermum maritimum*) has been detected on these shores; a plant better known as inhabiting a more eastern coast. In the cultivated grass fields may be seen the yellow rattle, rather conspicuous for its large and showy flowers. In the meadows grow the tall, purple, fimbriated orchis, and the delicate pure white species also, the bulbous arethusa, and other forms of floral beauty, which delight themselves in such spots. Nor wanting is the rich cardinal-flower on the plashy brink of the streams. The dry hill-sides afford the blazing

14*

star (*Liatris*), in August conspicuous by its purple spikes
of blossoms at the end of its long, wand-like stems ; while
in every copse, in each thicket, amid forest shades and in
the open pasture-land, burst forth, on returning spring, the
roseate blossoms of the *epigæa*, better known to our town's
folks as the MAY-FLOWER, and whose admiration of its
charming habits is only equalled by the associations which
its trivial and accidental name awakens.   This truly lovely
little plant is a hardy denizen of every northern state of
New England, and, appearing in bloom early in May, it is
familiarly known as the *May* flower, more especially in
New Hampshire, where it is the *first* flower of spring.
With us, when spring is unusually forward, in some favorable situation, it has been known to break forth from its
winter's sleep at the beginning or towards the middle of
April ; and to secure the first specimen of the first May
flower is considered a fortunate circumstance among its ad-
mirers.   A pleasing fiction obtains with some good people
hereabouts ; viz., that this little flower is peculiar to this
section of the country ; but truth, which always proves
stronger than fiction, has, however, reluctantly dispelled the
illusion.   None the less a favorite has the *epigæa* continued ; and, on any pleasant afternoon in spring-time, in
the streets of Plymouth, may be seen numerous children
and young persons bearing handfuls of these pretty blossoms, which they have culled with choice selection from the
neighboring woods and hills.   A curious and somewhat rare
plant, closely related to the *crowberry* or *crakeberry* of
alpine regions, flourishes with us in certain spots.   This
is an early flower, indeed, expanding its little and ob-
scure filaments in April, and reminding us, in its scien-

tific name, of a diligent investigator of New England botany.

The occurrence of *rare plants* in secluded spots and in narrow areas is a singular fact. Another instance of the kind besides that last mentioned, occurs in the linear-leaved sundew which was first detected there by the late venerable Judge Davis (as we are informed by Dr. Bigelow in his *Plants of Boston and its Vicinity*), several years ago ; and which very plant, since, has been one of the most interesting of this region. Bordering the ponds may be found *Sabbatia*, elegant with its bloom of every tint of color, from deep rose to purest white, the hyssop-leaved hedge-nettle, the humble *gratiola aurea*, with blossoms subject to variations, from its usual golden hue to paler yellow, and even to white, the rosy coreopsis, the narrow-leaved golden rod, etc., etc. Rising from the bottom of the shallower parts of the water may be seen xyris, with heads of yellow florets issuing from brown scales, frequently found of remarkable size ; the pickerel-weed, looking like spikes of blue hyacinths, and quite as pretty ; the white arrow-head, the curious little stems of the bladder-worts, covered with purplish or else with yellow flowers, while their finely divided foliage, kept from sinking by singularly contrived apparatus, is slightly fixed by delicate root-fibres in the softooze, or float at random and at pleasure. Of these, six or seven species may be found in close proximity. Entangled among them, perhaps, are the water-mill foils, the aquatic ranunculuses, with starry blossoms like flakes of snow, lying on the still surface, the glossy-leaved water-targets, curious species of sedges, bulrushes, and many other grass-like plants besides. And then, in drier situations, we have the tall, gorgeous fireweed, rivaling the garden phloxes, while to chance on a tuft of the orange-colored asclepias, which may be also found, this were delightful indeed.

To those who love to steal away into Nature's retreats, to sit listening to the perpetual sighing of the summer-breeze midst the pine branches, or to tread the white sanded margins of our crystal lakelets; to those, who love a walk for its own sake, or to cull flowers, or to forget their business or their cares for a brief space of time, there may be found, in and near this old town of Plymouth, sufficient inducements, besides even Forefathers' Rock, the memory of bygone days, the traditionary stories and cherished relics of the pilgrimage. Tracts of wild forests, which have never been cleared for cultivation, and in which the fallow deer yet roam at large, and the general features and outlines of what this spot was more than two centuries ago, will not fail to forcibly remind them of that primitive wilderness in which Freedom sought an asylum and a resting-place.

PLYMOUTH HARBOR. — The harbor is protected by a beach, three miles in extent, about one mile from the wharves. This beach is much reduced from its original width by the inroads of the sea. It was originally well wooded ; but, notwithstanding the fines early imposed to prevent depredation, the trees have all disappeared. Towards the northern part of it, within sixty or seventy years, there was a thick swamp, covered with pine, cherry and other trees. It abounded also with beach-plums and grapes. In 1764 two small breaches were made by the sea near this swamp, requiring twenty pounds for repairs. Dec. 25th, 1778, a severe storm greatly increased these breaches, and a hedge-fence was made for its protection. In 1784 a heavy gale, with a high tide, carried off most of the trees. In 1785, the General Court made a conditional grant of five hundred pounds, but through inability the town could not comply with its conditions. In 1806, a township of land was granted, on condition that the town raise five thousand dollars for repairing the beach. In 1812, a lottery was granted, the proceeds of which, amounting to sixteen thousand dollars, were applied for repairs. Previous to the year 1806, more than forty thousand dollars had been expended without any aid from government. An appropriation, made by the General Government in 1824 and 1825, of forty-three thousand, five hundred and sixty-six dollars, which sum was judiciously expended under the direction of Lieut. Chase and Col. Totten, of the United States Engineer department, has resulted in the preservation of this important barrier to the ocean, which, otherwise, must long since have been nearly destroyed. It still requires vigilant attention.

The severe storm in April, 1851, combined with the high course of tides occurring at the same time, occasioned considerable injury near the southerly part of the beach. We cannot but trust that government, following in the track of former days, will not suffer this indispensable barrier against the ocean to disappear for want of that care it requires to save our harbor from inundation.

An appropriation of one thousand dollars made and expended by the town, and also one by the United States of five thousand dollars, have, in some measure, repaired the injury sustained; but a further sum of fifty thousand dollars would probably be required to insure permanent security.

The GURNET, at the entrance of the harbor, contains about twenty-seven acres of good land. Of the original growth of wood nothing remains. It is the extreme point of Marshfield beach, and distant from the main land about seven miles. A light-house was erected by the then province of Massachusetts, on this point, in 1768, costing six hundred and sixty pounds, seventeen shillings, which was consumed by fire on July 2d, 1801 ; and that now standing was erected by the United States in 1803. It has two lights, about seventy feet above the sea.

SAYQUISH, an Indian name signifying clams, is a headland, connected with the Gurnet by a narrow neck, and contains about fourteen acres. Between the Gurnet and the western point of Sayquish, the cove is formed, which was " full of breakers," from which the shallop of the Pilgrims, when driven by tempest, narrowly escaped destruction. At Stage Point, within this cove, Mr. William Paddy and Mr. John Hewes erected fishing-stages about the year 1643, near which bass were seined. Clark's Island, a little to the north of Sayquish, has already been described.

COW YARD. — This place, from the arrival of the Mayflower to the present time, has served as a most convenient place of anchorage, between Beach Point and Clark's Island ; distant from town one and a half miles. The name arose from the fact that a cow-whale was taken there in early times.

BROWN'S ISLAND is about one-half a mile north by east of Beach Point. Though now under water, it was porbably covered with trees when the Pilgrims arrived, and was one of the " two islands " of the harbor mentioned in their first history. This is confirmed by the statements of elderly persons now living, who, in their early days, discovered the stumps of trees there. The island being so near the anchorage-ground of all strangers who visited New England for many years, the trees were perhaps soon converted into fire-wood, leaving it exposed to a rapid destruction from the violence of easterly storms. Its name was probably derived from Peter Brown, who came in the Mayflower, as there was no person then living in the colony so likely to give it that name. According to Gov. Winthrop, Oct. 6, 1635, two shallops were cast away upon "Brown's Island," near the Gurnet's nose, and the men on board were all drowned.

PONDS. — The number of ponds in Plymouth is estimated at two hundred; and the map of Plymouth, by S. Bourne, Esq., contains about one hundred and twenty, a considerable portion of which would, in most other parts of our country, be designated as lakes. They cover, as is generally estimated, three thousand acres in extent. The most attractive of these are *Billington Sea*, already described; *South Pond*, four miles from town, abounding with white and red perch. *Murdock's Pond* is a quarter of a mile west of the village. *Half-way Pond* is ten miles southerly. *White Island Pond* is north-westerly of the last named, and covers about six hundred acres. *Great Herring Pond* is fifteen miles south, on the borders of Sandwich. *Long Pond*, two miles in length, six miles from town. *Clam Pudding Pond* is seven miles south, on the Sandwich road.

The general features and scenery of these lakes are picturesque and beautiful, affording the most agreeable resorts in summer, for fishing and other amusements.

HILLS. — *Pinnacle Hill* is near South Pond. *Sentry* and *Indian Hill* are on the sea-shore of Manomet.

Paukopunnakuck is the Indian name of a hill called *Breakheart Hill* by the early planters. It is ten miles

from town, on the formerly travelled Sandwich road.
The name was appropriately applied at a period in our
early history when governors and other officers of
government travelled on foot from Cape Cod and back
again, in the discharge of their arduous duties to the
country.

Monk's Hill is a few miles from town, within the bounds
of Kingston. It rises three hundred and thirteen feet
above the ocean, in the midst of a widely-extended forest,
and commands a fine view of the ocean and interior. It
is called in the Old Colony Records " Monts Hill Chase,"
a name supposed to have been applied to a hunt in England.*

Mountain Hill is near Goose Point. *Sparrow's Hill*,
two miles from town, derives its name from Richard Sparrow, who was an early settler, and had land assigned
him there. He moved to Eastham, and died there about
1660.

" *Steart's Hill*," so called by the first planters, is directly below the farm now owned by Mr. Barnabas Hedge,
on the sea-shore, and is supposed to have been named from
" Start's Point, a place near Plymouth, in England." The
house of Gov. Prence stood a little south of that occupied
by Mr. Hedge, and the place was called Plain Dealing,
which name extended, it is believed, to Kingston line. It
would seem desirable to revive this ancient name of a place
which was owned at different times by several distinguished
men among the first planters.

---

* The author of " New England Wars," whose youthful footsteps
so often traversed the woodland scenery of his native hills, has
availed himself of this spot as the place of interview between a
venerable Puritan, whose daughter had been taken captive by the
Indians, and King Philip, the renowned warrior of Pokanoket.

BROOKS. — These are five in number, on the north side of the town. Near the third brook dwelt Deacon Hirst, in 1640, who there established the first Tannery in Plymouth.

Welkngsly Brook is half a mile south of the town, where Secretary Morton dwelt, and justly claims historical interest, in connection with his valuable labors, in compiling the history of New England and our early church records, and recording the transactions of the commissioners of the United Colonies.

CHILTONVILLE, formerly called EEL RIVER, about three miles south-east of the town, was so named from the abundant supply of eels it affords. Near it, on both sides the river, was a garrison-house during Philip's war. The house, which stood near that now owned by the Rev. Mr. Whittemore, was occupied by William Clark; and, on Sunday, the 12th of March, 1676, it was attacked by the Indians, and some persons were killed and several houses burnt. It is worthy of remark that this was the only serious attack made on Plymouth by the Indians, though it had frequently been threatened during its early history.

Elder Faunce resided on the road leading to Eel River Bridge, and his amiable character and great age attracted many distinguished visitors on their way to and from the Cape.

TOWN RECORDS. — These were commenced in 1638, at which time no settlement had been made beyond the town limits; and the Old Colony Records contain most of the municipal regulations which were previously adopted. The first entry in the Town Records relates to a division of cattle which had considerably increased from a single heifer,

15

given in 1624, to begin a stock for the poor, by James Shirley. Mr. Shirley was one of the Merchant Adventurers
of London, an influential and devoted friend of the colony,
as appears from his correspondence with Gov. Bradford. It
would be gratifying to learn more of this early benefactor
of Plymouth than history yet affords. It is also desirable
that the recommendation of Judge Davis, in a note to the
Memorial, should be executed by the town, in designating
some street or square by his name, in token of grateful remembrance. The records of the town are plainly written,
and in a good state of preservation.

THE OLD COLONY RAIL ROAD. — The completion and
opening of this Road occurred on the 8th of November,
1845, and it is now well patronized by the public. The
distances from Boston on the road, are as follows : Dorchester, 4 miles ; Neponset, 5½ ; Quincy, 8 ; North Braintree,
10 ; South Braintree, 11 ; South Weymouth, 15 ; North
Abington, 18 ; Abington, 19¼ ; South Abington, 21 ; North
Hanson, 23¼ ; Hanson, 24¾ ; Halifax, 28 ; Plympton, 30 ;
Kingston, 33¼ ; Plymouth, 37½ miles.

HOTELS. — The Samoset Hotel, erected by the Rail Road
proprietors, but now owned by an association of gentlemen,
occupies a most favorable situation at the end of Court-
street, directly opposite the depot. It commands a fine
view of the harbor, bay, and surrounding highlands. In the
rear, at a short distance, it has the attractions of hill and
woodland scenery, affording agreeable and convenient walks.
It is fifty by eighty feet, constructed in a handsome style
of architecture, and of perfect finish in every part. The
sleeping-apartments are pleasantly situated, and well contrived and furnished in every respect to promote the comfort
of visitors.

There are three other public houses,— one kept by Mr. John Bradford, in Leyden-street, who has kept the same continuously from November, 1809; and, for aught we know, may be as old an innholder as any in the state, and of whom it may truly be said that neither man nor beast has failed to receive their just requirements at his hands, guided by a conscientiousness and fidelity of rare exemplification. Besides this, another, called the Mansion House, is kept by Mr. N. M. Perry, at the corner of North and Court streets, and another in Leyden-street, owned and kept by Mr. Zaben Olney, principally designed for private boarders; while, as a restaurateur, the attractive saloon of Ballard may justly claim public patronage.

AGRICULTURE AND HORTICULTURE. — As a farming town, Plymouth possesses, as might be expected from the character of its soil, but few natural advantages, and the inhabitants have generally found other modes of employment more profitable. The cleared lands are about five by one and a half miles in extent. On this subject, a friend engaged in agricultural pursuits, observes, " that the sea, by equalizing the temperature through the year, gives us mild winters and a long season." There is an old standing prejudice that nothing on the New England coast will grow; and we are sorry to see that Mr. Downing, in his very pleasant book on the fruits of America, falls in with this popular error. Nothing is more certain than that excessive coldness of the atmosphere is injurious to vegetation; but with us the east wind serves only as a *balance to the broiling summer sun.* It also retards vegetation in the spring, and thus saves us from late frosts, often so destructive in the interior of the state. On the whole, we are thankful for the east wind. The land is of easy tillage, and from the numerous swamps and the contiguous shores of the sea, may be readily supplied and enriched.

The fruits exhibited by the Old Colony Horticultural Society, in September and October of 1845, were of the first excellence, and have never been surpassed in New England. Skill and industry have never failed from the east wind or any other point of climate. Indeed, there are many indications that the art of gardening will not only receive more attention than it has done in former times, but take the place of other employments.

The horticultural establishments of Messrs. Benjamin M. Watson, John Washburn, and Coomer Weston, abound in many excellent varieties of fruit and other trees, well deserving the attention of purchasers.

MANUFACTURES. — The following statement is extracted from the returns of the Marshal, dated June 1, 1850 :

Robbins Cordage Co., annual product seven hundred and fifty tons tarred cordage and Manilla, valued at $160,000; forty-eight hands employed. Plymouth Cordage Co., annual product eight hundred tons cordage, valued at $180,000; seventy hands employed. Holmes & Barrows' Cordage Co., annual product fifty-three tons cordage, valued at $10,000; eleven hands employed. Benj. Diman, cordage, lines and twine, valued at $2,500; three hands employed. Charles B. Irish, cordage, lines and twine, valued at $3,300; five hands employed. Robert Cowen, cordage, lines and twine, valued at $4,250; five hands employed. Plymouth Wool and Cotton Factory, duck, valued at $80,-000; eighty hands employed. Nathaniel Russell & Co.'s Iron Works, nails, plates, rods, etc., valued at $95,000; fifty hands employed. All other kinds of iron manufactures

valued at $56,000; thirty-seven hands employed. Boot
and Shoe Manufactories : — S. Blake & Co., 120,000
pairs boots and shoes, value $85,000; two hundred hands,
male and female. Dunham & Lamman, 21,600 pairs boots
and shoes, value $25,000; thirty hands, male and female.
Daniel J. Lane, 100,000 pairs boots and shoes, value $60,-
000; one hundred and sixty hands, male and female. Benj.
Bramhall, 1,000 pairs boots, value $2,500. John Wash-
burn, stoves and tin ware, valued at $6,000; four hands
employed. Wm. R. Drew,. stoves and tin ware, valued at
$8,000; seven hands employed.

Since the year 1851 some changes have occurred. The
business of Samuel Blake & Co. is now conducted by John
Churchill; that of Dunham & Lanman, by each party on
his own account; and the names of Wm. Morey and Henry
Mills should be added to the list.

The Rolling and Slitting Mills and Nail Factory, at Chiltonville, were recently purchased by the lately incorporated
company called the Russell Mills. This company is now
erecting the requisite buildings, one of which is one hundred
and eighty-four feet by fifty-four, built of brick, two stories
high, and the other of stone, seventy by forty-four feet, designed for the manufacture of cotton duck, and arranged for
the reception of forty looms. We learn with pleasure that
the Cotton Factory water privilege on the upper part of
Town Brook, so long disused, will soon be employed for
manufacturing purposes.

Besides the manufactures above detailed, an establishment
for ready-made clothing is conducted by Mr. Johnson Davie,
and several others for stock-making; product estimated at
about one hundred and fifty thousand dollars. The assessors
are now engaged in taking the census and statistics of the

town, and we regret that the result of these labors could not
be had in season for this publication.

COMMERCE AND THE FISHERIES. — One of the inducements held out by the Pilgrims to King James the First,
when they applied for a patent, was the prospect of advantage to the crown from the establishment of the fisheries in
America; and though his Majesty would not wholly swallow
this *bait* in exchange for *toleration*, he was so far inclined
to its taste, "as to connive at them if they would carry
themselves peaceably." The want of sufficient capital prevented the first settlers from doing much in this business;
and the manufacture of lumber, and traffic with the natives,
were the earliest principal sources of income. The enterprise of Isaac Allerton, however, accomplished much in this
respect; and Gov. Winthrop observes, in his history, that
February 1st, 1633, Mr. Allerton fished with eight boats at
Marblehead. That the fisheries did not for some time increase to the extent anticipated, appears from the fact that
in 1628, when the colony trade was purchased for six
years, and assumed by eight of their number, the whole
amount of shipping was "the pinnace, bass-boat, and shallop at Manomet."

In 1670, the valuation of fish-boats was, four at twenty-
five pounds; two at eighteen pounds; one at twelve
pounds; in all, one hundred and forty-eight pounds sterling. From this period the fisheries increased more
rapidly, and in 1770 amounted to about seventy sail, from
thirty to forty-five tons each, navigated by from six to eight
men.

The number of merchant-vessels employed in the Liver-
pool trade from 1755 to 1770, was three brigs, amounting
to four hundred and seventy tons. At this period, only one

vessel, Capt. Worth, sailed from Boston in the same trade, excepting a schooner owned by Samuel A. Otis, Esq., which made her outfits at Plymouth. Other vessels in the merchant-service at this time have been estimated at twenty.

The number of vessels engaged in the fisheries in 1854,— taken from the Custom-House books,— was 52. Tonnage, 3,778$\frac{32}{95}$; men employed, 412; product, ———. Bounty paid, $14,860,40. The number of vessels employed in 1855 is 52.

CENSUS OF PLYMOUTH AT DIFFERENT PERIODS. — In a work on New England, by Capt. John Smith, published in 1631; which may be found in the Massachusetts Historical Collections, vol. III., third series, he says, under date of 1624 : "In the plantation there is about one hundred and four-score persons, some cattle, but many swine and poultry." In 1629, when the colony charter was granted, the number of inhabitants mentioned in that instrument was three hundred; and Smith, before quoted, when speaking of Gov. Winthrop's colony, in 1631, estimates the number in Plymouth at between four and five hundred persons. De Rasieres, in 1627, stated the number of houses at fifty.

In 1701 a division of lands was made among two hundred and one freeholders of Plymouth. Estimating their families at six each, the population would be 1,206, an estimate probably not far from the truth. In 1643, the males from sixteen to sixty years of age, capable of bearing arms, were one hundred and forty-six. One in the score was the rate of military service. In 1646, the freemen and townsmen (voters) were seventy-nine; 1670, fifty-one; 1683, fifty-five; 1689, seventy-five.

In 1764, including seventy-seven colored persons and

forty-eight Indians, the number of inhabitants was 2,225; 1776, 2,655; 1783, 2,380. According to the United States census in 1790, 2,995 ; 1800, 3,524; 1810, 4,228; 1820, 4,348; 1830, 4,758; 1840, 5,281. The population, as returned June 1, 1850, was 6,026.

The present population may be safely estimated at 6,500, — and more nearly, perhaps, at 6,700,— and the dwelling-houses at 1,083.

PUBLIC SCHOOLS. — The first allusion to the subject of education appears in the first volume of Church Records, page 27, under date Feb. 25th, 1623 ; previous to which, some adversaries of the colony, residing in London, had preferred certain charges against the church, which were sent over to Gov. Bradford. One of the charges was, " Children not catechized nor taught to read ;" which was answered as follows : " This is not true in neither part thereof, for divers take pains with their own as they can. Indeed, we have no common school for want of a fit person, or, hitherto, means to maintain one, though we desire to begin." The record states that all the charges were answered and duly sent to London, greatly to the shame and confusion of all those who had been instrumental in so groundless a slander.

In the year 1635, Feb. 11th, it appears from the Old Colony Records, that " Benjamin Eaton, with his mother's consent, is put to Bridget Fuller (the widow of Dr. Samuel Fuller), being *to keep him at schooll two years,* and employ him in such service as she saw good, and he may be fit for."

It thus appears, from the above and other instances of a similar nature, that great care was taken that apprentices should have due attention in respect to the common branches of educati n Gov. Bradford himself had the charge of Thomas, the son of Robert Cushman, and also of his sons-in-law, Thomas and Constant Southworth; all of whom were afterwards highly distinguished in colonial affairs. Alice, the second wife of Gov. Bradford, as we learn from undoubted tradition, was earnest in the promotion of female education, and proved herself indeed a mother in Israel.

The first instance of legislation on the subject of Free Schools is found in the court proceedings of 1663, as follows : " It is proposed by the Court unto the several townships in this jurisdiction, as a thing that they ought to take into their serious consideration, that some course may be taken that in every town there may be a schoolmaster set up to train up children to reading and writing." At this time forty-two years had elapsed from the first settlement of Plymouth. Previous to this period, the colony was principally indebted for the means of education, to the learned and venerable clergy, who preferred nonconformity and exile, rather than adapt their consciences to the requisitions of unrighteous power. In every new settlement the first object was to establish public worship and secure an able minister; and the flock under his charge were not left without an earnest endeavor to impart at least the knowledge of the Scriptures, and ability to read them. These efforts, under every disadvantage of poverty and severe labor, paved the way for the school-house.

In 1670 a grant was made by the government of the Colony " of all such profits as might or should annually accrue to the Colony, from time to time, for fishing with nets or seines at Cape Cod, for mackerel, bass or herrings, to be improved fcr and towards a *free school* in some town of this jurisdicth m, provided a beginning were made within one year from the grant."

"Cape Cod, therefore" (observes the late S. Davis, Esq.), "which afforded the first shelter to the Pilgrims in 1620, at a subsequent period, as we have stated. from our Records, afforded also the first fund for the education of their children."

Present State of Public Schools. — With a population of over 6,000, Plymouth has thirty-two public schools, numbering 1,482 scholars. The town raises the liberal sum of $8,500 annually for their support. A considerable amount is also expended for private tuition and private schools.

In the year 1854, the town, by a decided vote, abolished the school-district system, and, by an equitable arrangement, assumed all school-buildings and school-property belonging to each district; and all the schools are now conducted, as nearly as may be, under one uniform system.

In addition to the School Committee is employed a School Superintendent, with a salary of eight hundred dollars, whose duty it is to devote himself to the supervision and welfare of the schools.

The schools in Plymouth village, and to some extent in the villages of Chiltonville and Manomet, are graded and clássified into primary, second, third and fourth grades, besides the Grammar School and the High School.

The High School numbers about one hundred scholars, and is conducted by a male as principal, and a female assistant. Chemistry, philosophy, physiology, algebra, and the higher branches of mathematics, are here taught; also the Latin, Greek and French languages.

Scholars are here fitted to enter upon the still more liberal studies of the college, or prepared to go out into the

various avocations of life, mercantile, maritime, or mechanical.

The old town is, therefore, fully up to the age in the
system, arrangements, and generous provision, for the support of public schools. Thus is honored, in the right spot
of all others, the memory of the Fathers, by fostering with
a careful and liberal hand the small streams of intelligence
which shall swell the fountain of knowledge to bless the
children of the present and coming generations.

PUBLIC BUILDINGS. — The Court House, standing in
Court Square (in early times called Framing Green), was
built in 1820, and is fitted up in the best manner, for
accommodating the courts of law, and the public officers of
the county ; having fire-proof apartments for the safe-keep-
ing of records. The jail and dwelling-house attached to it
were built about the same time. The first prison was
erected in 1641, and was twenty-two feet by sixteen, two
stories high, and stood near Prison Brook, in Summer-
street, where the house lately owned by Nathaniel Russell,
Esq., stands. The second jail stood in the same street, on
the lot owned by Capt. Ichabod Davie ; and the third where
the Court House, above described, stands. It is gratifying
to remark, that though the size of these necessary instruments of terror to evil-doers has been successively enlarged,
there seems to have been,· for many years past, great
improvement in their management.

House of Correction. — The House of Correction was
built, in the year 1853, from the plan furnished by, and
under the supervision of, Jonathan Preston, Esq., of Boston, architect. Until 1853, a part of the jail was used as
a House of Correction.

The building is of brick, of fifty feet by thirty-eight, with

stone foundation, and rustic corners of granite. It is built
in the most thorough manner, at a cost of about fifteen
thousand dollars. Its cells and interior arrangements are
constructed after the most approved model. It has thirty-
two cells, intended to accommodate one person only in
each. The building is so constructed that there may be
shut off about one-third part, or less, as is needful, for the
female inmates, by means of heavy iron doors, and so separate them entirely from the males. It has two work-rooms,
covering the entire size of the building in the upper story ;
one for the male and the other for the female inmates.

The manufacture of shoes has been successfully introduced as a means of employment for the inmates, who
number usually from twenty to thirty persons.

The Town House, occupied by the courts of law for the
county till the year 1820, was built in 1749 ; the Country
House, so called in the records, having previously stood on
the same lot.

Alms House. — In 1826, the town purchased several
acres of land on the south side of Town Brook, and erected
a spacious brick building, costing about five thousand
dollars, which affords comfortable accommodations for all
whom the changes of life compel to secure the aid which
humanity extends to the unfortunate in our day, so strik-
ingly in contrast with the narrow system prevalent in many
places some fifty years ago, when *public* charity, in this
respect, had hardly attained the dignity of a virtue.

Davis Hall. — This extensive and costly structure,
situated in Main-street, was erected in 1854 by Charles G.
Davis, Esq., whose liberality and zeal for the improvement
of Plymouth are so justly appreciated by the public.

The front building is of brick, four stories high, forty-six feet wide, and about fifty-five feet deep, and has nine-teen rooms in it, occupied for various purposes. A small hall in front, in the third story, forty-six by thirty. In the rear is a large hall, forty-six by ninety-two, with ante-rooms and a rostrum, sixteen by twenty-two. There are galleries, sixteen feet deep, at each end of the hall. The hall is about twenty-four feet high in the centre of the ceil-ing, and eighteen feet high at the eaves. It is lighted by eight circular windows, on each side, near the ceiling, directly beneath the cornice, made to open and close on hinges by means of pulleys. It is capable of seating com-fortably twelve hundred persons. It is heated by Chilton's large furnace, and lighted by gas, arranged horizon-tally around the hall, about twelve feet from the floor. The entrance to the hall is by an easy staircase, ten feet wide, with rails. There is a cellar under both buildings. It was erected throughout by Plymouth mechanics. Messrs. Churchill and Dunham were the masons, and Comfort Bates the carpenter.

One of the best arranged and most commodious Post Offices in the country is on the first lower floor of the build-ing. A daguerreotype saloon in the fourth story, with a skylight fourteen by twenty, is occupied by Mr. Stephen Lucas.

FINANCIAL AFFAIRS. — The amount of taxable estate in 1855 is, personal, $1,329,900.00 ; and of real estate, $1,738,183.33⅓. Total, $3,068,083.33⅓.

At a town meeting held April 2d, 1855, the sum of $23,800 was appropriated for the following purposes :

For the support of Schools, . . . $8,600.00
For Highways and Bridges, ... 3,800.00
For the Poor, ... 2,600 00

16

For the Insane Poor, ... 1,000.00
For Assessors and Assistant, . . . 250.00
For Treasurer and Collector, . . . 450.00
For Fire Department, ... 2,200.00
For Discount on Taxes, ... 1,500.00
For Sexton's Salary, ... 85.00
For Town Debt and interest thereon, . . 1,600.00
For Contingencies, ... 315.00
For Building New Road, . . . 2,200.00

                             $23,800.00
The Town's part of County Tax, . . 2,475.27
The Town's part of State Tax, . . . 1,966.50

     Total, ... $28,241.77

BANKS, &c. — *Old Colony Bank.* — Capital, $150,000. Jacob H. Loud, President; George G. Dyer, Cashier.

Plymouth Bank. — Capital, $150,000. I. L. Hedge, President; I. N. Stoddard, Cashier.

Plymouth Savings Bank. — Nathl. Russell, President; Allen Danforth, Treasurer. Depositors, 3,803. Deposits, $705,936.32.

Old Colony Insurance Company. — Capital, $50,000. Wm. Nelson, President; Wm. S. Danforth, Secretary.

Plymouth Loan and Fund Association. — Leander Lovell, President; Wm. H. Nelson, Secretary and Treasurer; Nathl. Brown, Vice-President.

Plymouth Five Cent Savings Bank. — Jason Hart, President; Daniel J. Robbins, Treasurer.

CHURCHES. — The number of churches in the whole town is eleven : of which five are Congregational, one Baptist, one Universalist, two Christian, one Episcopal, and one Methodist Episcopal.

The multiplication of sects in modern times, while doubtless tending to preserve the rights of conscience unimpaired, not unfrequently renders the liberal support of an able ministry burthensome, and sometimes impracticable. Protestantism, therefore, might do well to consider its actual position, and more earnestly study the things that make for peace, cherishing that enlarged charity which recognizes a brother, not from the stamp of his creed alone, but the divine graces of a pure life ; and in no case calling down fire from heaven to consume the adversary. [See Ap. p. 195.]

SUNDAY SCHOOL. — This valuable auxiliary to the instructions of the pulpit is now connected with most of the churches in town, and the number of children receiving the benefit of its teaching is probably more than nine hundred.

The Sabbath is still regarded with veneration by our citizens generally ; and, though relieved from much of the gloom and severity of discipline connected with its observance in former time, is but rarely violated in a manner disturbing the church-going habits of our population.

TEMPERANCE. — This subject excited early attention; and in 1816, an able report of a committee appointed by the town, appears on the records, suggesting various methods to check the progress of intemperance. Those who have labored in this cause may justly rejoice in the fruits of their persevering efforts. Many have been redeemed from the dominion of the most inveterate habits of intemperance, which long seemed incorrigible, and now rejoice with joy unspeakable, in the renovation of a new life.

MILITARY. — The improved legislation of the state has

judiciously changed the old organization of the militia; and the Standish Guards, originally organized under an act of the legislature, dated August 25th, 1818, and named in honor of Miles Standish, the veteran hero of 1620, afford all the defensive preparation required in times of peace. Charles Raymond, Captain; Charles C. Doten, Clerk.

NEWSPAPERS. — The *Plymouth Journal*, edited and printed by N. Coverly, was commenced in March, 1785, and continued till June, 1786. It was published too near the metropolis to find sufficient encouragement to justify its continuance, particularly at that period of individual embarrassments. The Old Colony arms, four men kneeling, implumed hearts in their hands, on a field quarterly, was its head ornament; legend, Plymouth, *Novanglia*, *sigillum*, *societatis*, 1620. The motto (selected by Rev. Dr. Robbins) was, *Patrum pietate ortum filioram virtute servandum*.

The *Old Colony Memorial* was commenced May 4, 1822, and the *Plymouth Rock* in 1837; the former issued on Saturday, and the latter on Thursday of each week.

CEMETERY. — Oak Grove Cemetery is situated west of the village, about three quarters of a mile from the Court House. It contains sixteen acres, possesses much natural beauty, and is appropriately laid out with various avenues and walks. The corporation was organized May 15th, 1841. The Grove was consecrated Sept. 12th with religious services and address. About one hundred and fifty lots have been sold; many of which have been improved and ornamented, particularly during the last year.

John Atwood, Jr., President; B. H. Holmes, Treasurer; Samuel H. Doten, Secretary.

PLYMOUTH GAS COMPANY. — Capital, $40,000. Incorporated April 8, 1854. Gas was introduced in November last, and is fast becoming a favorite mode of illumination among our citizens.

Isaac L. Hedge, President; John J. Russell, Clerk and Treasurer.

ORNAMENTAL TREES. — The compact settlement of the central part of Plymouth has left but little room for the cultivation of ornamental trees. The elms in Town Square, at once appropriate and ornamental, were brought from Portsmouth, and set out by the late Thomas Davis, Esq., in the year 1784. The linden-trees, so beautiful in summer, in the garden and in front of the dwelling-house now occupied by Abraham Jackson, Esq., in North-street, were set out in 1760, by the late George Watson, Esq., having been brought from Nova Scotia.

Those in front of the dwelling-house owned by the heirs of the late Charles Jackson, Esq., were set out not far from 1760, by Miss Penelope Winslow, whose father, Edward Winslow, Esq., built and owned the house, and afterwards removed to the British Provinces.

The elms at the residence of John Russell, Esq., were set out by the late Samuel Jackson, in 1790. Those standing in the front yard of Nathaniel M. Davis, Esq., were set out, in 1783, by the late William Watson, Esq.; and two in Court Square, by the late Capt. James Nickerson, in 1792.

For the thrifty range of trees extending through Court-street to the Samoset hotel, the public are mainly indebted to the liberal and enterprising efforts of Andrew L. Russell, Esq.

INDIAN NAMES. — The sources of information respecting

16*

the *signification* of Indian names are quite limited. Those
in relation to the colony are mostly derived from the inves--
tigations of the late Samuel Davis, Esq. Accomac, Plymouth, or *Accaumuck*, signifies to go by water, and is applied
to places where it is more convenient to go by water than
land. *Cantaugeanteest*, Watson's Hill. *Patackosi*, the
name of Town Brook, from *Tackosi*, "short, narrow."
Coatuit, the name of Half-way Pond. *Agawam*, a part
of Wareham. *Kitaumet*, Manomet Ponds. *Cummaquid*,
Barnstable. *Paumit*, or *Pamet*, part of Truro. *Matta-
keese* or *Mattachiest*, Yarmouth. *Mattakeset*, Duxbury.
Nauset, Eastham. *Namasket*, Middleborough. *Monamoy*,
Chatham. *Capawack*, Martha's Vineyard. *Manamoos-
keyin*, Abington. *Shaume*, Sandwich. *Satuit*, Scituate.
Tionet, from *Taunek*, the "Crane." *Pimesepoesc*,
"provision rivulet," a compound phrase from *pime*, food;
the latter part little river,— a place visited by Governor
Bradford in 1622 to procure corn, and now called Manomet
river, running into Buzzard's Bay.

FIRE DEPARTMENT. — In the year 1758 a fire-engine
was procured from London by the town, and subsequently
another by subscription. By means of successive efforts
made during the last ten years, the fire department, grad-
ually assuming a far more extended organization than
previously existed, has become highly efficient and successful in its operations, on many occasions of imminent danger
from threatened conflagration, and may, therefore, justly
claim, not only an adequate support, but the grateful confidence and approbation of the public.

It is now composed of two hundred and two men,— ten of
whom are engineers,— three suction-engines with forty men,
and a hose-carriage, with three hundred feet of hose to each;

one tub-engine with forty young men, a hose-carriage with three hundred feet of hose, and a bucket-carriage, with fifty-five buckets. There are two hydrants of force pump; one at the Arch bridge, and the other at the dam of the Robbins Cordage Company, with three hundred feet of hose, and a company of eight men to each hydrant; and a hook and ladder carriage, with a company of sixteen men; all of which are in good working condition.

George Simmons, Chief Engineer; Charles Raymond, Clerk.

PLYMOUTH WATER WORKS. — By an act of the General Court, passed Feb. 15, 1797, Joshua Thomas and others were constituted a corporation for the purpose of conveying water by subterranean pipes into the town, by the name of the Plymouth Aqueduct. The first recorded preliminary meeting on the subject was held July 27th, 1796. By an agreement executed Sept. 14th, 1796, between the Company and Mr. Caleb Leach, the main pipe was to be of cedar logs, one-third thereof to be ten, one-third, nine, and one-third eight inches, the bore to be two and five-eighth inches, commencing near the bridge at the foot of Deep Water Pond, to extend about six hundred rods, the trench to be three feet deep; the whole to be completed on the first day of July, 1797, to be paid four dollars per rod. On the 5th of June, 1797, it was voted "to write Mr. Leach, at Boston, to expedite the finishing of the cross-pipes;" and the water was probably introduced in the autumn of that year.

The late Samuel Davis, Esq., writing on this subject in 1815, observes, "This work was performed by Mr. Caleb Leach, who then lived in Plymouth, now of Oswego, New York, whose talents, as a self-taught mechanic, are of the

very first order ; to these talents it is that Boston, and the
city of New York, etc., are in a degree indebted for the like
convenience."

Mr. Leach, as we learn from Mr. David Turner, a son
of the late Capt. Lothrop Turner, invented the first screw-
bit for boring pumps; previous to which the common
pod-auger had been used for that purpose.   The first auger
of this kind made by Mr. Leach is now in possession of Mr.
Turner, and measures twenty inches pod, bore two and five-
eighth inches, with a shank of five and a half inches.

Mr. Leach was a native of Halifax, served in the revolution ; and, returning home for a while, removed to Plymouth
about the year 1790.   After leaving Plymouth, his eminent
mechanical skill found a more enlarged sphere of action in
the State of New York, proving highly beneficial to the
community, and honorable to himself.

For a more particular description of the works, now in
process of construction, see Appendix G.

GEN. WOLFE AND LORD NELSON. — The two following
incidents of our early history, connected with the distinguished names of Wolfe and Nelson, are here inserted as
deserving attention ; the first of which is copied from the
Notes on Plymouth, by the late Samuel Davis, Esq.

"1745. This year a full company was raised in Plymouth for the expedition against Louisbourg; and it is
remarked they were the first for that service who appeared
at Boston, whence they embarked and served with credit on
that memorable occasion.

"The captain of this company, Sylvanus Cobb, continued
in Nova Scotia, where he had the command of a government
sloop ; and in 1758, was selected by General Monckton to

conduct General Wolfe to a reconnoitre of the fortress previous to its second capture. As they sailed into the harbor, no one was allowed to stand upon deck but Cobb at the helm, and Wolfe in the foresheets, making observations, while the shot were flying around. The latter observed they had approached as far as he wished for his purposes. Capt. Cobb, however, made yet another tack; and, as they hove about, Wolfe exclaimed with approbation, ' Well, Cobb; I shall never doubt but you will carry me near enough !' This anecdote of the hero of the plains of Abraham we give as well attested.

" There was something, it is said, in Capt. Cobb which gained the esteem of the great man we have named. He was born in 1709, at Plymouth. He was son of Elisha Cobb, and descended from Henry Cobb, who appears in Plymouth as early as 1633. Ebenezer Cobb, the greatest instance of longevity in this vicinity, was his uncle. He accompanied the expedition to Havana, and died there in 1762."*

" In 1782, Lord' Nelson, then a lieutenant in command of his majesty's ship Albemarle, while cruising along the Massachusetts coast, captured the schooner Harmony, of Plymouth, owned by Thomas Davis, and commanded by Nathaniel Carver, both of that town. After some days' detention on board ship, as pilot in the intricate navigation of the coast, Capt. Carver was released. Upon his return home, Mr. Davis at once determined to make an effort to recover his vessel; and together with Capt. Carver, took a boat well freighted with fresh meats and other accepta-

---

* The frankness and affability of General Wolfe have been often mentioned by those who saw him on this occasion ; striking traits of the true heroic mind in all ages and all countries.

ble presents, and boarded the ship, which was still cruising in the bay. Nelson received them politely, and invited them to his cabin, where he entertained them with as bountiful a repast as his larder afforded. Upon their return to the deck the schooner was alongside, having been signalized during their visit to the cabin, subject to their orders. Upon their leaving the ship, Nelson placed in the hands of Capt. Carver a certificate, the original of which is in possession of Wm. T. Davis, Esq., a copy of which follows :

" ' These are to certify that I took the schooner Harmony, Nathaniel Carver, master, belonging to Plymouth ; but, on account of his good services, have given him up his vessel again.

" ' Dated on board His Majesty's ship Albemarle, 17th August, 1782, in Boston Bay.

" ' HORATIO NELSON.' "

APPENDIX.

A.

GOV. BRADFORD'S LOST HISTORY.

THE following letter, very obligingly written by Charles Deane, Esq., of Boston, in reply to inquiries made of him respecting the long-lost manuscript history of Gov. Bradford, presents a full statement of the circumstances which led to the restoration of this invaluable work, which we doubt not will unfold in detail many interesting occurrences of early times, and impart fresh interest to the curiosity of historical research :

BOSTON, July 16, 1855.

"WILLIAM S. RUSSELL, ESQ., —

"DEAR SIR : You inquire of me for some information relative to the recent discovery or *recovery* of the long-lost manuscript history of Gov. Bradford, and I cheerfully comply with your request. On the 17th day of February last, the Rev. John Stetson Barry, who was at that time engaged in writing the first volume of his History of Massachusetts, since published, called upon me, and stated that he believed he had made an important discovery, being no less than Governor Bradford's manuscript history. He then took from his pocket a printed duodecimo volume, entitled, 'A History of the Protestant Episcopal Church in America, by Samuel, Lord Bishop of Oxford. Second edition. London : 1846' (which he had a few days before borrowed from a friend), and pointed out to me certain passages in the text, which any one familiar with them would at once recognize as the language of Governor Bradford, as cited by Morton and Prince ; but which the author of the volume, in his foot notes, referred to a 'MS. History of the Plantation of Plymouth, &c., in the Fulham Library.' There

191

were other passages in the volume, containing new matter, which were referred to the same source. I fully coincided with Mr. Barry in the opinion that this Fulham manuscript could be no other than Bradford's History, either the original or a copy of it, — possibly it might prove but a fragment of it, — and that measures should *at once* be taken to cause an examination of it to be made.*

"Being in correspondence with Rev. Joseph Hunter, F. A. S., of London, a distinguished antiquary, who has taken a great interest in the early history of the Pilgrims, and has made valuable contributions thereto, with the concurrence of Mr. Barry, I addressed him a note on the very day above named, in which I stated some of the circumstances detailed here, and requested of him the favor to ascertain what this Fulham MS. was ; and if it be proved what we hoped it was, to have a copy taken for publication in the Collections of the Massachusetts Historical Society, the next volume of which came under my charge as chairman of the publishing committee. This note, in which I enclosed an original letter of Governor Bradford, as a means of verification of the manuscript, I forwarded by the steamer of the 21st February from New York.

" On the 12th of March, Mr. Hunter addressed me a letter in reply, stating that he had made application to the Bishop of London, who has charge of the Fulham Library, for leave to inspect the manuscript, preliminary to a request for a copy of the same for the Society ; and that he was in daily expectation of hearing that it had been brought to London. On the 19th, one week after, he wrote to me again, saying that he had had an opportunity of inspecting the MS. at the house of the Bishop of London, in St. James' Square. He says : ' There is not the slightest doubt that the manuscript is Governor Bradford's own autograph. Not only is there a sufficient degree of correspondence between the handwriting of the manuscript and that of the letter which you transmitted to me, but there is the attestation of the family, written in 1705, stating that it was given by the Governor to his son, Major William Bradford ; and by him to *his* son, Major John Bradford. There is, also, in the handwriting of Prince, a memorandum dated June 4, 1728, showing how he obtained it from Major John Bradford. It also appears to have been in the New England Library ; and, finally, the written pages are two hundred and seventy, the number named by

---

* At the same time Mr. Barry stated to me that he had called the attention of our mutual friend, Dr. N. B. Shurtleff, to these references ; and that he concurred in his views respecting them.   C. D.

Prince,' etc. Mr. Hunter also stated that the Bishop had granted him the favor to take the volume home, and to make whatever extracts from it he pleased, or to copy the whole. ' So that all difficulties of that kind are removed, and the Society is perfectly at liberty to have a copy made for its use from which they may print, if they think it expedient to do so.'

"A copy of this precious volume is now in progress, and we hope soon to receive it.

"It may, perhaps, be interesting to state that, in a more recent letter received from Mr. Hunter, he says that there is connected with the manuscript, though, of course, making no part of the history, a rather long piece, 'being Hebrew roots with English explanations.' That 'it is in Governor Bradford's handwriting, and therefore shows his attention to such studies.' This confirms what Cotton Mather says of Bradford.

"I am, dear sir,
"Your friend and obedient servant,
"CHARLES DEANE."

Although Mr. Deane, in the foregoing letter, discloses no opinion as to what further may be expected from Governor Bradford's history, in addition to the copious extracts made by Prince and Hutchison, there is good reason to believe that much incidental matter exists there, which they could not incorporate in their respective works. The following extracts from the Church Records, volume I., page 22, show at least that, in relation to the transactions between the Merchant Adventurers and the Pilgrims, much may be expected of great value :

"In the foregoing five chapters the reader may take a view of some of the many difficulties our blessed predecessors went through in their first achievement of this weighty enterprise of removal of our church into these American parts ; the immediate following relations in Mr. Bradford's Book, out of which divers of these matters are re-collected, do more especially concern the conditions of their agreement with several Merchant Adventurers towards the voyage, etc., as also several letters sent to and fro, from friend to friend, relating to the premises, which are not so pertinent to the nature of this small history. Wherefore, 1 shall here omit to insert them, judging them not so suitable to my present purpose."

17

B.

MONUMENT TO THE PILGRIMS.

THE following description of the proposed monument in honor of the Pilgrims was obligingly prepared for this work by Hammatt Billings, Esq., the eminent designer, of Boston, with whom the magnificent plan originated. It is gratifying to announce that active measures will soon be adopted to execute this great work, which has already excited a deep interest in the community.

"The National Monument to the Forefathers, which is just about to be commenced under the auspices of the Pilgrim Society, is intended to be the grandest work of the kind in the world. Raised in commemoration of the great starting-point in our history, it is the idea to make it, as far as possible, worthy of the great event which it will record.

"In size it will be the greatest of modern works, and only equalled by those vast monuments of Egyptian power and grandeur which remain to us, the most wonderful triumphs of mere mechanical power. It is to be built of massive blocks of granite, and will be eighty feet at the base, and a little over one hundred and fifty feet high. The plan of the principal pedestal is an octagon, with four small and four large faces; from the small faces project four buttresses or wing pedestals. On the main pedestal stands a figure of Faith. One foot rests upon the Forefathers' Rock; in her left hand she holds an open Bible; with the right uplifted, she points to heaven. Looking downward, as to those she is addressing, she seems to call them to trust in a higher power. This figure is to be of granite, and will be seventy feet high.

"On each of the four smaller or wing pedestals is a seated figure; they are emblematic of the principles upon which the Pilgrims proposed to found their Commonwealth. The first of these is Morality. She holds the Decalogue in her left and the scroll of Revelation in her right hand; her look is upward towards the impersonation of the Spirit of Religion above. In a niche, on one side of her throne, is a Prophet, and in the other one of the Evangelists. The second of these figures is Law. On one side of his seat is Justice; on the other Mercy. The third is Education. In the niche, on one side of her seat, is Wisdom, ripe with years; on the other, Youth led by Experience. The fourth figure is Freedom. On one side Peace rests under his protection; on the other, Tyranny is overthrown by his prowess. Upon the faces of these projecting pedestals are alto-reliefs representing scenes from the history of the Pilgrims. The first is the departure from Delft-haven; the second, the signing of the social compact; the third, the landing at Plymouth; the fourth, the first treaty with the Indians. These reliefs are to be in marble, as susceptible of greater delicacy of treatment. The four figures on these pedestals are to be of granite, each thirty-four feet high. The figures in the panels eight feet.

" On each of the four large faces of the main pedestal is to be a large panel for records. That in front will contain the names of all who came over in the Mayflower; behind, the events of the voyage. On one side, the events previous to sailing from Delft-haven; on the other, early events of the colony. Below these are to. be smaller panels, to contain the dedication of the monument, names of officers of the Pilgrim Society, etc., and such other records as may be considered of sufficient consequence.

"Within the monument will be a chamber twenty-six feet in diameter, with a stone stair leading up to the platform, upon which stands the principal figure. From this platform, which will be over eighty feet above the entrance at the ground, all the principal localities in the early history of the colony of Plymouth may be seen almost at a glance. The anchorage-ground of the Mayflower, the location of the Rock where the first Pilgrims landed, Captain's Hill, at Duxbury, etc., etc.

" Around the monument, a space of nine acres, making a fine square, is to be kept open forever."

C.

CHURCHES.

THE Church Covenant adopted by the first church of Plymouth, and the first Protestant church in America, is copied from the records now in the keeping of the writer. Neither history nor tradition affords any information as to what became of the Leyden Church Records; and *research in England* might possibly restore them.

"1676. The war continuing, and also sickness, the Church set apart April 19th for fasting and prayer; and also May 30th, for the same grounds. The General Court in June, being sensible of the heavy hand of God upon the country in the continuance of war with the heathen, appointed a day of humiliation to be kept, 22 day of it, and added thereto a solemn motion to all churches to renew a covenant engagement to God for reformation of all provoking evils. The church attended that day of prayer, and then the elders appointed a church meeting to be on June 29th. The church then all met. Our church meetings were ever begun and ended with prayer (the pastor ordinarily beginning and the elder concluding therewith). After prayer for God's direction and blessing in so solemn a matter, a church covenant was read, and the church voted that it should be left upon record as that which they did own to be the substance of that covenant which their fathers entered into at the first gathering of the church, which was in these words following: .

"In the name of our Lord Jesus Christ, and in obedience to his holy will and divine ordinances, we, being by the most wise and good providence of God, brought together in this place; and, desirous to unite ourselves into one congregation or church, under the Lord Jesus Christ, our Head, that it may be in such sort as becometh all those whom he hath redeemed and sanctified to himself, we do hereby solemnly and religiously, as in his most holy presence, avouch the Lord Jehovah, the only true God, to be our God, and the God of ours, and do promise and bind ourselves to walk in all our ways according to the rule of the Gospel, and in all sincere conformity to his holy ordinances, and in mutual love to, and watchfulness over, one another, depending wholly and only upon the Lord our God to enable us by his grace hereunto."

The present settled ministers of Plymouth are as follows: 1st Church, James Kendall, senior pastor, Geo. S. Ball, colleague pastor; 2d Church, D. H. Babcock; 3d Church, Joseph B. Johnson; Benjamin Whittemore, Russell Tomlinson, Universalist; Robert B. Hall, Episcopal; William Kelley, Methodist Episcopal.

The Rev. Adiel Harvey, having accepted the place of superintendent of schools, he resigned his charge of the ministry in the Baptist church.

D.

DRUILLETES' VISIT TO PLYMOUTH.

FROM a manuscript narrative in French, recently discovered in Canada East, by Mr. John G. Shea, — a translation of which by him has

been presented to the Massachusetts Historical Society, — it appears
that Father Druilletes, the author, a Jesuit missionary to the Abnaquois Indians on the Kennebec, made a visit to Boston and Plymouth
in the latter part of the year 1650, to negotiate a colonial union, which
had been proposed by New England, and which Canada now accepted,
in hopes of procuring aid against the Iroquois, who had just overthrown the Hurons, the early allies of the French; and also to solicit
aid for the Abnaquois.

He came to Boston, accompanied by John Winslow, whom he met at
"Koussinoc," now Augusta. After spending some days at Boston
and vicinity, and seeing the governor and some of the distinguished
men, in furtherance of the object of his mission, he went to Plymouth,
in company with Winslow, where he arrived on the 22d December, the
day after he left Boston. He says, Winslow "lodged me with one of
the five farmers* of Koussinoc, named Padis.† The governor of the
place, by name John Brentford,‡ received me with courtesy, and appointed the next day for audience; and then invited me to a fish dinner,
which he ordered on my account, knowing that it was Friday. I met
with much favor at this settlement; for the farmers, and, among others,
Captain Thomas Willets, spoke to the governor for the good of my
negotiations," etc.

He spent not over two days at Plymouth, returning to Boston on the
24th December. By February he had returned to his station on the
Kennebec.

Respecting the above proposition of the French, so far as it relates to
the Plymouth colony, we find in the court orders, Vol. II., the following
record:

"Bradford, Governor, 1651. Whereas, a request was made last
winter by a Messenger from the French at Canada, to assist them
against the Mowhakes; or, at least, to have libertie to go up through
these parts for their more commodious encountering with the said Mowhakes, the Court declare themselves not to be willing either to aid them
in their design, or to grant them libertie to go through their jurisdiction
for the aforesaid purpose."

The Trading-house of the Plymouth Colony was established in 1628,
and their chartered jurisdiction extended fifteen miles each side of the

* Those who farmed the trade on the Kennebec.
† William Paddy.
‡ William Bradford was then Governor.

17*

river Kennebec; and the route described, to the Mohawk country, was more direct than any other. The Iroquois, as stated in Documentary History of New York, under date of 1665, "are composed of five nations, of which the nearest to the Dutch is that of the Mohawk, consisting of two or three villages, containing about three to four hundred men."

Those who are accustomed to regard the Puritans of 1650 as severe, unbending, and "even morose" in their deportment, may find in this brief narrative an evidence of courtesy and true politeness, not only deserving of admiration, but which might extort commendation from the most polished adherent of the Chesterfieldian school itself.

_____

E.

PLYMOUTH COLONY CHARTERS.

THE following extracts are copied from a publication of Charles Deane, Esq., called "The First Plymouth Patent," printed for private distribution, in November last:

"It is well known that when the Pilgrims landed at Plymouth, in 1620, they had no patent or charter authorizing them to make a settlement there. They had intended, before leaving Holland, to plant near the Hudson river, and had secured a grant accordingly from the Virginia Company. Finding themselves beyond the bounds of their patent, which, therefore, become 'void and useless,' on the return of the Mayflower, in May, 1621, they made application, through the Merchant Adventurers, to the President and Council of New England, established at Plymouth, in the county of Devon, for a grant of the territory on which they had unintentionally settled.

"Mr. Weston, in a letter to Governor Carver, dated London, July 6, 1621, sent by the Fortune, writes : ' We have procured you a Charter, the best we could, better than your former, and with less limitation.' (Prince, Vol I., page 114). Judge Davis, in a note on Morton's Memorial, page 73, remarks : 'This intimation refers to a patent from the President and Council of New England to John Peirce and his associates, which was in trust for the company. It was probably brought in this ship [the Fortune], and was a few years since found among the old papers in the Land Office at Boston, by William Smith, Esq., one of the ' Land Committee. It bears date June 1, 1621.' This original instrument, after it was used by Judge Davis, appears to have been lost or mislaid for a number of years, as Dr. Young, in his Chronicles of the Pilgrim Fathers, page 235, remarks : ' I have sought for the original in vain in the archives of the State. It was never printed ; and, it is to be feared, is now lost.'

"Fortunately, however, this ancient memorial of the Pilgrims h'.s been recently recovered at Plymouth, where it most appropriately belongs, among some papers which were once in the possession of the late Judge Davis.

"It may not be deemed uninteresting to state, that this *first* Plymouth patent, now for the first time printed, is the *first* grant, of which we have any record, made by the great Plymouth Company, which had received its act of incorporation seven months before, viz., on the 3d of November, 1620.

"The second patent (which is not extant) was obtained April 20th, 1622, as appears from one of the memoranda, furnished me by Rev. J. B. Felt, from the State Paper Office in London.

" The difficulties concerning this second patent were finally settled by an assignment of it by Peirce to the Merchant Adventurers for *five hundred pounds*.

"The original of the third patent, granted 13th January, 1629, O. S., to William Bradford and his associates, is preserved in the office of the Register of Deeds at Plymouth. This has been frequently printed. In this grant their territorial limits are defined, which was not the case in the first patent.

"A patent of *Cape Ann*, dated January 1, 1623, O. S., was granted to the Plymouth people by Lord Sheffield, a member of the Council of New England. This place, used for a time for their fishing stages, they soon after abandoned. The patent is extant, and will soon be published.*

" The terms and conditions of the grant which the Pilgrims procured from the Virginia Company at London, for a settlement about the Hudson river (alluded to above), and which was taken out ' in the name of Mr. John Wincob, a religious gentleman, then belonging to the Countess of Lincoln,' are not known."

* It has been recently published by J. Wingate Thornton, Esq., of Boston, in a work containing many interesting historical facts in relation to the early settlement of Massachusetts.

F.

STANDISH'S SWORD.

THE sword of Standish has recently attracted much attention from many scientific and antiquarian gentlemen, who have visited Pilgrim Hall, on account of the peculiar and yet undeciphered inscriptions on its blade, none of whom, however, seem able to determine the place of its manufacture, or the significance of the figures. With a view, if possible, to ascertain the matter, a fac-simile of the sword was lately taken, plainly indicating the inscriptions, which was sent to a young gentleman of this town, now at the University of Gottingen, in Germany. It was submitted to the inspection of several distinguished scientific men in that quarter, and, among others, to the celebrated Baron Humboldt, of Berlin, in Prussia; but, thus far, no interpreter has appeared to expound the mysterious characters of this antique memorial of the military chieftain of 1620.

The whole length of the sword is 39¼ inches; the average width, 1¼ inches; the hilt or handle, 5¼ inches; the cross at the hilt, 4¼ inches, and the cross and guard are of brass. It has but one edge, the blade being slightly curved, and nearly through its whole length is fluted, having three rather narrow and shallow channels. Within the space of ten inches from the hilt, on both sides of the blade, several inscriptions appear, among which the figures 1149 are perfectly distinct.

G.

WATER WORKS.

FOR many years past the citizens of Plymouth have felt the importance of procuring a supply of pure water, the old aqueduct being in a decayed condition, and no longer adequate to supply the increased demand of a growing population. This consideration, in connection with another, of perhaps equal importance, that of guarding against the emergencies of fire, led to an application by the town to the Legislature for authority to construct suitable water works. This application was successful; and the town, by an act passed in 1854, and another in 1855, was duly authorized to proceed in the matter. The statement below, furnished by Charles O. Churchill, Esq., one of the Water Commissioners, gives a brief view of the works which are now in process of construction:

" The water is to be brought from Little South Pond, a distance of 13,065 feet, or about two and a half miles.

" Ground was first broken May 19th.

" The contract for laying pipe is made with the Jersey City Water and Gas Pipe Co.

" Main pipe, ten inches; pipe through Main-street, eight inches; other streets, from six to two inches. To extend to Kingston line on the north, and to Wellingsly village at the south.

" There are to be thirty fire-hydrants; and the facilities for extinguishment of fires will be equal, if not superior, to any place of the same size as Plymouth.

" The head of water will be about one hundred and ten feet above Water-street, and sixty-one above Main-street.

" A reservoir, capable of holding one million of gallons, will be built on the hill north of the Episcopal church.

" The route for the main pipe from South Pond to the village is graded, so that there is a gradual descent from the pond to the point of distribution.

" Cost of the works, completed, not far from $85,000."

H.

TABLE OF LONGEVITY.

THE following list, exhibiting the longevity of some of the first planters of the Old Colony, is mostly copied from the Old Colony and Church Records:

Those having an asterisk prefixed arrived in some one of the first four ships, namely, the Mayflower, Fortune, Ann, or Little James. The rest mostly arrived before the year 1632; and John Rogers and Hope Nelson were native-born.

Names.	Time of decease.	Age.
* William Brewster, ...	April 16th, 1644	84
William Thomas,*, ...	August, 1651	78
* Julian Kempton, widow of Manasseh Kempton, Feb. 19, 1664–5		81
Gabriel Fallowell, ...	December 28, 1667	83
John Dunham (Deacon), ...	March 2, 1668–9	80
* Alice Bradford (widow of the Governor), . .	March 26, 1670	80
* John Howland, ...	February 24, 1672–3	80
* Thomas Prence, ...	March 29, 1673	73
* Elizabeth Warren (widow of Richard Warren), October 2, 1673		90
Thomas Tupper (of Sandwich), ...	March 28, 1676	98
Anna Tupper (Sandwich), ...	June 4, 1676	90
Priscilla Cooper (sister of Gov. Bradford's wife		
Alice), ...	Dec. 29, 1689	91
Dorothy Brown (Swanzey, wife of John Brown), . . .	1675	90
* Edward Bangs, ...	1678	86
Phineas Pratt, ...	April 19, 1680	90
* Nathaniel Morton (Secretary), ...	June 29, 1685	73
Robert Finney (Deacon), ...	January 7, 1687	80
Mary Carpenter (sister to Gov. Bradford's wife), . . .	1683	90
* John Alden, ...	September 12, 1687	89
* Experience Mitchell, ...	1689	80
* Thomas Cushman (Elder), ...	December 10, 1691	84
John Dunham (son of the Deacon), ...	1692	79
Anna Lettice (widow of Thomas Lettice), . . .	July 3, 1687	81
* Elizabeth Howland (wife of John Howland), ...	1687	81
Samuel Eddy (Swanzey), ...	1688	87
George Watson, ...	January 31, 1688	87
Andrew Ring, ... '.	1692	75
John Thomson (of Middleborough), ...	June 16, 1696	80
Mary Thompson (wife of the above), ...	March 21, 1714	88
William Pabodie (of Little Compton, early of		
Duxbury), ...	December 31, 1707	88
Elizabeth Pabodie (sometimes spelt Peabody,		
wife of the above, and daughter of John		

* The following is copied from the grave-stone of William Thomas, Esq., in the old burial-ground at Marshfield; and is, we believe, the oldest grave-stone in the Old Colony:

"Here lies what remain of William Thomas, Esq., one of the founders of New Plymouth Colony, who died in yᵉ month of August, 1651, about yᵉ 78th year of his age."

Names.	Time of decease.	Age.

Alden and Priscilla Mullins, who came in
the Mayflower), ... May 31, 1717 94
John Rogers* (Barrington, son of John
Rogers, of Duxbury), ... June 28, 1732 92
James Pitney (of Marshfield), ... March, 1663 80
Phebe Finney (Plymouth), ... December 9, 1710 92
Hope Nelson (of Middleborough, widow of
Thomas Nelson, a native of Barnstable
county), ... December 7, 1782 105
* Mary Cushman (widow of the elder), ... 1690 90
* Thomas Clark (once supposed to have been
the mate of the Mayflower), ... 1697 98
Elizabeth Eddy (Swanzey), ... May 24, 1689 82
Richard Wright, ... June 9, 1691 83
Patience Whitney (widow, and mother of Elder Faunce), . 1692 77
George Bonum, ... April 28, 1704 95
Samuel King, ... August, 1705 90
James Cole, ... 1709 85
John Doane, first of Plymouth, removed to Eastham in 1644, and died
there in 1686, aged perhaps 95. (See Savage's Genealogical Diction-
ary, Vol. I., p. 55.)

* From a reliable source the following is extracted: "June 28th, 1732. At
Barrington died our grandfather, John Rogers, Esq., after about ten days'
sickness, in the ninety-second year of his age (91 years, 5 months). He had
been blind nine years. He left two children, Bradford and Searl, and twenty
grandchildren, sixty-nine great-grandchildren, and one great-great-grandchild,
— ninety-two in all. All these sprang from his first wife, whose maiden name
was Elizabeth Peabody."

NOTE.— In the next generation many instances of longevity might be collected. Elder Thomas Faunce died in 1745, aged 99 years. His daughter,
Patience Kempton, died at New Bedford, in 1779, aged 105 years and six
month. Ephraim Pratt, grandson of Joshua Pratt, one of the first comers at
Plymouth, died at Shutesbury, Worcester county, in 1804, aged 115. Ebenezer
Cobb was born in Plymouth, and died at Kingston, in 1801, aged 107 years, and
was of the third generation. John Alden, a descendant of John Alden who
came in the Mayflower, died in Middleborough, in 1821, aged 102. Three of his
children, two daughters and one son, were living and dwelt under the same
roof in Middleborough, whose average age was 84 and one third years.
Widow Abigail Bryant died in Plympton, Feb. 21, 1821, aged 99 years, six
months, and ten days.

APPENDIX TO THE THIRD EDITION.

Names of passengers on board the ship Mayflower, and of those of the party who died during the winter and spring of 1621, taken from Governor William Bradford's Manuscript History, as published by the Mass. Historical Society in 1856, vol 3. Fourth Series. Alphabetically arranged for convenient reference.

Alden, John
Allerton, Isaack
    Mary, his wife .... died.
    Bartholomew ⎫
    Remember   ⎬ their children.
    Mary   ⎭
    John... died.
Billington, John
    Elen, his wife
    John   ⎱ their sons.
    Francis ⎰
Bradford, William
    Dorothy, his wife..................................... died.
Brewster, William
    Mary, his wife
    Love   ⎱ their sons.
    Wrasling ⎰
Britterige, Richard................................... died.
Browne, Peter
Butten, William, in Samuell Fuller's family .... died.
Carter, Robart, in W. Mulline's family................. died.
Carver, John.. died.
    Kathrine, his wife .... died.
Chilton, James...................................... died.
    ————, his wife.................................. died.
    Mary, their daughter
Clarke, Richard..................................... died.

Cooke Francis
    John, his sone
Coper, Humility, in Edward Tilley's family
Crackston, John... died.
    John, his sone
Doty, Edward, in Steven Hopkins' family
Eaton, Francis
    Sarah, his wife.. died.
    Samuell, his sone
Ely,
English, Thomas... .... died.
Fletcher, Moyses.. died.
Fuller, Edward.. died.
    ———, his wife... died.
    Samuell, his sonne
    Samnell
Gardenar, Richard
Goodman, John.. .... died.
Holbeck, William, in William White's family................ died.
Hooke, John, in Isaack Allerton's family.................. died.
Hopkins, Steven
    Elizabeth, his wife
    Giles
    Constantia
    Damaris } their children.
    Oceanus, (born at sea)
Howland, John, in John Carver's family
Langemore, John, in Christopher Martin's family............died.
Latham, William, in John Carver's family
Litster, Edward, in Steven Hopkins' family
Margeson, Edmond.. died.
Martin, Christopher.. died.
    ———, his wife... died.
Minter, Desire, in John Carver's family
More, Jasper, in John Carver's family...................... died.
    Richard, in W. Brewster's family
    ———, in W. Brewster's family......................... died.
    Ellen, in Edward Winslow's family.................... died.
Mullines, William .... died.
    ———, his wife... died.
    Joseph
    Priscila } their children.
Priest, Digerie.. died.

Prower, Salomon, in Christopher Martin's family................. died.
Rigdale, John.. died.
    Alice, his wife... died.
Rogers, Thomas.. died.
    Joseph, his sone
Samson, Henry, in Edward Tillies'family
Sowle, George, in Edward Winslow's family
Standish, Myles
    Rose, his wife... died.
Story, Elias, in Edward Winslow's family .... died.
Thomson, Edward, in William White's family .... died.
Tillie, Edward .... died.
    Ann, his wife... died.
    John.. died.
    ———, his wife... died.
    Elizabeth, their daughter
Tinker, Thomas.. died.
    ———, his wife... died.
    ———, his sone.. died.
Trevore, William
Turner, John.. died.
    ———, his sone.. died.
    ———, his sone.. died.
Warren, Richard
White, William.. died.
    Susana, his wife
    Resolved
    Peregriene, (born a ship board) } their sones
Wilder, Roger, in John Carver's family....................... died.
Williams. Thomas.. died.
Winslow, Edward
    Elizabeth, his wife..................................... died.
    Gilhart
A maid servant in John Carver's family, name unknown.

This list of Governor Bradford's gives one hundred and four names. It includes the names of two children born on the passage, and the name of William Butten who died at sea.

The number of deaths is fifty-two, including the death of William Butten.

Governor Bradford, at the close of his History, page 455, remarks, that " Of these one hundred persons which came first over in this first ship together, the greater halfe died in the generall mortality, and most of them in twc or three months time. And for those which survived, though some

were ancient and past procreation, and others left the place and cuntrie, yet
of those few remaining are sprung up above 160 persons, in this thirty
years, and are now living in this presente year, 1650, besides many of their
children which are dead, and come not within this account.

" And of the old stock (of one and other) there are yet living this present
year, 1650, nere thirty persons. Let ye Lord have ye praise, who is the
High Preserver of men."

The following memoranda are in a later hand, on page 455:

" Twelfe persons liveing of the old stock this present yeare, 1679. Two
persons liveing that came over in the first shipe, 1620, this present year,
1690, Resolved White and Mary Cushman, the daughter of Mr. Allerton.
And John Cooke, the son of Francis Cooke, that came in the first ship, is
still liveing this present yeare, 1694; and Mary Cushman is still living, this
present year, 1698.

We here subjoin the two notes of Charles Deane, Esq., the Editor of
Bradford's History, appended to the Document from which the foregoing
list is taken. See pages 447 and 455, of Bradford's History. " To the gen-
ealogist, the value of this list of passengers of the Mayflower, preserved
by Governor Bradford at the end of his history, cannot be overestimated.
Prince made but a partial use of this interesting record. Taking the list of
signers to the compact, in the order in which the names appear in the Memorial, he has given the *number* of which each family was composed, without always indicating the individuals who make up that number   Resort
has therefore been had, hitherto, to other sources for information, and much
has been left to conjecture. No perfect list has ever been made out. Two
names in this record (Trevore and Ely) do not appear in Morton's list of
signers. They are not included in any of the families, and appear to have
been overlooked by Prince in estimating the number of passengers." —
Bradford, pp. 77, 90; Prince, 1, 85, 86.

It appears, on an examination of this list, that of the one hundred and
two passengers of the Mayflower who arrived at Cape Cod, fifty-one died
within a few months. This number includes Mrs. Carver, who died in the
early part of the summer, within five or six weeks after her husband, who
died in April. The name of John Goodman, which is in this list of deaths,
appears also among those who shared in the division of land in 1623-4. An
error therefore exists either in this list or in the Colony Records.

It seems proper to state that the communications of the Hon. H. C.
Murphy, respecting the Leyden Records, first appeared in the Historical
Magazine, published in New York and Boston, by C. Benjamin Richardson,
Esq., in the numbers of that valuable periodical, for the months of September, November, December, 1859, and January, 1860. Mr. Richardson, in
reply to a note addressed to him on the subject, obligingly tendered the
unrestricted use of these communications for this work, the first of which
is copied nearly entire, and the more important parts of the second and

third, with no alterations, except a classified and alphabetical order of the names, to secure a more ready reference. The information obtained through the zealous efforts of Mr. Murphy is matter of just congratulation, and may encourage the hope that other diplomatic representatives of the United States will emulate so laudable an example.

THE PILGRIMS AT LEYDEN.

"I have visited Leyden several times for the purpose of looking over the early records of that temporary abode of the founders of New England, with a view of gleaning further information in relation to their residence in Holland. In prosecuting these researches, I have been kindly assisted by W. J. C. Rammelman Elsevir, Esq., a lineal descendant of the celebrated printer of that name, and a gentleman of great intelligence and private worth, who is the keeper of the archives of the city; and by Mr M. Keyser, a resident of Leyden. Thus aided, I have been able to recover some few facts in the personal history of the pilgrims and forefathers in Holland, which cannot be otherwise than interesting to their descendants, as well as historically valuable to all who would inform themselves of the condition of the life of those who led the mighty movement of New England colonization. There is no fact, however slight, relating to them, which may not throw light upon some side or the other of that movement, or serve to correct misapprehensions or wrong inferences, which many writers are very apt to draw from other facts. Thus, Mr. Hunter, in his ' Collections concerning the Founders of New Plymouth,' says (p. 115) that Dorothy May, the first wife of William Bradford, was probably a daughter of a Mrs. May, a member of Johnson's Separatist church, of Amsterdam, who is spoken of not very respectfully, by Ephraim Pagitt, in his Heresiography. Why Mr. Hunter should have gone out of his way to make a fling at Dorothy May, I know not, unless it was to make a more striking comparison with Alice Southworth, the second wife; but this is certain, that his remark is altogether gratuitous and unfounded, as she and her parents were residents of Leyden.

"In addition to the personal details which are now given, I have been enabled to discover the precise residence of the minister, John Robinson, where the meetings of his congregation were probably held. The deed or *transpoort brief* of the property was found entered in one of the volumes of the Stadhuis, and, with some other particulars in regard to Robinson, will be the subject of another paper for your magazine.

"Some matter in relation to Elder Brewster may form a third, which, with the others, I venture to believe, will be deemed suitable for publication in your valuable repository. H. C. M.

" THE HAGUE, *June* 1, 1859."
18*

" The first record to which we will direct attention is that of the mar
riages, registered at the Stadhuis, or City Hall, of persons not in communion
with the Dutch Reformed Church. It is not always easy to distinguish
Robinson's congregation, for there are many marriages recorded of English,
who were members of another congregation of dissenters, who had come
from England to Leyden, and were more numerous than the others. In fact
one of the difficulties which explorers of the past history are subject to still,
is the continual confounding of the two congregations. Another difficulty
in the record is the orthography in which the names are given. The register or clerk spelt them according to his own ear, and the powers of the
Dutch alphabet. The consequence is, that there is hardly a name, either
of a person or place, of English derivation, correctly spelt. Still, in most
of the cases, the English name shines through the Dutch covering sufficiently distinct. In those cases in which we have not been able to recognize
it, we give the orthography as it is in the record, and in italics.

" The minute of each marriage is very full, giving, as it were, a succinct
history of the previous condition in life of both parties. It furnishes the
date of the first publication of the banns, and of the marriage the names of
the parties to the ceremony, the occupation of the bridegroom, the places
of birth of both, their previous condition as to marriage, whether widowed
or not, and if widowed, the name of the deceased, and is accompanied by
the names of two or three friends on each side, to prove their identity. The
names which occur, of the pilgrims, are not very numerous, though there is
a goodly number of them, and some of the most distinguished.

" For convenience, the names are arranged alphabetically, the initial
letter of the names of the vessels (viz: M., the Mayflower; F., the Fortune;
A: the Ann,) indicating the one in which the party came."

M. ALLERTON, ISAAC
        " 1611.   October 4, November 4.   ISAAC ALLERTON, young man,
    (that is, having never been married before,) of London, in England,
    accompanied by Edward Southworth, Richard Masterson, and Ranulph
    Tickens, as witnesses, with
        " MARY NORRIS, maid, of Newbury, in England, accompanied by
    Anna Fuller, and *Dillen* Carpenter, as witnesses."
        Isaac Allerton, who, upon the death of John Carver, the first gov-
    ernor of the colony, was chosen assistant, was, as we learn from an-
    other record, a tailor.
M. BARKER, ELIZABETH, married EDWARD WINSLOW.
F. BASSETT, WILLIAM
        " His banns were published first with Mary Butler, on the 19th of

March, 1611; but she died before the third publication. He soon found, however, another bride.

" 1611. July 29, August 13. WILLIAM BASSETT, Englishman, widower of Cecil *Lecht*, accompanied by Roger Wilson, and Edward Goddard, with

" MARGARET OLDHAM, maid, from England, accompanied by Wybran Pautes, and Elizabeth Neal."

In the division of the lands by the General Court of the Colony, on the 22d of May, 1627, the name of the wife of William Bassett is given Elizabeth Bassett, as there are two of that name mentioned in his family.

M. BRADFORD, WILLIAM

" 1613. November 8, November 30. WILLIAM BRADFORD, fustian maker, young man, of Austerfield, in England, with

" DOROTHY MAY, of *Witzbuts*, in England. Is not identified; but presents a certificate."

Dorothy May was drowned on the 7th of December, 1620, in Cape Cod Harbor. Her father is mentioned by Roger White in a letter from Leyden, to Governor Bradford, in 1625.

A. CAREY, SARAH, married JOHN JENNE.

CARPENTER

AGNES, married SAMUEL FULLER. She did not live long.

JULIA ANN, married GEORGE MORTON.

F. CHINGELTON, MARY, married ROBERT CUSHMAN.

F. CUSHMAN, ROBERT

" 1617. May 19, June 3. ROBERT CUSHMAN, wool carder, of Canterbury, in England, widower of Sarah Cushman, accompanied by John Kebel, with

" MARY CHINGELTON (Singleton?) of Sandwich, widow of Thomas Chingelton, accompanied by Catharine Carver, (wife of John Carver.)"

The name of Cushman is spelt *Coetsman*.

M. DINGBY, SARAH, married MOSES FLETCHER.

M. FLETCHER, MOSES

" 1613. November 30, December 21. MOSES FLETCHER, smith, of England, widower of Maria Evans, accompanied by William Lysle, and William Bradford, with

" SARAH DINGBY, also of England, widow of William Dingby, accompanied by Sarah Priest and Margaret Savery."

Moses Fletcher died in the general sickness. His name is spelt in the Record, " Moyses Fletjear." The diphthongs ch and sh are unpronounceable by a Hollander.

FULLER

M. ANNA, married WILLIAM WHITE.

M.   SAMUEL

"1613. March 15, April 30. SAMUEL FULLER, say (silk) maker, of London, in England, widower of Elsie Glascock, accompanied by Alexander Carpenter, William Hoyt, his brother-in-law, Roger Wilson, and Edward Southworth, with

"AGNES CARPENTER, maid, of Wrentham, in England, accompanied by Agnes White and Alice Carpenter, her sister."

Samuel Fuller was the future physician of the Colony. Agnes, his wife by this marriage, did not live long, and he married, as we will presently see, his third wife in Leyden. Alice Carpenter became the second wife of Governor Bradford. She came to America a widow.

"1617. May 12, May 27. SAMUEL FULLER, saymaker, widower of Anna Carpenter, accompanied by Samuel Lee, his future brother-in-law, with

M.   "BRIDGET LEE, maid, of England, accompanied by Joos Lee, her mother."

A.   GOODALL, MARY, married RICHARD MASTERSON.

A.   JENNE, JOHN

"1614. September 5, November 1. JOHN JENNE, young man, brewer's man, of Norwich, in England, living in Rotterdam, accompanied by Roger Wilson, with

"SARAH CAREY, maid, of Moncksoon, in England, accompanied by Joanna Lyons."

M.   LEE, BRIDGET, married SAMUEL FULLER.

      MASTERSON, RICHARD

"1619. November 8, November 26. RICHARD MASTERSON, woolcarder, young man, of Sandwich, in England, accompanied by William Talbot and John Ellis, his brother-in-law, with

"MARY GOODALL, maid, of Leicester, in England, accompanied by Elizabeth Kibbel and Mary Finch."

M.   MAY, DOROTHY, married WILLIAM BRADFORD.

A.   MORTON, GEORGE

"6 July, 1612, 23d July, 1612. GEORGE MORTON, Englishman, of York, in England, merchant, accompanied by his brother, Thomas Morton, and Roger Wilson, as witnesses, with

"JULIA ANN CARPENTER, maid, accompanied by her father, Alexander Carpenter, her sister, Alice Carpenter, and Anna Robinson, as witnesses."

M.   NORRIS, MARY, married ISAAC ALLERTON.

F.   OLDHAM, MARGARET, married WILLIAM BASSETT.

M.   PRIEST, DEGORY

"1611. October 4, November 4. DEGORY PRIEST, of London in England, accompanied by William Lysle, and Samuel Fuller, as witnesses, with

SARAH VINCENT, of London, widow of John Vincent, accompanied by Jane *Diggens* and Rosamond Jepson, as witnesses."

Degory Priest died in the general sickness, which carried off so many of the first comers, shortly after his arrival in America. His wife did not accompany him in the Mayflower. It appears, by a subsequent minute in this record, that she married again on the 13th of November, 1621, with Goddard *Godbert,** and is there called " Sarah Allerton, widow of Degory Priest." She was probably related to Isaac Allerton, as we find the marriage of the latter on the same day as hers with Degory Priest.

A. TRACY, STEPHEN

" 1620. Dec. 18, 1621, Jan'y 2. STEPHEN TRACY, saymaker, young man from England, accompanied by Anthony Clemens, with

" TRIFASA LE——, maid, of England, accompanied by Pruce Jennings."

VINCENT, SARAH, married DEGORY PRIEST.

M. WHITE, WILLIAM

"1612. January 27, February 1. WILLIAM WHITE, wool-carder, young man, of England, accompanied by William Jepson and Samuel Fuller, with

ANNA FULLER, maid, of England, accompanied by Rosamond Jepson and Sarah Priest."

William White died shortly after reaching America, and his widow became the second wife of Edward Winslow, whose first marriage we find on our record.

M. WINSLOW, EDWARD

" 1618. April 27, May 16. EDWARD WINSLOW, printer, young man, of London, in England, accompanied by Jonathan Williams, and Isaac Allerton, with

ELIZABETH BARKER, maid, from *Chatsum* (Chester), in England, accompanied by Jane Phesel, her niece, and Mary Allerton."

There are others of Robinson's congregation in this record, who did not emigrate to America, as we may judge from the names of the witnesses. Thus, William Brewster is given as a witness on behalf of William Pantes, fustian maker, from near Dover, on his marriage with *Wybra* Hanson, maid, on the 4th of December, 1610, on behalf of Raynulph Tickens, young man, of London, with Jane White, maid, of *Bebel*, on the 11th of April, 1611, and for William Buckrum, block maker, young man, of Ipswich, with Elizabeth Neal, maid, of Scrooby, on the 17th of December, 1611.

* The inventory of *Godbert Godbertson* was presented to the Court at Plymonth, October 25, 1633; and his wife, *Zarah*, in another place is called the sister of Isaac Allerton.

William Bradford is, in the same manner, witness at the marriage of Henry Crulins, bombazine worker, widower, of England, residing at Amsterdam, with Dorothy Pettinger, maid, of *Moortel*, on the 20th of November, 1613; and John Carver appears in the same capacity, on behalf of John *Gillies*, merchant, of Essex, widower of Elizabeth Pettinger, on his marriage with Rose Lysle, maid of Yarmouth, on the 23d of March, 1617.

We will conclude this paper with some extracts from the book of admissions to the right of citizens, or freemen, of Leyden. The number of pilgrims who obtained this privilege, was only three, as follows:—

(1.) "1612. March 30. William Bradford, Englishman, admitted upon the proof and security of Roger Wilson and William Lysle."

(2.) "1614. Feb'y 7. Isaac Allerton, Englishman, of London, admitted upon the proof and security of Roger Wilson and Henry Wood."

(3.) "1615. Nov. 16. Degory Priest, hatter, of England, admitted upon the proof and security of Roger Wilson, say draper, and Isaac Allerton, tailor." H. C. M.

NOTE BY THE AUTHOR.—It appears from a document found by Mr. Murray, addressed to the Hon. Burgomaster of the city of Leyden, which we have not room to copy entire, that on the 12th of February, 1609, "Jan Robartshe (Robinson) minister of the divine word, *and some of the members* of the Christian reformed religion, born in the Kingdom of Great Britain, to the number of one hundred persons, or thereabouts, men and women, represent that they are desirous of coming *to live in this city*, by the first day of May next, and to have the freedom, thereof, in *carrying on their trades without being a burden* in the least to any one, which request was granted."

We have already given the different trades pursued by those of Robinson's congregation who were married at Leyden, and emigrated to America in the first four ships. We now furnish, from the same source, a list, with their trades, and places of birth, of some of them who did not embark in the Mayflower, the Fortune, the Ann, or the Little James. Sometimes the particular city is named; at others, only the country from whence they came:

Berry, Zachariah, from England.

Buckram, William, from Ipswich, block maker.

Butler, Samuel, from Yarmouth, merchant.

Butterfield, Stephen, from England, silk worker.

Carpenter, Alexander, father of Gov. Bradford's second wife, and of George Morton's wife, trade unknown.

Clemens, Anthony, trade unknown.

Chandler, Roger, from Colchester, silk worker.

Codmore, John, from England, ribbon weaver.

Cullens, Henry, from England, bombazine worker; he lived at Amsterdam.

Ell's, John, trade unknown.

Fairfield, Daniel, from Colchester, silk worker.

Ferrier, Samuel, from Caen, Normandy, silk worker. (This is an instance of the admission of a Frenchman into the congregation. We gather this from the fact that he married Mildreth Charles, maid, from England, on the 16th May, 1614, having on that occasion two of the congregation, namely, Roger Wilson, and Samuel Fuller, as witnesses.)

Gillies, John, from Essex, merchant.

Gray, Abraham, trade unknown.

Hatfield, Thomas, from England, wool carder.

Hoyt, William, trade unknown.

Jennings, John, from Colchester, fustian worker.

Jepson, Edmund, from England, bombazine worker.

    Henry, from England, silk worker.

    William, trade unknown.

Keble, John, trade unknown.

Lee, Samuel, from England, hatter.

Marcus, Isaac, trade unknown.

Marshall, Henry, trade unknown.

Nelson, Robert, from England, haize worker.

Nes, Israel, trade unknown.

Pantes, William, from Dover, fustian maker.

Parsons, Joseph, from Colchester, silk worker.

Pickering, Edward, from London, merchant.

Reynolds, John, from London, printer; he lived at Amsterdam.

Robinson, John, from England, minister.

Simons, Roger, from Sarum, mason.

Smith, Robert, trade unknown.

    Thomas, from Bury, wool carder. He married Anna Crackston, daughter of John Crackston, one of the company of the Mayflower.

Southworth, Edward, from England, silk worker; first husband of Governor Bradford's second wife.

    Thomas, (brother of Edward,) trade unknown.

Spoonard, John, from England, ribbon weaver. John Carver attended as a witness to his marriage, 9th December, 1616.

Talbot, William, trade unknown.

Tickens, Raynulf, (brother-in-law of Robinson,) trade unknown.

Warrener, Robert, from England, wool carder.

White, Roger, (brother of Mrs. Robinson,) trade unknown.

Wilkins, Roger, from England, wool carder.

Williams, Jonathan, trade unknown.

    Thomas, trade unknown.

Wilson, Henry, from Yarmouth, pump maker. John Carver attended as
    witness to his marriage on the 16th May, 1616.
    Roger, from England, silk worker.
Wood, Henry, trade unknown.

" These lists might be much extended, but we have confined ourselves,
for the present, to such as most distinctly appear to have been connected
with Robinson's congregation prior to the sailing of the last four ships. A
close scrutiny would, we doubt not, double the number. An interesting
question presents itself, as to what became of these numerous families. At
first the congregation at Leyden consisted, as we have seen, of about one
hundred persons, men and women; subsequent accessions from England
and other sources increased the number to about three hundred souls in
1620, of whom it is said not more than one half went to America. After
the death of Robinson in 1625, there does not appear to have been any
minister among them. Some of his flock, like his own children, became
absorbed in the Dutch population, though there is not at this day more than
three names of families in Leyden, bearing any resemblance to those above
given. It would seem probable, therefore, that a number of them subsequently went to America, for which reason we have thought it useful to add
the last list. It cannot be doubted, however, that all the members of the
community pursued useful trades.' None of them appear to have been rich;
but in so far as they were able, by their avocations, to gain their own support, they were independent, especially as they had every opportunity and
advantage that the Dutch residents themselves possessed, namely, freedom
of trade and protection of the laws for their property, persons, and religion.
It is not, therefore, empty diplomatic language, when Governor Bradford
repeats, in a second letter in October, 1627, to the Governor and Council at
New Amsterdam, that ' we acknowledge ourselves tied in a strict obligation
unto your country and state, for the good entertainment and free liberty
which we had, and our brethren and countrymen yet there have and do
enjoy under our most honorable Lords the States.' "   H. C. M.

    GEORGE SUMNER, ESQ., in his very interesting " Memoirs of the Pilgrims
at Leyden," (Mass. Hist. Coll. vol 9, third series,) says he is disposed to
believe that the religious assemblies of the Pilgrims at Leyden were held
in some hired hall, or in the house occupied by Robinson, though he was
not able to discover anything more in relation to the dwelling of the minister, than a statement, in the record of his burial, that he lived near the belfry, which adjoined St. Peter's church. The question which he here
suggests is an interesting one in more than one aspect, and principally as it
goes to show, according as it may be determined either one way or the
other, whether the Pilgrims received any consideration from the Dutch
authorities, and whether they were held in any particular estimation by
them."

" We intend to present, as it were, a supplement to Mr. Sumner's investigations, having ascertained some facts which escaped his observation; we mean the exact site of Robinson's house, its dimensions and history, as derived from the existing records. These facts tend, in a remarkable degree, it appears to us, to strengthen Mr. Sumner's conjecture as to that house being the place of worship, and also to show the limited means at the command of the Pilgrims at the time of their settlement in Leyden. There is a space of two years, or a little more, between the time of the arrival of Robinson and his flock in Leyden, and the purchase of this house, in which he afterward lived until his death. There is nothing to show where he resided during that short period; but on the 5th of May, 1611, *a transport brief* or deed was made to him, in conjunction with three others of his congregation, of the house and piece of ground in question, nearly opposite the belfry, which stood in the rear of St. Peter's church, and fronting on Pieter's Kerckhoff, or the Clock Steech, (literally translated *Bell Alley*,) a street between twenty and thirty feet wide. The consideration to be paid was three thousand two hundred dollars, of which eight hundred dollars were paid down, and the balance secured by a *casting brief*, or consideration lien, upon the property, and was to be paid in annual instalments of two hundred dollars each. Now the fact that the title was taken in the name of four persons, in connection with another circumstance disclosed in another record, namely, that Robinson was the only one of the four who lived in the house, goes to show that the purchase was for a general object, of which the pastor was the leader. This deed was found recorded in Register M. M. page 105 of indemnifications, (*Protocollen van Waerbrieoen,*) and was doubtless so recorded as a security to the grantor for the balance of the purchase money. It will be found curious to the general reader, as a specimen of Dutch conveyancing. We preserve the names of the different parties, according to the orthography of the original deed. It reads as follows: —

" We *Pieter Arentsz Deyman* and *Amelis Van Hogeveen*, schepens in Leyden, make known that before us came Johan de Lalaing, declaring for himself, and his heirs that he had sold, and by these presents does sell to *Jan Robinszn*, minister of God's word of the English congregation in this city, *Willem Jepson*, *Henry Woed*, and *Raymulph Tickens, who has married Jane White*, — jointly and each for himself an equal fourth part, — a house and ground with a garden situated on the west side thereof, standing and being in this city on the south side of the *Pieter's Kerckhoff*, (grounds of Peter's church,) near the Belfry formerly called the *Groene poort*, (Green gate,) Bounded and having situated on the one side, eastwardly, a certain small room which the *comparant* (the appearor or grantor) reserves to himself, being over the door of the house hereby sold; next thereto is *William Simonsz van der Wilde*, and next to him the residence of the *Commandarije;*

19

and on the other side, westwardly, having the widow and heirs of *Huyck van Alckemade* and next to him the comparant himself, and next to him is the *Donckere graft*, (the Dark Canal,) which is also situated on the west of the aforesaid garden, and next to it is the *Falide Bagynhoff* (Veiled Nun's cloister,) extending from the street of the Kerckhoff aforesaid to the rear of the Falide Bagynhoff before named; *all and so* as the aforesaid house is at present built and made, used and occupied, with everything thereto attached, (*aert ennagelvast*, — fastened to the ground or nailed,) to him the comparant belonging, subject to a yearly rent charge of eleven stivers and twelve pence payable to the *Heer van Poelgeest*. And he, the comparant, promises the afore-said house and ground, upon the conditions aforesaid, to warrant and defend from all other incumbrances with which the same may be charged, for a year and a day and forever, as is just, hereby binding thereto all his property, movable and immovable, now owned or hereafter to be owned by him, with-out any exception. Further making known that he, the comparant, is paid for the aforesaid purchase, and fully satisfied therewith, the sum of eight thousand guilders, the last penny with the first, and that with a purchase money lien, — two thousand guilders being paid down, and five hundred guilders to be paid in May, 1612, and annually thereafter until all be paid. And this all in good faith and without fraud.

" In witness of these presents we have set our seals the 5th of May, 1611.

(" Signed.)   J. SWANENBURCH."

The grantees in this conveyance, besides Robinson himself, were mem-bers of his congregation, as we find by the record of marriages. None of them went to America. Jepson bought out the interest of the others on the 13th of December, 1629, after Robinson's death. He is described in this second conveyance as a carpenter. Tickens was the brother-in-law of Robinson, whose wife Bridget was the sister of Jane White. Roger White, who communicated from Leyden to Governor Bradford the death of Robin-son, was the brother of Mrs. Robinson. From the circumstance that Jane White's name is mentioned in the deed, it may be inferred that the money for Tickens's share came from her. Tickens is described as a looking-glass maker. In 1637, Jepson, who had become the sole owner, having died, the property was conveyed, by guardians of his children, to Stoffel Jansz Ellis, and thus ceased to be held any longer by the Brownists.

The house was taken down, with a number of others, in 1681-3, for the. purpose of erecting a *hofje* or *hof* for the Walloons, still remaining called *Pesyn's hof*.

The other record to which we referred as showing that Robinson alone resided in the house, — excepting, of course, the room over the door, reserved by Johan de Lalaing, — is a list of those rated for a poll tax on the 15th of

October, 1622, in the Bon, or Wyk; that is, a small district set off for muni-cipal purposes, called the Seven Houses. The only persons mentioned as living in this house are those composing Robinson's family, making with himself, nine in all. They are named as follows:—

"JOHN ROBINSON, Minister.
 BRUGITTA (Bridget) ROBINSON, his wife.

James
Brugitta
Isaac
Mercy
Fear
Jacob
} Robinson's children.

Mary Hardy, maid servant.

"The only further mention of any portion of the family that we have noticed, is the marriage of the daughter Bridget on the 10th and 26th May, 1629, to John Gryuwich, student of theology, young man. On that occa-sion, Robinson's widow attended as a witness.   H. C. M."

THE COURT-HOUSE.

The present Court-House was erected in the year 1820, and was 68 feet in length by 46 feet in breadth. It was remodelled and enlarged in 1857, by au addition of 39 feet in length, and 46 in breadth, making the entire length of the present building 102 feet, and the width 56 feet. The walls were raised six feet above the old structure, and the whole covered with mastic, in imitation of freestone.

Two entries extend from East to West, through the building, to which access may be had, both in front and rear. In front there are two porticos, which are reached by flights of granite-stone steps. On the south entry are situated the offices of clerk of the courts, register of deeds, probate and chancery, and county treasurer. A stairway leads to the basement and second story. From the north entry, access is had to the court room, grand jury, witness, insolvent and probate court, and county treasurer's rooms. In the second story are situated the court law library, two jury, and two other rooms for the judges, and a stairway to the cupola. The court room is large and airy, being of the same size as the old structure, (60 by 45 feet,) and six feet higher in the walls, thoroughly ventilated in the ceiling and otherwise. The entire building is lighted by gas and heated by furnaces. The grounds connected with the building are enclosed by a substantial iron fence. The offices are all provided with fire-proof safes, five in number.

[The above account was obligingly prepared by James Bates, Esq., Sheriff of the County, and formerly of the Board of County Commissioners.]

PLYMOUTH COLONY SEAL.

Inquiries are frequently made as to the origin, design, and significance of this ancient symbol of Old Colony sovereignty, and the object of this brief notice is to satisfy public curiosity.

The first intimation respecting a colony seal appears in a letter from Robert Cushman to Gov. Bradford, dated December, 1624, in which he says, " Make your corporation as formal as you can, under the name of the society in Plymouth in New England." The Plymouth Colony Charter, from the Council of New England to William Bradford and associates, dated Jan. 13, 1629, among other provisions, authorizes " the said William Bradford, his associates, his heirs and assines att all tymes hereafter to incorporate, by some usuall or fitt name and title, him or themselves, or the people there inhabitinge under him or them." Here was the first legal grant of authority to use a seal within the jurisdiction of New Plymouth. The best engraving of the seal extant, is that found in the recently published volumes of court orders and grants of land, edited by Nathaniel B. Shurtleff, M. D.

The only description of the seal known to the writer, is that of the late Samuel Davis, Esq., in the following words: " The Old Colony arms, four men kneeling, implumed hearts in their hands, on a field quártely, was its head ornament; legend, Plymouth *Novanglia, sigillum, societatis,* 1620." We are therefore led to conclude, that the true object of this ancient memorial of bygone days, was designed to indicate the fixed purpose of the fathers to engage, with united heart and hand, in the great work assigned them by the providence of God, that of establishing the civil and religious institutions, which so justly claim and receive the grateful homage of their posterity.

Under the tyrannical administration of Sir Edmond Andros, in 1686, the original seal was purloined from the Old Colony archives, and the governor, Thomas Henckley, was requested, in behalf of the court of 1689, " to endeavor the regaining of our publique seal, if it may be, and if otherwise, to procure a new one, and the colony to defray the charge of it." It was, however, never recovered, and its further uses were terminated by the union of the Plymouth and Massachusetts colonies, in the year 1692.

CUSHMAN MONUMENT.

" On the 16th of September, 1858, the ardently hoped for consummation of the wishes of the Cushman family took place at Plymouth, when the monument, which they had erected on Burying Hill, in memory of their venerated ancestry, was consecrated at a family gathering, with exercises and ceremonies worthy of the occasion.

" The monument is a massive and tasteful structure; built of smoothly-hewn granite, of the finest and most durable quality, and is highly creditable to the skill and faithfulness of the contractors.* Its form is that of an obelisk, with plainly champered edges, having a Grecian base, standing upon an ornamented pedestal, also champered to its base, and containing sunken panels. The pedestal rests upon two square plinths, and the whole structure upon blocks of hewn granite, occupying the whole space inclosed by a quadrangular fence, constructed with large stone posts, and substantial iron rails. The whole height of the monument, including the stone blocks upon which it stands, is about twenty-seven and one half feet. The base of the pedestal is about five feet square; and of the lowest plinth about eight feet. The space within the railing is about twelve feet square."

The Fort Hill, so called in early times, afterwards named Burial Hill, the southwesterly side of which forms the site of this monument, is fraught with the most interesting associations to every thoughtful mind. Here the first military post was built, in 1622, to protect the humble dwellings on both sides of Leyden Street, below; the lower part of it designed for public worship, the upper part for mounting the artillery required for defence. Near by repose the ashes of the Pilgrims, while the

" Bay, where the Mayflower lay,"

widely expanding its silvery flood, rivets the glad vision of the observer. Here,† once assembled for public worship, Winthrop, Governor of Massachusetts, Wilson, pastor of the first church of Boston, Roger Williams, assistant pastor of Plymouth Church, with elder Brewster, Gov. Bradford, Winslow, and others of the pilgrim band, in spiritual communion. The monument itself is highly creditable to the skill and taste of all concerned in its erection, and presents the only adequate memorial yet reared in honor of any individual among the pilgrims of 1620. We learn that the requisite funds were obtained from the descendants of Robert Cushman, — amounting to $2,500, an instance of liberality and enterprise as rare as it is landable.

* E. R. & C. Mitchell.
† See Gov. Winthrop's visit to Plymouth in 1632.

19*

EARLY CORRESPONDENCE OF THE PILGRIMS.

The following letters were obtained in the year 1851, from the late Judge Nahum Mitchell, of East Bridgewater, whose valuable researches have so largely contributed to the illustration of our early history. The early domestic correspondence between the Pilgrims is mostly lost, and for that reason alone, to say nothing of the excellent spirit they manifest, these letters are highly interesting. The note of explanation, which follows the letters, was prepared by Judge Mitchell.

Loving and kind Uncle,—

My hearty and kind salutation I do here desire to tender unto you, hoping and wishing your and your's well being, both in soul and body. I shall here communicate unto you a sad dispensation of the Lord toward me, in the taking away from me out of this life, my most dear and tender mother, the which unto me indeed is a great loss, not only missing her most tender affection to me and over me, the which is very much, but also the godly example of piety, by the which, as by her counsel and godly persuasions, she did labor to bring me, and us all here with her, to see and experience more and more the sweetness of walking in the ways of God, in obeying of him and in keeping close unto him, the missing of which you may easily judge, cannot but be sad unto us here. Nevertheless we do desire, seeing it thus is the will of our God to administer unto us, having appointed unto all once to die, to labor to be contented, and to submit unto the will of our God, considering the goodness of the Almighty, even in this providence, the which, had it been long before, would have been more sad, in respect of my minority and young years: it being always her desire to see me to come to age before she should depart this life, the which mercy the Lord hath granted unto us, for I am now 23 years of age, and able sundry years ago, through the mercy and goodness of the Lord my God, to subsist in the world by my father's trade, the which, indeed, is a good consideration, and gives me occasion to awaken my soul, and yet to be thankful to God, especially when I mind the sadness she was in of late, being very weakly, out of which the Lord has delivered her, having taken her out of this sad and toilsome life, a world of misery, and has brought her to the kingdom of his dear Son, to an inheritance immortal in light. She deceased this life on the 25th March, 1662. Thus, most loving uncle, I have communicated my sad thoughts, and do further acquaint you, that I have received a letter from you, bearing date 23 April, 1661, in the which I understand concerning all your healths, at the hearing of which I am very glad. I do also wish my cousin Elizabeth much joy with her daughter that God has given her to her 6 sons. I do also wish my cousin Sarah much joy in her married estate. And as touching your enclosed letter, for Mr. Preserved May, I have delivered it, and do return an answer. And now, as touching my two sisters, and their husbands and children, they are well, and do most heartily remember their loves unto you and their cousins, and I pray remember me most kindly to your wife, and unto all my loving cousins, the which by name I cannot. I also pray you, Uncle, do so much as to present my respects and my sisters', and their husbands', to my aunt Jean Gunn, and my cousin Joseph, and acquaint her concerning my dear mother's departing. I would have writ to her also, but I wanted time, the ship being to go away; and pray my Aunt and cousin to write, and not to fail. And I pray do you also not fail to write, and so commending you all to the Lord's tuition, I rest and remain wherever I am   Your very loving cousin,

THOMAS MITCHELL.

In Amsterdam, 24 July, 1662.

Uncle, yet a word, the which, perhaps, you have not heard of, the which is the decease of Mr. John May, and Uncle Dickens, who died both about half a year since.

The superscription is "For to be delivered unto his loving Uncle, Mr. Experience Mitchell, dwelling in Duxbury town, New England. To be sent."

[Written, probably, in the early part of 1690.]

Loving cousin, Edward Mitchell.

Sir: Your letters of July and October, 1689, are come well to hand, and I am very glad to hear of your welfare, as also that there is a way discovered of sending letters, with much more security of not misbearing, than heretofore, for truly, it cannot but be a desirable thing for friends to converse, one with another, the which, when it cannot be personal, as ours cannot. Providence having otherwise disposed of the bounds of our habitations, then to supply by letter, what cannot otherwise be done. And the more desirable is it to maintain correspondence with such as are not alone tied in friendship together by the bonds of nature, but have besides that, and above that, a better and nearer, yea, a lastinger nearness and relation one unto another, to wit, such as are children of one father, have one Saviour, and life by one Spirit, being by the same all joined together to that one body, whereof Christ, our Lord, is head, and have all one divine nature, and shall all meet together, and be ever with the Lord. These things unite better than natural ties, and truly—[wanting]— for in your lines I perceived a favoring and a relishing of the things of God. The Lord maintain, keep up, and perfect the good work he hath began, and that to the day of the Lord. Your kind token, the otter's skin, I received, and thank you heartily for it. As for trade together, I at present say only this to it, that there requires more estate than I have; besides that little that God in his mercy hath given me is employed in a stocking trade; but that which is of great consideration, also, is, that I am informed there are sometimes great losses by New England commodities. This is all I can say to it at present, but if time should present —[the rest of the letter is wanting, but there is on the back of it the following postcript.]

Cousin, I here, by Mr. John Carter, send you two fowling pieces, they say very good and exact. They cost seven gilders apiece; the one accept as a token. As to the estate of things in Europe, they are full of confusion, and it looks bad with religion. But the time is coming, when God has accomplished his work on Mount Zion, that he will reckon with their and his enemies, and then will their deliverance be. Even so let it be, O Lord.

One more farewell in the Lord.   THOMAS MITCHELL.

The two foregoing letters were copied from the originals, in the hands of William Mitchell, now (March 9, 1851,) living in Bridgewater, in his 91st year, and who is of the 6th generation from Experience, inclusive. Copied by N. M., who is in his 83d year, and of the 5th generation from Experience, inclusive.

Experience lived and died at Joppa, in E. Bridgewater, and on the farm now owned by Charles Mitchell, great-great-grandson of Experience, and which has remained in the family from the beginning; each descendant before Charles, viz: Edward, Edward, Cushing, lived and died on the same farm; and the wills of all, Experience included, are preserved.

LETTER OF GOV. WILLIAM BRADFORD TO MARY CARPENTER.

We copy, from the New England Historical and Genealogical Register, a letter communicated by Frederick Kidder, Esq., of Boston, which appeared in that valuable journal for July, 1860, page 196. We are not aware that it had ever been previously published, and gladly place it by the side of those next above.

Loving Sister.

We understand, by your letter, that God hath taken to himself our aged mother, out of the troubles of this tumultuous world, and that you are in a solitary condition, as we easily apprehend. We thought good, therefore, to write these few lines unto you, that if you think good to come over to us, you shall be wellcome, and we shall be as helpfull unto you as we may, though we are growne old, and the countrie here more unsettled, than ever, by reason of the great changes that have been in these late times, and what will further be, the Lord only knows, which makes many thinks of removing their habitations, and sundrie of our ministers (hearing of the peace and liberty now in England and Ireland) begin to leave us, and it is feared many more will follow. We do not write these things to discourage you, (for we shall be glad to see you, if God so dispose,) but if you find not all things here according to your expectation, when God shall bring you hither, that you may not thinke we dealt not plainly with you. This bearer is to come as near you as Dorchestere, and hath promised to see this letter safely conveyed to you, and if you cane write or send to him, he will give you the best directions and furtherance he can, about your coming over. His occation will be most at London. He dwells here with us, and is to return this next year. He is a brother to Mr. Winslow. But we conceive your best and easiest way will be to come from Bristol, if there be any passage. And if you cannot pay your passage, agree with the master, and I will pay it here.

We have sent letters formerly, wch we perceive have miscarried, but I hope this will come safe to your hands. The rest of your friends are all in health, blessed be God. We hope you will have such opportuuities, as your passage will be comfortable. Thus desiring the Lord to keep you and bring you in safetie, with our love remembered unto you, we take leave, and rest,

Your loving brother and sister,

WILLIAM BRADFORD.

PLYMᵒ, August 19. 1664.*

To his very Loving Sister | Mary Carpenter at | Wrington in Somersetshire some 8 | myles from Bris | toll these be | d'd.

This letter to be left at the | House of Joseph Leggat near | the sign of the rose in Ratcliffe | street in Bristoll to be conveyed as above said.

NOTE. The death of Mary Carpenter is recorded in the church records as follows: —

"1687. Mary Carpenter, (sister of Mrs. Alice Bradford, the wife of Governor Bradford) a member of the church at Duxbury, died in Plymouth, March 19–20, being newly entered into the 91st year of her age, — never married." This agrees with the copy taken from Winsor's history of Duxbury, as quoted by the N. E. G. Register, page 195, excepting the *date*, which should have been 1687, instead of 1667. Gov. Bradford, in his list of passengers who came in the Mayflower, observes (writing in 1650) that " Gilbert Winslow, after diverse years abroad here, returned into England, and died there."

Priscilla Wright, the widow of Wm. Wright, another sister of Gov. Bradford's wife, Alice, m. Dea. "John Cooper, Nov. 24, 1634; removed to Barnstable, and was dismissed from the church there," 8–18, 1683, to Plymouth Church,

* "This is so in the Copy, but it must be an error; probably the original read 1644, or 1646, as there is internal evidence that the letter was written about that time.

according to a memorandum copied from the Barnstable Church Records, by
Amos Otis, Esq. She died "Dec. 29th, 1689, in her 92ond yeare." Another
sister, — Julian, m George Morton, who died in 1624, and she probably m.
Manassah Kempton previous to 1627, and died in 1664, aged 81 years. It was
for a long time fully believed that Bridgett, the wife of samuel Fuller, who
came in the Mayflower, was also another sister, but the researches of Mr.
Murphy, show that her maiden name was Bridgett Lee, and a third wife, and
that his first wife was Anna Carpenter, another sister, whose age we have not
ascertained. The united age of the four first-named sisters, amounts to 343
years, averaging 85¾ years ; presenting not only a remarkable instance of longevity in a single family, but a cluster of worthies, whose honorable lives
adorned with the graces of piety and intelligence their own age, and may justly
claim the homage of ours.

————

JOHN HOWLAND.

In the second edition of this work, on page 48, an occurrence on board
the Mayflower, respecting John Howland, was related, being an extract
copied from a fragment of Prince's MS. annals, which extract differs considerably from the language of Gov. Bradford, when narrating the same
event, and the text, as now corrected, conforms to the last-named authority.

On page 67, the inscription copied from the gravestone of John Howland,
requires correction by the statement of Gov. Bradford, that "John Tillie
died a little after they came ashore; and their daughter, Elizabeth
married, and hath issue, as is before noted." The uncertainty of tradition
(though in many cases important,) was, perhaps, never more apparent than
in the present instance, it having been firmly believed for more than two
centuries, that he married the daughter of Gov. Carver, and that too,
through successive generations, distinguished both for intelligence and longevity. The births of John Howland's children do not appear on the Plymouth Colony Records, and are not accurately known. The following extract from the Historical Magazine, for January, 1860, page 6, seems reliable, and give the birth of Lieut. [Jabez] Howland, and is otherwise interesting, and is as follows: —

" A fragment of Judge Sewall's journal, during his judicial circuit in the
Old Colony, in 1702, reads thus: Saw Lieut. Howland upon yᵉ Roade, who
tells us he was born Feb. 24, at our Plymouth. Visit Mr. [Isaac] Robinson, who saith he is 92 years old, is yᵉ son of Mr. Robinson, pastor of yᵉ ch.
of Leyden part of wᶜʰ came to Plimᵒ, but to my disappointmenᵗ he came

not to New-England till y⁰ year in w⁰ʰ Mr. Wilson was returning to Engld [1631] after y⁰ settlem⁰ of Boston, 1 told him was very very desirous to see him for his Father's sake, and his own. Gave him an Arabian piece of Gold to buy. a book for some of his Grandchild."

BURYING HILL.

In addition to what appears on pages 62, 8, and 4, respecting this spot, we are gratified to announce that the exact site of the ancient watch-house, built at the time of Philip's war, (1675), was recently ascertained. Its dimensions correspond with the town records, being 12 by 16 feet on the ground, and about 15 feet high, for a particular description of which, the reader is referred to a note on page 64. Guided by traditionary information, and the minute description contained in the records, this interesting memorial, after the lapse of 185 years, stands revealed, forcibly reminding us of the conflicts and horrors of savage warfare.

The northwest corner is about 14 inches below the surface of the ground, and nearly coincides with the southeast corner of the Judson monument. The stone of this corner, and the brick layer on the same, forming part of the foundation of the building, still remain, and also the stone foundation of the fireplace, about 2 feet square. Some small pieces of glass were found, which doubtless belonged to the two small windows, a piece of fused lead, a few large board nails, a fragment of iron, and quite a number of bricks, some of the latter, from their coarse and more ordinary appearance, seeming to have formed a part of the watch-house, built in 1643, at which time bricks are first named in our records. The watch-house above described was enclosed with palisades, one hundred feet square, the latter, without doubt, designed to shelter a large part of the population, in case of any sudden or dangerous emergency. The four corners of the site of this relic of colonial warfare, are designated by posts of granite.

POWDER-HOUSE.

This ancient memorial of the Revolution has yielded at last to the inroads of time, and the impatience of modern innovation, and by a vote of the town was ordered to be removed in May last. It was built in 1770, under the direction of Thomas Foster, Elkanah Watson, and John Torrey, a committee of the town. It was originally built of brick, but some 40 years ago was covered with materials of wood. A slate stone, of an oval form, was inserted in the brick work on the easterly side of the door, 2 feet in width by 1½ feet in height, on which a Latin inscription was chiselled, and above this, on the top, the form of a powder-horn and cartridge, and at the bottom a cannon mounted on a carriage. The decay, and loss of several letters and words of the inscription, render its accurate translation difficult. It stood near the western entrance to the hill, and its site is now occupied by ornamental trees.

DISTANCES FROM PLYMOUTH TO OTHER PLACES.

The following distances, in the vicinity of Plymouth, are taken from the data of the U. S. Coast Survey.

DISTANCES.

From the spire of Plymouth Courthouse

To the Gurnet Lighthouse, in a direct line, 4 65-100 miles.

To the north extremity of Plymouth Beach, in a direct line, 1 68-100 miles.

To the centre of the island in Billington Sea, in a direct line, 1 75-100 miles.

To the summit of Captain's Hill, Duxbury, in a direct line, 4 miles.

To the Kingston Railroad Depot, by main road, nearly 4 50-100 miles.

To the house of Daniel Webster, Marshfield, by main road, nearly 11 91-100 miles.

To the Duxbury Postoffice, by main road, nearly 8 82-100 miles.

To Green River Harbor, by main road, nearly 12 64-100 miles.

Length of Gurnet Beach, north and south, nearly 4 40-100.

Total length of Gurnet Beach, nearly 6 54-100 miles.

Length of Plymouth Beach, nearly 2 50-100 miles.

Width of entrance to Plymouth Harbor, 1 26-100 miles.

Total shore line of Billington Sea, including islands, 4 29-100 miles.

Greatest length of Billington Sea, 1 83-100 miles.

The water surface, or area of Billington Sea, is 67-100 of square miles, equivalent to 428 8-100 acres.